Praise for *Zetas Till We Die*

"Betrayal, deceit, and friendship—*Zetas Till We Die* has it all. Mystery mixes with timely social commentary and the unbreakable bond of sisterhood to deliver an engaging, can't-put-it-down thriller that twists and turns through these women's lives then and now, making you wonder how well you know anyone."

—Darby Kane, bestselling author of *Pretty Little Wife*

"*Zetas Till We Die* is a riveting and brilliantly crafted thriller with so many twists, you'll be whipping through its pages. I couldn't put it down, and I never saw *that* ending coming."

—Nicola Sanders, author of *Don't Let Her Stay*

Praise for *Perfect Little Lives*

"*Perfect Little Lives* is a seductive thriller that tackles contemporary issues of racism and social justice with an engaging storyline. Excited to have these new voices in the genre."

—L.S. Stratton, author of *Not So Perfect Strangers*

"What starts as a slow burn quickly heats up when a relentless heroine searches for the truth about her mother's murder. *Perfect Little Lives* exposes the truths hidden behind the closed suburban doors in a suspense you won't want to miss."

—Jaime Lynn Hendricks, bestselling author of *I Didn't Do It*

Praise for *Someone Had to Do It*

"A disturbing peek into the world of privilege. *Someone Had to Do It* is a tense page-turner that had me yelling out loud at the characters."

–**Lucinda Berry, bestselling author of *The Secrets of Us***

"A juicy, brilliant treat of a thriller that combines sexy fashion-world glamour with salient points about privilege, racism, and the corrosive effects of extreme wealth. Somehow, *Someone Had to Do It* manages to be both a scathing critique of our late-stage capitalist hellscape, and the perfect mental escape from it. I couldn't put it down!"

–**Layne Fargo, author of *They Never Learn***

THE HOUSE GUESTS

Also by Amber and Danielle Brown

Someone Had to Do It
Perfect Little Lives
Zetas Till We Die

THE HOUSE GUESTS

AMBER AND DANIELLE BROWN

GRAYDON HOUSE

Recycling programs for this product may not exist in your area.

ISBN-13: 978-1-525-80990-3

The House Guests

Copyright © 2025 by Amber Brown & Danielle Brown

Branch illustration © busurman/stock.adobe.com

All rights reserved. No part of this book may be used or reproduced in any manner whatsoever without written permission.

Without limiting the exclusive rights of any author, contributor or the publisher of this publication, any unauthorized use of this publication to train generative artificial intelligence (AI) technologies is expressly prohibited. Harlequin also exercises their rights under Article 4(3) of the Digital Single Market Directive 2019/790 and expressly reserves this publication from the text and data mining exception.

This is a work of fiction. Names, characters, places and incidents are either the product of the author's imagination or are used fictitiously. Any resemblance to actual persons, living or dead, businesses, companies, events or locales is entirely coincidental.

® is a trademark of Harlequin Enterprises ULC.

Graydon House
22 Adelaide St. West, 41st Floor
Toronto, Ontario M5H 4E3, Canada
www.GraydonHouseBooks.com

HarperCollins Publishers
Macken House, 39/40 Mayor Street Upper,
Dublin 1, D01 C9W8, Ireland
www.HarperCollins.com

Printed in U.S.A.

To everyone who screams at the screen,
but would still trip running from the killer.

THE HOUSE GUESTS

chapter **one**

The downers started a few months after my mother forced me to watch her blow her brains out. That's abrupt, I know. But that's how it was for me too.

I didn't see the Beretta in her hand until the muzzle was shoved deep down her throat. She bought it at a pawn shop with the three hundred dollars she stole from the purse of an elderly patient at the nursing home she cleaned Monday and Thursday nights. Her fingers were always thickly calloused from the strenuous manual labor, but they were still in good enough condition to pull the trigger back. All it took was one tiny squeeze, a barely perceptible motion, and like an empire that had been doomed for decades, she fell. We'd once been connected by a tough, bloody cord filled with oxygen and nutrients, and somehow I was suddenly standing barefoot in a black-red pool of her still-warm blood, connected again, but impotent; there was no way to sustain her life as she had done for me when we were bonded in that sacred, primordial way.

The miasma of the smoky gunpowder and the metallic tang of the blood took weeks to fade away. She dedicated her last words to hurting me in only the way a mother can hurt her daughter. She first used the word *hubris* in a way that didn't make grammatical sense. But the part that resounds in my head whenever it gets too quiet, when the stars are shining their brightest, is when she said she wished she would have gone to the clinic when she had the chance. It was in no way a novel sentiment. I can't begin to compile the number of ways she shared this with me, some of them artful and ingenious, other versions crude and bare. Nothing brought my mother more pleasure than reminding me what a mistake I was, not even her vices, the ones she swallowed, snorted or shot up. She would always sling her regret as an insult, as if I had any autonomy or involvement in her decision to bring me to term and eject me into this wretched world. The ecstasy my suffering brought her rivaled the joy she took in holding me in her arms for the first time. If I had been able to accept her apathy for what it was while she was alive, maybe the cruel way she orchestrated her gory demise wouldn't have scarred me so deeply. Down past all the layers of my skin, under the muscle and the tendon, inside the bone and the marrow, deep down to my blood, poisoning the substance most essential for life.

And her gruesome final bow isn't even the worst thing she ever put me through. I was the one who had to get down on my knees and clean up the sanguinary mess—bleach first, then medical-grade antibacterial soap that burned my eyes. The police didn't send anyone with vans and plastic jumpsuits to protect their clothing wielding professional cleaning supplies. My sweat amalgamated with her blood as I scrubbed, creating this nauseating fantasia of swirls, and it dawned on me that it was the most intimate thing we'd done since I'd crawled into her hospital bed and spooned her after one of her overdoses three years ago.

Her funeral was closed casket because of how much brain matter escaped her skull, and was attended by four people. Two were a couple in their twenties who clearly had had too much to drink and stumbled out after the welcoming remarks were made. I sat stiff-backed in the front pew like a ballerina en pointe wearing a navy dress she liked. It had a Victorian-prim neckline and an equally demure just-below-the-calf hem. She'd never complimented me in it, but I could sense her fondness by how mean she was to me once when I came by her apartment with it styled with a pair of pointed pumps that were a size too small.

The other attendee was a man I'd only met forty hours before the service. He was extremely tall and sweaty and smelled faintly of mothballs and mispronounced her name during the eulogy six times. By the fifth, he stopped giving any effort into even remembering how many syllables it had.

My mother, Genevieve, an ode to her creole grandmother, was six feet tall, painfully thin and as tough as a rusted nail. Eating was never easy for her and she rarely slept. I never saw her without a lit Camel between her fingers, which were long and birdlike. When she sucked on her cigarettes, her gaunt cheeks would look so severe, it seemed like the bones would poke through her skin. She was no angel. She was more of an Eve, the last syllable of her name when mispronounced, though the downfall of the many people that can be traced back to her is actually justified. She was smarter than she ever gave herself credit for, much smarter than most, and maybe that's why she grew addicted to solitude and was repelled by the thought of engaging with people by the time she was thirty. I could say she was troubled, but that would be a bit too kind.

My temple gently knocks against the thick panel of glass supporting the weight of my foggy brain, and then I feel the weight of a hand on my thigh. For a second, I panic. I don't know where I am or what time it is. Hard, steady rain drums against the windshield, pelts the roof, makes the car rock. I blink deliberately a few times, willing my brain to recalibrate, and then slowly and all at once everything around me comes into focus. I recognize the slick, clean interior of Eli's oversized SUV, and relax at the feel of his hand on my leg, warm and strong.

"Hey, babe. Iris." He leans my way, his fingers brushing against my temple to move a chunk of curls from my cheekbone so he can see me better. "We're here."

I glance out the window, confused as to how we got here so fast. I've always loved the drama of thunderstorms, their fierce choreography in the sky. Tonight's is holding its breath, waiting. No thunder yet. Only the promise of it.

In the dark, the lake is haunting and melancholic, and I think we'll get along great. The dark water is punctuated by countless tiny ripples, each drop creating a fleeting, silvered splash. The property is much larger than I was expecting and seems to be accessible only by a single meandering road that cuts through the dense forest. From what I can see, the road is unpaved, just gravel and dirt, barely wide enough for one vehicle, flanked by dense undergrowth and tall pines and firs, their trunks thick with age like all the men in Eli's bloodline.

I squint through the downpour and make out the edges of the house. It's enormous and completely isolated. There's not a neighbor in sight or even within shouting distance. The seclusion is both tranquil and menacing. It's a moonless night, and the sky is almost pure black now that we're miles out from the city. This is a different kind of dark, much different than city dark. City dark is a soft kind of dark, a deep charcoal versus this void-like blackness. This is the kind of dark where you can't tell where the sky ends or begins, the kind of dark that makes you strain your ears.

I've always known Roman and Garrett's family was loaded, but this is even more than I expected. I sit for a moment, my breath catching as I take in what looks like a massive wrap-around deck on both levels. There's thousands of square feet, not enough to get lost in but enough to find plenty to do in. The front façade is lined with floor-to-ceiling windows, a battalion of glass that shimmers in the rain.

I try to imagine what it would have been like to grow up with relatives who had beautiful escapist homes like this to make pilgrimages to during the heady summer months, but it seems so preposterous that this sort of spontaneous aphantasia happens, and my mind goes blank. I would have settled for a balanced breakfast every morning and a ride to school so I wouldn't have had to catch three buses just to get across town.

"I fell asleep?" I ask Eli, because it seems so improbable. I need to hear him confirm it.

I've been in a bardo state of delirium for the past few months. My voice constantly sounds like I'm on day three of a disorienting December chest cold. Insomnia is amber, and I'm the arthropod frozen in its luminous resin.

On the rare night I manage to fall asleep, my rest is plagued by horrific nightmares. Sometimes my mother is there, sometimes she's not. One time I dreamt all of my friends were lined up on a roof and I was tied to a chair being forced to watch as a woman in a garish red satin ball gown blew off their heads one by one. There was another one where I was running naked down an abandoned alley with a huge open wound on my forehead, blood gushing down my face as some guy in a Lotus stopped to stare at me, but I kept running until there was nowhere else to go. I wake up most nights with balled fists, sweat pooling, my heart pounding, fighting battles in a war that can never be won.

"Only a couple minutes," Eli says, but still it's hard to believe, like I've skipped a chunk of time. Not time that would have been used in any productive manner, but all time is created equal, and that's my favorite thing about the proverbial hourglass controlling everyone's fate.

I can't even remember the last time I fell asleep on my own. Not alone—without chemical assistance. The past few weeks have been grueling, a constant battle with the relentless chaos in my head. These days even an hour of uncorrupted sleep is a gift to deeply cherish. So many nights I lie limp in bed, staring at the ceiling, or nothing, or the inside of my head, or Eli's soft expression, willing sleep to rescue me from my haywire thoughts. And every morning I am heavy with fresh disappointment and stale exhaustion. It doesn't matter how much I toss and turn, how much I try to "relax." It's like my body has forgotten how to rest.

I've tried everything. Warm milk before bed even though I find milk revolting, reading, avoiding screens, meditating, sound machines, lavender-scented pillow spray. At the height of my desperation, I was scammed by glorified placebos—healing crystals, homeopathic sleeping pills, sleep-enhancing teas, acupressure mats, detox foot pads. I kept the crystals because they're pretty, but tossed everything else after months of trying my best to delude myself into thinking they were helping. I even went to a psychic with a jarring coffee-and-cigarettes drawl, even though I know psychics are nothing more than exceptionally skilled cold readers, not actual conduits of the supernatural.

Every night I'm defeated by my own psyche. I just lie there next to Eli, blinking as my mind careens nonstop. Every day blends into the next, a never-ending, exhausting loop, my head a foggy, muddled mess. There are no edges, just one amorphous blob of time. Yesterday, I left my keys in the freezer. The other day, I forgot my department head's name during a team meeting and had to fake illness as an excuse to bolt out of the room. Last month, my boss called me into her office because I'd missed another important deadline. I tried to defend myself, reminding her of my mother's death and promising I was doing my best. At first, she seemed receptive. But then her head started to shake, and I could feel the air thickening in the room. "It's been almost a year. I'm sorry, but you need to get it together," she finally said with a sympathetic smile that seemed overperformed. I couldn't blame her.

The dizzy spells come without warning. I'd held my head for a moment, trying to steady myself, and when I'd looked up, two guys from accounting, their suits too tight, were staring at me. I had laughed it off, said something about a wild night at a bachelorette party, but their expressions told me they didn't buy it.

The rain is unrelenting, pouring without pause, no sign of stopping soon. I reach up and flick the overhead light on, the soft click filling the silence. I squint at the empty console behind the gearshift, lift the worn pocket Bible that's been wedged in the slot. But there's nothing beneath it. Eli always reads the same verses from Matthew and Philippians when he's anxious, over and over. A mantra, a prayer. Something to keep him grounded.

"Babe," I say, scanning the surface of the dashboard again. "My glasses. Where . . ."

"Haven't seen them," he says, not with an actual shrug but with one in his tone, and I'm startled by his lack of urgency. "Check your bag."

"No, I . . ." I inch up further in my seat to see if they slid behind me while I was asleep. "Why would I pack them? I put them right . . ."

I split my thighs and feel around at the space by my feet, but my hand doesn't bump into any of the glass or acetate I expect. I open the glove compartment—a little too roughly, I can tell by the way Eli flinches—and shuffle mostly useless junk around that he swears might come in handy one day. When it's obvious I've struck out again, I go back under the seat with my hands just to double-check. I look in the back, but I find nothing. I tug at my hair, wanting to pull it out, knowing there's no way we can go back for them now.

"You haven't slept in two nights," Eli reminds me, his voice a mix of concern and careful warning.

"Three," I say, correcting him with a sigh of frustration. "And what, I look it?"

He doesn't take the bait. He waits for me to meet his eyes. "Remember that time? Right after it happened, you didn't sleep for a whole week, and you—"

"What happened to never bringing that up?" I snap, and before the sound of my own voice registers, I regret losing my cool. As much as I try to control it, I always get like this when I'm sleep-deprived, but also, he swore he'd never mention this again. It's only a slight betrayal, but it feels cavernous at a time when I need him the most. Still, I remember all the times he's been more than patient with me, and I promise myself I'll do better.

"Just saying." Eli rubs my knee. "You got that prescription for a reason."

The car goes quiet and I don't know how to respond. It feels like an accusation, an attack. But it's only a fact, as basic as I have curly hair and I have wide feet.

After the incident at work, Eli talked me into seeing a doctor. I consulted a myriad of therapists who gave perfunctory evaluations, and then I moved on to taking psychiatrists on a trial run until I found one who actually listened to me, who made an effort to understand all the hues and nuances of my situation instead of broad-brushing. It only takes a few words to make someone feel human, but just one moment of silence can reduce you to a statistic or inevitability. Eli drove me to every appointment in case I wasn't in the head space to drive myself home. I was terrified of taking the pills my doctor prescribed at first. I was so anti-drug, I hadn't even swallowed a Tylenol capsule before. I knew I couldn't get addicted to acetaminophen, but even slight dependency terrified me. It still does. I refuse to take my prescription until I've gone over three days with no sleep.

"Just pop a couple so you can sleep tonight and wake up refreshed," Eli says gently, his tone soft as he does his best to weave calm into the space between us. "Yeah? Come on, we came all this way. You deserve to enjoy yourself for once."

I want to talk to Eli about my mother, but every time I recall a memory or tell a funny story, he never smiles or laughs. He tells me I was abused and neglected and asks me if I've spoken about it to my therapist yet, and then the mood is ruined. He's becoming apathetic, though he tries his best to disguise it under a veil of feigned normalcy. I snapped at him one time over something silly and called him useless, and we didn't speak for two days. I've also forgotten to meet him for dinner a couple of times when we've made plans, my mental clarity gone haywire. Even though he said it was fine after I apologized profusely, I could sense his frustration through the phone. It's like I'm only halfway here, a part of me always drifting, searching for sleep that seems to be a continent away.

I search Eli's bright hazel eyes. In the sunlight, they have specks of topaz in them. "How am I supposed to enjoy myself without you?"

"I know, babe." He reaches over the console and strokes my arm with the pad of his thumb. "Wish I could stay."

I nod and do my best to appear phlegmatic and self-possessed. I don't want him to see the truth. I don't want him to know I'm crushed, that I desperately want him to stay with me. Escort me upstairs. Hold me until he falls asleep, his arm hooked tight around my rib cage, protecting the part of me that protects my heart.

At its inception, this last-minute staycation seemed like a long overdue respite. I really wasn't keen on leaving the house at all, especially since my job had gone partly remote, but Eli convinced me that this lake in the middle of nowhere would be the perfect antidote to my unrelenting ennui. He said it was just what I needed to lift my spirits and finally carve myself out of the block of stone that has held me captive for almost a year. He said the lake house was beautiful—*chalet*, I think is what he called it.

I immediately packed my bag. It was the perfect opportunity for us to spend some quality time together with no distractions and have a chance to reconnect. Eat too much. Hold hands. Catch each other staring. Talk about nothing and everything. There were also phrases like *romantic walks along the lakefront* and *balmy nights* he'd used. I could practically smell the lake when he was done pitching it to me. I pictured us christening every room in the house over the course of the week, getting creative with it. He's been quickly moving up at his company, putting in ungodly hours to get the promotion he's had his eyes set on for months, and finally he was going to carve out time for us to spend together. It's been six years since we first got serious. I figured he was planning on proposing in front of all of his friends. Not my preference, but the answer would have been an effusive, iridescent yes. I saw the diamond on my finger. Princess cut. Imagined the weight. The sparkle. The minor inconvenience it would cause whenever I dug around in my purse. I cried thinking of how I'd cry when he said those four words, flashing his beautiful teeth, a smile twinkling in his eyes. I imagined the open layout of our future house, the laughter of our future babies.

Eli told me yesterday about the change of plans, that he'd be driving up to Boston so he can spend time with his grandmother in the hospital. Kidney failure, the second time in two years. This time it's looking worse than before, a full recovery much more unlikely. It felt too selfish to ask him to stay in New York, to bring up any of my reservations about staying at the lake without him, to make this about me when his grandmother is in a hospital bed, fighting for her life.

And it's not that I don't like his friends. Three years in a row, we picked a spot on the map and spent the week together, all seven of us crammed into suites and rentals, frolicking, partying, drinking—so much drinking—and dancing. Cancun, Whistler, then Maui. It was supposed to be an annual tradition, but last year everyone was too busy to convene, all of our schedules impossible to align even in the languorous summer months—weddings, babies, a funeral. I thought the tradition had been severed with last year's hiatus. Or maybe I'd hoped it had been until a few weeks ago, when Garrett invited us to drive up here to the lake. Eli said yes even before he relayed the invitation to me. But this is who they are, and I've learned to expect nothing more and nothing less. Eli always does everything Garrett says. He was his wide receiver in college, and the *jump, how high* dynamic has always bled into their relationship off the field.

Garrett was the quarterback in college, Eli was the MVP, but Roman was the crowd favorite. If he hadn't torn his ACL junior year, he would have been drafted in one of the early rounds, and his ego would probably be as big as his biceps. I think there's a piece of him that still hasn't recovered from the tragic and abrupt end to his dream, and I've always deeply empathized with the pain of watching his lifelong ambition being shattered in only a few seconds. One wrong pivot and it was over.

Lauren and Gia have been cheering together since they were eight. Violet tutored the guys, meaning they paid her to write their papers, but the relationship was more sister-brothers than transactional, and still she's indispensable to them even though there are no more GPAs to maintain. She was always the one to sit with me at the games and the only one who has consistently checked in on me since the funeral, her texts always thoughtful and sincere.

Even though they've all been nothing but kind and welcoming to me—the girlfriend, the outsider, the one who still fumbles over football lingo, the only one not from a two-parent household in a cushy cul-de-sac in the middle of suburbia—every time I've been around them without Eli, the feeling of wearing someone else's shoes suffocates me. They don't quite fit. We've all kept in contact since graduation and are only spread out across the tri-state area. But I still don't know any of them outside the context of Eli. Sometimes,

I'm not even sure if I know *myself* outside the context of Eli anymore.

"I would take some," I say about the pills, my tone glaringly noncommittal even to my own ears, "but I didn't bring any with me."

"I packed them for you," Eli says so flatly, I'm too stunned to respond.

He reaches into his back pocket and hands me a silver key on a small metal ring. I stare at it, confused and still a little speechless. It's the key to the house; I can figure that much with my scrambled brain, but I thought he'd carry my bag in, and I'm still trying to figure out why he packed my medication when I didn't ask him to.

I purposefully left them behind, figuring if I could get sleep anywhere, it would be in a place that gets darker than my moods. Have I been that awful lately? What is he trying to say? I've been going to therapy twice a week for the last month instead of my usual once, preparing for next week, the one-year anniversary of my mother's death.

I watch as Eli reaches into the back seat for my bags, my thoughts crashing into each other like tectonic plates. Against my own will, I think of the deer. I see her slack face, her wide eyes. And then all the blood.

I see my mother's blood, the brain matter slithering down the wall.

chapter
two

I can still see everything from that night, the one Eli swore he would never speak of again. I can hear the shrill sound of my tires screeching, the deafening thud of the impact. I can smell the cool night air, almost taste it. I hadn't been going that fast, only ten over the speed limit, but it was late and dark and I'd been nodding off the whole day.

    By the time I stumbled out of my car and ran around to the front, the doe was splayed on the ground like a spilled shadow, her delicate legs bent in all the wrong directions. Blood gushed out as she heaved with shallow, desperate breaths. I rushed to her side, dropping to my knees instinctively, tears welling in my eyes. I tried to pump her chest, tried to do whatever I could to resuscitate her. I barely remember any of it, the feral sounds she made, the ones I made, just my hands trembling like the heart of a captive bird and covered in the cruelest red. I screamed at her, for her, begging her to stay alive. The words ripped from my throat and left my throat raw. But it was no use. She just stared up at me with huge, glassy eyes, blood pooling beneath her limp body.

I stayed on the ground until Eli pulled over on the side of the road. I told him to bring towels, but he forgot. He said I'd scared him and he'd run out of the apartment and jumped straight into his car. My clothes were soaked all the way through, tears still falling down my face when he crouched down to get a good look at me. He pried me away from her still body, then helped me up to my feet. I looked at her one last time, her eyes still open and petrified.

Just like my mother's were.

The most haunting déjà vu.

The whole ordeal sent me into a spiral for weeks. The guilt capsized the little sleep I'd been getting during pockets of the day—never at night—and it feels like I've been sinking ever since. The image of that sweet doe wouldn't leave me. It was like every time I remembered her eyes, they got sadder and sadder. I just couldn't stop thinking about a helpless dappled fawn or two somewhere near, waiting for a mother who would never come home. My heart broke at the thought of the additional pain and suffering my recklessness could have inflicted. I kept myself medicated for an entire week, swallowing a couple of pills every few hours or so. It was the only way to macerate the images in my head, haunting me, suffocating me.

"Sure you'll be okay by yourself?" I ask Eli, secretly hoping he tells me that actually, he needs me by his side. "I can go with you to the hospital and—"

"Babe, don't worry. I'm good. You need this. I want you to enjoy yourself, get some rest." Eli gives me another smile, his teeth stark white against the night, and the whole world seems to light up for a moment.

I swear, I must have fallen in love with him during one of those smiles. I force one back, wondering how I got so lucky. He helped me through the darkest time in my life with undying patience. He cried with me, cooked for me, held me, took care of me better than my mother ever did. He was there for me when I was at my worst, and he's still thinking of me, putting me first.

I reach over and run a hand over his soft hair turning slick in the humidity. "It's okay if you're not, you know."

Eli nods and reminds me that he has the care package I prepped, that he'll give it to his grandmother once she's up. I take the key from his hand, though a part of me can't help feeling like I should be there with my presence, not just sending along baked goods and a card.

If I'm honest, it stings a little that he doesn't want me close during this crisis. I could help. I *want* to help, to feel significant to him in this way. It's one thing for someone to be there for you, another for them to allow you to be there for them. His capacity of truly caring for other people, of selflessness, is one of the reasons I fell so hard for him. His love for his family is unrelenting. Biblical. To him, family is not just kin; it is an altar he worships at with the utmost piety. I've seen the depths of his devotion. They are more of a tribe than a unit, and I was hoping I was getting closer to being initiated. As much as I admire his dedication to his grandmother, it only leaves me wondering where I fit in. All these years, all these sacrifices, and I still have no ring on my finger.

Every time I gently try to broach the topic of marriage, he conveniently avoids it, spiraling into a sermon about the institution itself, turning a simple question into a philosophical debate. He dissects marriage as a concept, never once letting the conversation brush against the reality of us. Of what it would mean for him to ask, or for me to say yes. His epistolary ruminations are a temporary reprieve, but the hollow, bottomless yearning always returns in the quietest moments, haunting me while we're in bed, Eli inches away deep in repose, dreaming while I fester. Wondering if my heart will always be the one that beats harder, that gives more, that breaks first.

Eli tilts his face, his eyes shutting as his lips press into mine. I kiss him, thinking he's going to draw back right away, but he opens my mouth with his, slowly. Purposefully. All the tension inside me drains away in an instant.

We both pull away at the same moment, startled. Like a faucet being twisted, the rain shuts off. I take it as a good omen. I may be running on empty and without my glasses, but this will be a good week full of rest and relaxation even if Eli is hundreds of miles away. He passes me my bag from the back, and I close the door. Immediately it feels like I've stepped into an overactive sauna. The heat in the city was stifling, but out here it's wet and thick, the humidity like a wall.

As Eli turns his car around, I glance at the water and take in the woodland. The isolation. The quiet. It won't last long. Not once the others arrive and get a few drinks in. Eli is convinced that Garrett and Lauren have calmed down a notch since having their two-year-old. I doubt it. Something happens when the six of them get together. All inhibitions fly out the window. When Eli's with them, a completely different side of him comes out, one I never see when it's just us. Violet is a riot, and Roman is down for anything. Gia is always trying to prove she's cooler than everyone, and there's no dare Lauren won't take to get Garrett to drool over her recklessness.

Ready to head back down the road, Eli slides his window down.

"Give your grandma a kiss for me when you get there, okay?" I say, shouldering my duffel.

"I'll call you as soon as I check up on her."

"Love you."

"Love you."

I blow him a kiss with my hand, and he makes a show of returning it.

When I step into the house, a faintly stale smell lingers in the air, making me wonder how long this Uncle Nolan has been gone, if this isn't his primary residence and he has another home somewhere closer to civilization. The entryway is lined with large boots and jogging sneakers. I fumble around for the lights, everything dark and out of focus. I manage to find a set of switches that make a few recessed lights in the ceiling flicker to life. The large open room slowly reveals itself.

The furniture is all dark, heavy wood, just like the floors. The monochromatic palette makes the room feel both intimate and oppressive. A dog-eared book lies face down on the coffee table next to a mug, stained with old remnants from lattes and espressos. A small craftsman table and a pair of mismatched chairs frame the panoramic view of the lake. A deck of cards and a wooden chess set are stacked on top, and knowing Eli's friends, both will be put to good use, though only if the stakes involve nudity and wild dares.

I head to the other side of the room and flick on another light just beside the massive stone fireplace. The head of an enormous buck mounted above the mantel comes into focus, and I lurch back, a scream caught in my throat. I force myself to exhale, to stay calm. It's dead. The deer is dead. But it looks so alive, the eyes shiny and lifelike. I stare at it, the humongous antlers, doing my best to avoid the eyes. It looks nothing like the doe I hit, but just as close to life. When I squint, I see a few small stains marring its dull fur, dark blotches that look like patches of dried blood. I quickly flick the light back off, then the others, and pad toward the stairs.

The old oak floors creak and groan beneath my feet like a grizzled elderly man. Climbing up the stairs feels like moving through sludge, my head starting to pound from the minor exertion because of my lack of sleep. My equilibrium almost sends me back down the stairs mid-ascent, but I catch my balance at the last second and grip the banister with a tight fist to make it to the top. As I turn at the landing, I miscalculate, and my shoulder crashes into an edge of the wood-paneled wall. A sharp pang boomerangs down to my fingertips and back up my shoulder, but I grit my teeth and push through it, rubbing the sore spot with my fingers as I drag myself down the hall.

There are four bedrooms on the upper level, the biggest one sitting at the back, slightly removed from the others. I leave the primary suite for Garrett and Lauren and push inside the one farthest from the stairs, hoping it'll be a quiet alcove. I click on the bedside lamp and sink onto one of the twin beds. Apart from a large dresser topped with a few books and random knickknacks, there isn't much going on. Inside the closet there are a few plaid shirts hanging, untouched and collecting dust. I toss my bag onto the other bed, hoping Violet and Gia share a room so I can have this one to myself.

I slip out of my shoes, pull off my top, step out of my shorts and climb under the floral sheets, a groan escaping my mouth as the mattress conforms to my vertebrae. A small mechanical clock on the nightstand ticks with every second, the sound so loud in the silence, at first I think I'm imagining it. I cut the light off and ease my heavy lids over my eyes, willing myself to drift off.

I was born and raised deep in the lights and pulse of the city. This kind of quiet is overwhelming. It's more of a hush than silence; it has a heaviness to it, a presence. I'm hoping it lulls me to sleep. As I turn on my side, my mind drifts to Eli. I know I shouldn't, but I can't stop thinking of how much better this would be if he was here. Having this entire house all to ourselves for the week. Lazy morning swims on the lake. Slow, sunlit boat rides. Good bad food on the deck. Enjoying each other's quiet, no distractions. Time to reflect, reminisce, fall in love again.

chapter
three

Two hours later, I lie still, my body heavy with exhaustion, more awake now than when my back first hit the mattress. I'm in the same position, arms folded over my rib cage like a corpse, eyes locked on the dark ceiling but seeing nothing. I let out a long sigh of defeat, then climb out of the bed. I shuffle through my duffel until I find the plastic baggie of round white pills Eli stuffed into one of the side pockets.

When he mentioned them, I felt affronted. It seemed like such an undignified thing to do, to remind me that I'm now dependent on a synthetic substance to regulate my nervous system just to be able to perform the most basic human function. But now that I see the little pills, I'm relieved he had the forethought. He knows me better than I know myself, and I'm undecided on whether that's indicative of a sensitivity in him or a flaw in me.

I don't bother getting dressed before I head down to the first level for water. I take slow, measured steps in the dark, keeping a palm against the wall to steady me down the hall. Somehow, even with my hand on the banister, I manage to miss the last step and end up a crumpled mess at the bottom landing. I don't feel the searing pain in my knee until I'm back on my feet. It's hard to put all of my weight on my leg, so I limp as I feel my way into the kitchen. There is no view of the lake from this side of the house, though the large windows continue to allow the outside in.

For a moment, the remoteness gets to me. I'm glad to be away from the noise of the city, but my fall could have been worse. If I'd fallen from the top step, I might have broken bones. I could have gotten myself fully incapacitated with my clumsiness or even knocked unconscious, leaking blood, no one around to hear my scream for help.

The kitchen is small but functional. I don't bother figuring out where the lights are. I open a few cabinets until I slip a hand in one and make contact with a collection of mismatched enamelware crammed into one of the lower shelves, along with a stack of tumblers. I turn on the faucet, but the nozzle's missing entirely, leaving only a rusty thread where it should be. The water pours out in a steady stream, thick and sluggish, tumbling down in a wide, slow cascade. I fill my glass and toss two pills into my mouth.

I suck in a deep breath after I swallow, shutting my eyes for a second. A wave of exhaustion rolls through me, but I keep them shut and try to envision myself sleeping in a heavenly place like my therapist recommends. I picture myself lying in a grassy field beneath a night sky filled with stars; a colorful garden in full bloom, monarch butterflies fluttering around, the heady scent of wild jasmine enveloping me; cozying up in front of a crackling fire, Eli rubbing my feet, his features glowing in incandescent light. Just as it seems to be working, the thoughts in my head quieting to a whisper, the hum of a car engine jolts me out of my brief daze.

It sounds large, like a truck of some sort, and shuts off with a sputtering sigh. My body goes still, my bare feet anchored to the tiled floor. No one else is supposed to be arriving tonight. We'd all agreed to arrive tomorrow; Eli only decided last-minute to drop me over here tonight since it was on the way up to Boston.

I whip my head in the direction of the front door even though a wall stands between us, the muscles in my body fully alert again. I strain against the dark for any more sounds, voices, footsteps. Somewhere close by I hear the gentle click of a car door being shut.

I scurry down the narrow hall and cross into the living room as quietly as I can, but it's empty. The front door is shut. I inch deeper into the space and make sure I locked it behind myself. I did. I whip around and peer through the large windows. The lake looks the same, but now a white pickup sits parked out front, its monstrous off-road tires covered in muddy sludge from the rain.

Someone else is here.

None of Eli's friends drive a pickup. They're all coming together in Garrett's Jeep.

I back away from the windows and rack my brain, trying to remember where I put my phone. I can't remember carrying it upstairs, pulling it out of my bag or setting it next to me on the nightstand. I run through every action I took since I stepped inside the house, and as soon as I get to when I kicked my sneakers off, a dull thump breaks the quiet.

The sound isn't familiar. I can't place it.

Another thump.

I freeze, holding my breath until a soft scraping sound follows. I lean forward, straining my ears to figure out where the sound is coming from. It sounds too faint to be coming from inside the house.

Just as I start toward the staircase to find my phone, the noise stops.

I do too. I turn around, just in case.

But I don't see anyone.

I listen as hard as I can. A beat passes, and then it starts again—steady now. A hollow, menacing rhythm that eclipses the noise of the dead silence out this way.

Thump, scrape. Thump, scrape.

It's coming from outside.

In the back.

I creep toward the eerie sounds, staying close to the walls and taking the turns as quietly as I can, but the old floorboards creak beneath my feet. The thumping grows louder as I inch toward the back, and I know I'm getting warmer, but my blood is getting colder. My hands tremble as I slip inside the room off the kitchen, a second living space anchored by what sort of looks like a fireplace and pool table. Large sliding glass doors with an unobstructed view of the pines span the wall. I inch closer, squinting through the darkness, but without my glasses everything is a blur, a fuzzy haze of abstract shapes and shadows.

I make sure most of my body is hidden by the wall and wince as I lean just enough to peek through the glass. As soon as my gaze settles on the only source of movement, I jump back. A silhouette of a man materializes outside.

My breath catches in my throat. My eyes strain as I try to make out the details of him. He's obscured by the dark, but I make out a pair of rugged, thick-soled boots and a tactical jacket, the hood flipped up. With his back to me, he picks up a large shovel about ten yards away from the outer edge of the deck. I've been on the sidelines so often that I can gauge distances with my eyes within an inch or two, but without my glasses, my depth perception is skewed. I've never met Garrett and Roman's Uncle Nolan; I have no clue what he looks like.

I take a few backward steps away from the glass, my legs moving on their own as I watch him build a pile of dirt next to him. It looks strenuous, but he's clearly determined.

My mind spins, immediately jumping to the worst. There's only one reason people dig holes: to bury something.

I shake my head and force myself to think more rationally. It could be something much more mundane. There could be a perfectly valid reason someone would be digging a hole in the dark, late at night.

But I can't think of one.

I keep my body in the shadows as best as I can, my eyes locked onto his every movement. The pile of dirt grows bit by bit, first a few inches, then a foot. He keeps going like this until he's exhausted. He straightens out, planting the shovel in the ground and taking a moment to catch his breath. I can't make out much about him other than his height—just above six feet. And then I notice something on his jacket.

I ease in front of the doors, my breath fogging up the spotless glass so I can get a better view of something dark on his left side. His arms are akimbo as he paces. His head is down and obscured by his hood. When he switches directions, I get a front view of his jacket again. A splattering of something dark. A stain that follows no pattern. Could be mud. Could be blood.

I swallow and continue to watch him, waiting for his next move.

He clicks on a flashlight and waves it down at the beginning of a pretty shallow hole. Definitely not deep enough to fit a body inside. I release a breath and keep watching, but his light doesn't help me much. I still can't make out anything that could identify him. Just as I start to take another breath, thinking that maybe he's finished, the man pauses, the shovel hovering in the air again, and for a moment, everything is still.

Then, as if sensing me, he turns, slowly.

I slide my back against the nearest wall as fast as I can, hard enough to knock the wind out of my pipes. My pulse rattles in my ears. I hold perfectly still, hoping he can't see me. I shut my eyes, count to ten, then try for twenty, but all I can see is red.

The deep, black-red of the blood spatter all over his clothes.

It *was* blood. It had to be.

I jump when I hear a sound, repetitive and rhythmic. But it's not the shovel scraping up the soil. I peek out and see that it's the sound of heavy footsteps. He's closer now. Heading for the doors. Heading for me.

I crouch down and duck-walk until I'm behind the sofa, the unofficial border between the rec space and the kitchen. I hold my breath and flatten out to a prone position, the lactic acid quickly building up in my biceps. But I move too fast. My head feels like it weighs more than a T. rex and spins.

And then I remember the pills.

They're starting to take reign, liquifying my insides.

Click.

The door opens.

Click.

It shuts.

My heart thumps as he crosses the room, the staccato of his boots like a stampede, every step louder than the one before. The faucet in the kitchen runs. I peek above the edge of the couch, just one eye. His back is to me as he holds a glass under the rushing tap, breathing heavily in gasps and swallows.

Before I lose my chance, I push through the sedation weighing me down and bolt from the room, my soles barely making a sound on the floor. I scurry through the unfamiliar, unlit house, searching for a hiding place. I stay on the balls of my feet as I creep to the end of the narrow hall. The floorboards in the kitchen creak under the man's weight as he moves around the room . . . pacing, maybe?

I glance toward the living room on my left, then the stairs on my right, and notice something I hadn't before.

Beneath the stairs, there's a small door.

It's a closet crammed with cleaning supplies and musty old coats. I slip inside, closing the door with a soft click, trying desperately not to make a sound as I shift things out of the way so I can sit. I press my back against the wall, trying to calm my racing heart. It doesn't take long before I feel my eyes getting heavy, everything muting to a low-frequency hum. My limbs feel heavier as a contrived weakness settles into my body.

Just as I give in to the buzzing warmth and let my head fall back against the wall too, my eyes pop open in panic. I left my glass of water on the counter. The man might see it. He'll know I'm in the house. He'll come looking for me.

I push myself up to an elbow. Maybe there's a lock on this door.

But I can't get up to my knees.

The fatigue pulls me down like an anchor. I close my eyes and hear his boots on the hardwood again.

Getting louder.

Closer.

chapter
four

I jerk awake with a gasp, and a dull throb pulses in my temples as I blink myself back into consciousness. I rub my eyes and see the culprit. Lurid, morning rays bleed through the crack under the door. The hard wood presses against my hip, unforgiving. I unfurl my body, my legs stiff and cramped from being in the fetal position for so long. I pull myself up from the floor, and my head crashes into the ceiling. I cry out in befuddlement, and then I remember.

I fell asleep in the closet under the staircase. I'm not home. I'm miles and miles upstate, far away from the city. There's a lake and a ton of trees, and Eli's friends are on their way to the house.

I inch the closet door open and peek through the crack. It seems impossible that the sun is out already, that I've slept here, on the floor, for the entire night.

Gone are the halcyon days when getting a full night's sleep was my designated prophylactic, an infallible method to waking up well-rested and ready for life, for love, for loving life. The only thing I ever feel on waking is relief from the agony my mind has put me through for hours and hours, glad it's over but still not ready for the day, stuck in a purgatory that's not death but is far from living.

I try to remember how I got here, but my mind is a blur, clouded by the soft pounding in my temples. I wait a few moments before stepping out into the hall, the house completely still and silent. When I grip the banister of the staircase, I almost jump out of my skin.

Another mounted corpse.

This time it's a taxidermy brown bear that hangs over the threshold to the hall that leads to the kitchen in the back. Part of me wants to run and call Eli to come take me back to Brooklyn, but the other part of me can't look away from the preserved cadaver's grotesque beauty, its large, jagged fangs on full display. I try to imagine the type of man who would hunt for his own entertainment or to bolster his precious ego. Who would so proudly showcase death and destruction in this way and feel no indiscretion or penitence. Who would be so unnecessarily cruel and nonchalant about setting traps for such majestic beasts. I think of the doe again, of how, for days afterward, I lay in bed consumed by guilt, and simply can't understand how someone can be so detached from life that it would feel appropriate to decapitate your bloodied prey and nail it onto the wall as decoration, a macabre souvenir.

I edge into the living room just enough to peer through the windows. The sun looks hot and dangerous already. My mother hated the sun. Blackout curtains covered every window in our house, and they remained drawn from sunrise to sunset. We didn't own any lamps. There was no light in our quiet little world. I didn't know any better until my roommate in college came home after lunch and asked me if

I was okay, did someone set up a camera or something, as she furiously opened the blinds and peered left to right, looking for a predator.

The lake is twice the size I estimated in the dark. The line of the farthest shore is so faint, I can't be sure that it even exists. The water is a vivid, cerulean blue, so lustrous it seems unreal. A light breeze creates the most gentle ripples on the surface. I wonder how warm the water is, then fantasize about a slow nude swim before the others arrive.

I head upstairs, and as I make my way to the top, a faint throbbing comes alive in my knee. Then I remember my tumble last night. I pause on the stairs and try to remember everything else that happened, but there's only bits and pieces I can recall. They return to me in distorted flashes. Climbing in Eli's SUV with my packed bags. Eli shaking me awake. Kissing him goodbye. Watching him drive off. Getting in bed. A drink of water. Then a hole . . . some kind of hole.

None of it really amounts to much. This is why I'm so conservative with the benzos. This happens every time.

Everything I pass on the way looks different from what I expected, now that it's all bathed in the bright daylight. Bigger. Older. The bedroom I find my duffel in looks more lived-in than I thought. There's a shabby white-painted bookshelf along the wall stuffed with an assortment of travel and fishing books, old board games and old fishing lures, bright golden light streaming in from the east-facing windows, which have an unobstructed view of the Catskills.

I grab my electric toothbrush from my duffel bag and try a few doors in the hall, forgetting which leads to what, and finally push into the bathroom. The mirror is covered in a light veil of hair and dust. A cluttering of old, half-empty bottles of amoxicillin, lisinopril and metformin line the pink-tile countertop. I turn on the tap, which sputters to life in sections, then brush my teeth. I rack my brain, trying to recall what happened leading up to me crashing in the closet, and when I do, I almost choke on the fluoride swishing around my mouth.

I drop my toothbrush and cling to the images in my head. Dirt. Out back. Blood. Rain and dirt. A man. His jacket covered in blood. A shovel in his hand.

The aggressive humming from my toothbrush's motor rips me from my train of thought. I click it off and do a sloppy job of rinsing before running into the room for my glasses. I scan the top of the nightstand. It's empty except for a silver lamp. I scan the other surfaces in the room, then frantically empty my bag, panic twisting deeper and deeper until I remember the last part.

I left them at home.

I hurry to the window, which has a partial view of the lake, but more importantly, a view of the gravel leading up to the house and the designated parking area. Both are empty. No white pickup truck.

He's gone.

Relieved I'm alone, I move back over to the bed and grab my phone. Eli didn't text me last night confirming he made it to his mother's house and still hasn't let me know how his grandmother's doing. He was supposed to let me know as soon as he got there. I call him, and he picks up on the second ring as if he's been waiting for me to call.

"Babe," I say, flipping through the contents of my bag again, spread out on the mattress. "I still can't find my glasses."

"Good morning to you too."

"Sorry. I'm just freaking out. I think I forgot them."

"You checked the inside pockets?"

I grab my duffel and unzip both pockets in the lining. They're empty. I wish I never came here. I shouldn't have let Eli talk me into staying here without him.

"They're not there," I tell him. "My eyes are hurting. Getting a headache."

"Did you sleep?"

I give up and slump back onto the bed. "Yeah. Took the benzos. How's your grandma?"

"Stable but unresponsive," he says, and with everything in me, I wish I could hold him and rock the trepidation out of his voice.

I clamp my eyes shut and for a moment forget about the man in the rain with the shovel. The blood I saw on his jacket. The hole he was digging. The complete isolation of this house. I want to tell Eli everything, beg him to come get me, but I can't. If I called him away from his grandmother and this was his last chance to spend time with her, I'd never forgive myself. I forget it all and pray his grandmother makes a full recovery. I don't know if our relationship could handle another loss so soon. He has been solid as a boulder throughout my turmoil, but this could be what breaks him.

"Are you there now?" I ask, breaking the silence.

"Yeah, my mom just got here." He sounds distracted for a second, then comes back on the line and asks if he can call me back later. I tell him I love him and end the call. Then it all rushes back like a tsunami.

I slip my feet into my sneakers and hurry down the stairs. On the way out the back, I notice the two empty glasses on the counter. One highball and one tumbler, a couple feet apart. My heart pounds at the sight, and I wonder if the man put two and two together. If he came looking for me after I passed out under the stairs.

The air is balmy and smells faintly of petrichor. My favorite smell in the world aside from the inside of Eli's work shirts. Dew glistens on the grass and the short, round bushes that rim the perimeter of the property, but I don't take time to revel in their poetry. I head past the grass to the dirt patch just before the forest, where I saw that man digging.

I'm shocked by how flat the area is. It looks like no one was back here at all. My head feels heavier and heavier atop my neck as I fail to find the hole, something, any indication of the hole that was dug up last night. There's no line of demarcation, even when I strain my eyes. I start to step away when I notice it, a patch covered with soil that's a slightly different hue of dark brown than the rest. I squat close to the ground and touch it, then the darker part next to it. The lighter patch isn't soaked through like the rest, as if it was dug up from deeper in the ground and put back on top.

My head jerks toward the front of the house as heavy-duty tires ease down the gravel path. I slowly move back to my feet, my heart pounding in my chest.

It isn't him. It isn't the man who was here last night.

Eli's friends are here, their voices loud even from inside the car. I take a steadying breath and brush my palms on my shorts, wishing Eli was here. He's less than a couple hundred miles away, but it feels like thousands.

I slip inside the house through the back door, overlapping voices filling multiple rooms as I make my way to the front. I step into the main room wishing I'd had the chance to shower before they got here, but no one notices me, too busy looking around and chatting among themselves.

"Holy shit," Violet says, chin up as she takes in the height of the ceilings, which are at least thirteen feet high. "This place is sick."

She wanders aimlessly as she takes it all in—the huge fireplace, the deer on the wall, then finally the breathtaking lakefront view. The last time I saw her, she'd shaved off all her hair and dyed it hot pink as it grew out. Before that, her hair had always been down her back in silky black waves. Now it's white-blonde with the roots grown out.

Garrett shoots her a grin, letting his duffel drop to the floor. "Wait till you see the hot tub in the back."

I didn't even notice a hot tub.

He looks the same as the last time I saw him, which was right after he'd become a dad, only he has more stubble on his face now. It suits him, gives him this rugged, all-grown-up edge. He's in a white T-shirt and cargos, all of his tattoos on display. He towers over Lauren, who's five-ten and just as svelte. They both seem to only be getting hotter with age.

"Are you serious?" Lauren scoffs, carrying nothing but her phone and a monochromatic Chanel bucket hat as her Hermès slides flip obnoxiously with each step. "We're literally in the middle of nowhere. No room service. No bottle service."

"At least you're serving cunt," Gia says, coming in behind her, and they cackle together.

She's wearing the kind of Levis cutoffs that make you look like you have a wedgie. I can see the smile lines under her ass and a hint of nipple through her tiny white crop top. She looks gorgeous, her features a perfect amalgamation of her parents, her mother German and her father Jamaican.

"You're such a snob," Violet says, rolling her eyes, the only one who ever calls Lauren out on anything.

Sometimes I admire her ballsy barbs. Other times I hope I'm never on the receiving end.

"Is that supposed to be an insult?" Lauren shoots back, and when she turns to the side, I see that she's thinner than she was even before the baby. Clearly she's been glued to her Peloton.

"Geez, you two are at it already?" Roman says before Violet can get a rebuttal out, strutting in through the front carrying a crate of beer.

A lot of men as tall as him have a habit of walking a little bent over, as though permanently worried they might bump their heads. But not Roman. He walks with a straight back, deliberate languid steps like he enjoys being ogled, sized up. He commands the space around him and is the first to notice me. But Gia cuts him off before he gets a word out.

"Hey, how'd you beat us inside?" she asks, looking me over, and I hate myself for not at least changing into fresh clothes.

I can't help but feel insecure with my bare face on display. It's been months since I've done more than SPF and lip salve, and without Eli here, there's no one to impress. But I can't help but feel a sour wave of inferiority engulf me in the presence of their poreless complexions, glowy cheekbones and overlined lips. I wish I had at least stained my lips and dabbed some concealer under my eyes to cover up the dark circles that have practically taken root.

"She didn't ride with us, birdbrain," Violet says, answering for me before I can respond.

Gia looks me over again, then cocks her head, a light bulb going off. "Oh."

I give her a small smile, but inside I can feel my anxiety settle into my limbs, knotting up in the pit of my stomach.

Gia and Lauren come off as harmless sweethearts with their bleached-white smiles, but really they're ruthless, more competitive than any football player they have ever cheered for. They exchanged tiny vials of blood with each other in middle school that they apparently got put into matching rings so they could be connected by blood like sisters, yet Gia is always quick to point out that she *doesn't get girls*. She also has a habit of saying everything in the form of a question.

"Hey, Iris. You good?" Violet asks, leaning in to hug me. Her eyes linger on mine as she pulls back.

"Yeah," I say, as Garrett adjusts the thermostat on the wall, dropping the temperature a few notches. "Eli dropped me off last night."

"Last night?" Garrett asks, coming my way now, Lauren on his heels. "Thought he was gonna drop you off this morning."

I take him in again—his three-hundred-dollar haircut, skin with a brownish glow almost as dark as mine. "He wanted to get to Boston late last night so he could be at the hospital when visiting hours started this morning." I pause. Then, because he doesn't respond, I say, "Hope it's cool."

"No, it's cool," he says, giving me a big smile. "Hope you're ready to party for the next seven days."

Before I conjure up enough enthusiasm to feign excitement, Roman catches my eye, narrowing the gap between us with languorous steps.

"Hey, Iris," he says in his husky voice, and flashes me his lopsided smile.

"Hey, Roman." I smile back.

The different hues remind me of the lighter patch of soil in the backyard.

There's a beat between us, his gaze lingering on mine. I expect him to say something, but he never does.

"Okay, I know what's different now," Gia says as if she's made a significant discovery, her eyes moving up and down my frame as she pushes him out of the way. "You look way sluttier without your glasses. Almost unrecognizable."

The way she's staring at me, it's clear she's expecting me to take that as a compliment, and while I don't take offense, I remember exactly why I didn't want to be here without Eli. When he's around, she's slightly less patronizing. It took a while for me to see past her sharp edges, beyond the snarky comments always disguised as sarcasm, but now I know her bitterness and hostility aren't personal.

We were all having poke and shaved ice our first night in Maui and she referred to her absentee millionaire accountant father as her "sponsor," and I instantly felt bad for her. After that, I saw past her venom and vitriol and made excuses for her petty jabs, backhanded compliments and all-around bitchiness.

"Uh-oh," Garrett says, playfully lifting a brow. "Wearing contacts now?"

"I can't. My astigmatism is too severe for—"

"Come on," Lauren says to Garrett, tugging on his hand with both of hers. "I want to see our room and *unpack*."

She looks up to Garrett, biting the corner of her lip, and it's obvious by the way she emphasized *unpack* with a little body roll that it's code for *undress*.

Lauren had been the kind of pregnant that you could only verify from the side. She did Pilates until late in her third trimester, but I think it was mostly the muscle memory from being athletic since she was a child that helped her get so slim so quickly. From what I've seen on her Instagram feed, her shift into motherhood has been effortless, but I know it must be hard finding alone time with a curious toddler painting the walls while you brush your teeth and dedicating the majority of their days to finding the most creative ways to die as soon as you turn your back.

"Hold on," Garrett tells her, and she pouts, but he gently removes her hands and turns to address everyone else. "Couple of house rules. Rule number one: No one is allowed to be fully sober at any point from now until Sunday morning. Rule number two: Anyone who brings down the vibe is subject to cruel and unusual punishment."

Everyone hoots and cheers, and I fight to not roll my eyes as I relinquish the last bit of hope I was clinging to that maybe they've all matured past the days of drinking themselves into twenty-four-hour comas in the name of having a good time. It's like they've instantly regressed back to when we were freshly legal with no responsibilities and undeveloped prefrontal cortexes. I was crossing my fingers, thinking maybe Eli was right, that things would be different now that Garrett and Lauren are parents and we all have respectable careers. Well, except for Gia. Her idea of a career is using men like her father to get what she wants, and to her credit, she's gotten pretty far with it. She's petite and fit and generally appealing in the way that men think all women should be—sweet, bouncy, elastic. It only makes sense that she uses what she's got to get what she wants. I've seen her in action. Every interaction she has with a man is a transaction, a carefully orchestrated performance. The gold Rolex and Cartier Love bracelet on her wrist were gifts from the one who has a helipad in the back of his property.

"By the way," Gia says to Violet, her voice suddenly sturdy with conviction. "*Birds* are smart. I saw a crow put a nut in the middle of the road once, wait for a car to run it over, then go back for it and voilà. A perfectly cracked nut."

Violet waves Gia off, then whips out her phone and snaps photos of the water. I watch Garrett and Lauren as they head up the stairs. He can't even keep his hands to himself until we're all out of view.

I catch up with them at the landing. "You said we have this place to ourselves, right?" I ask, thinking back to last night, still unsure of exactly what happened, what I saw, my memories still fuzzy around the edges.

I remember watching a man digging a hole. I remember him coming into the house for water, but everything after that I can't be certain of. The details are hazy, slipping away from me like sand through my fingers.

Garrett glances back at me. "Yup. All week."

I watch them turn the corner, then slip to the back of the house and peer out at the forest. This time I notice the large hot tub that could probably fit all of us comfortably, but my eyes don't linger there. I shift my gaze back to that lighter patch of soil. I think of the doe, of how out of it I was that night. I'd zoned out for a minute behind the wheel, maybe more. It felt like I was driving on a clear coast, nothing ahead but open road and an endless horizon stretching out before me until I slammed straight into her.

If it weren't for the mismatched patch of soil, I would chalk the man up to a figment of my imagination courtesy of my medication. But I know what I saw last night. I just need to know what he buried.

chapter
five

I push inside the bedroom I'm staying in and check my texts to see if there's an update from Eli. He's sent a bunch of messages. I scroll through them, and as I respond to one, out of the corner of my eye I notice my bag of pills right in the center of the bed for anyone to see. I reach for them, but before I get a chance to tuck them under my pillow, Violet's voice slithers from behind me.

"So . . ."

I whip around, shocked that she was able to slink inside the room behind me without me sensing her. The front of her T-shirt says *Drink Coffee, Tickle Pussies*.

"Eli's cool with us sleeping together?" she asks, teasing me.

I smile without showing my teeth, playing along because I know her flirting is only to get me to blush. "He trusts me."

"Well, it's not you he should be worried about," she whispers, glancing down at my hand. Her expression changes, a gleam of excitement flashing in her eyes when they lock back onto mine. "Oh, you're trying to party for real, for real."

She takes the baggie and lifts it to inspect the pills.

I snatch them back, a little too forcefully.

"Those are for sleep," I say, feeling heat cover my face.

"Okay, okay. Wanna help me bring in the rest of the stuff? Roman's moving the boat, and you know Gia doesn't lift anything over three pounds because she's afraid she'll get 'bulky biceps.'"

I'd rather not haul a bunch of heavy stuff, just like I'd rather she share one of the other rooms with Gia, but I also don't know how to tell Violet no, so I follow her downstairs.

When we step outside, Roman is in the Rubicon they all arrived in and is skillfully backing the boat to the edge of the dock with one hand on the steering wheel. When he climbs out, his shoulder-length hair sways in the gentle breeze, framing his face like a wild, untamed mane. He has the kind of intelligence that makes him the funniest guy in every room, very alpha nerd, always smells like soap and makes crispy empanadas that melt in your mouth and transport you across borders, oceans, longitudes and latitudes.

Violet and I work up a decent sweat as we carry all the boxes and bags of groceries into the kitchen. I set down the extra bottles of Hendrick's and Jack Daniel's with a groan, practically expecting my underused muscles to explode.

"Can't wait to get in the water," Gia says, digging around in one of the bags as soon as Violet sets it down.

"Oh, I'm going to *live* in that water for the next seven days," Violet says, which is unsurprising since she was a competitive swimmer until she graduated college.

Gia pushes more groceries around, then finally settles on string cheese. As soon as she gets one of the individual packs open, Lauren slithers into the room, a self-satisfied smile on her lips. Her hair is normally a darker shade of brown, but the summer has given her some natural highlights. I've barely soaked up any sun this year.

"Well, that was fast," Gia says, pumping the stalk of mozzarella in her mouth, toward her throat.

"I have it down to a science," Lauren says, hoisting herself up onto the edge of the peninsula.

"Guess I should have paid more attention in biology."

Lauren shrugs. "I could give three-hour lectures. Anti-evolution 101: How to not procreate and keep your husband happy."

"You still don't think you want another baby?" Gia asks, seeming appalled at this revelation.

"Two is enough. The little one is always biting me, screaming at me or throwing food in my face. Whoever wrote the pamphlet about being a boy mom is pulling a Frank Abagnale–level con. I would give him a chunk of my liver, but he's not getting any siblings."

"And the big one?" Violet asks, jumping in, and I realize they're talking about Garrett.

"He's even more work. He whines when he doesn't get his way, refuses to eat his vegetables and wants to be patted on the back for putting his dirty socks in the hamper instead of throwing them *right next to it*."

Violet catches my eye, her expression mirroring mine, and scoffs. "I may have crippling anxiety and chronic IBS, but at least I'm not hetero."

Gia huddles up with Lauren and tries to convince her that what this world really needs is another cherub-faced offspring from her favorite couple while Violet opens one cabinet, then another. I sneak out and head upstairs, hoping to catch Garrett alone.

The door to the bedroom he's sharing with Lauren is still shut when I get there, so I lean back against the wall. When he steps out a minute later, his head is down, both hands working on his fly. I push off the wall and he jumps back, startled, which startles me.

"Sorry," I say, giving him a moment to collect himself. "Scared you?"

"Nah, you're okay." He gives me a reassuring smile and leads the way back downstairs. "What's up?"

I follow close behind. "There was a truck parked out front last night." I pause to gauge his reaction, but he doesn't give much of one. "A white pickup. Maybe a Toyota. I couldn't see."

Garrett is quiet for a second, and then it hits him. "Oh. That's Uncle Nolan's."

I swallow, and all the words I was going to say next jumble in my head.

Garrett studies me for a beat. "What? Did he do something creepy?"

My heart plummets, every vision I have from last night flashing in my head in rapid succession. The hole. The shovel. The bloodstains on his jacket.

Scrape, thump.

Scrape, thump.

Scrape, thump.

"Something creepy?" I ask, treading lightly. I don't want to lead him into anything.

"I mean, he's definitely got a type," he says with a shrug.

"A type?" I echo, my voice low, cautious, though the unease is already curling in my stomach.

Garrett smirks. "Let's just say if *you're* in the room, he's noticing."

"Oh. No. He didn't see me." I pause, trying to figure out the right way to say this. "I was just getting a glass of water in the kitchen and I saw him. In the back. With a . . . shovel."

We reach the main room. Garrett slows and turns to face me. "A shovel?"

"It was actually kind of weird. He was digging a pretty big . . ." My words trail off when I see that we're no longer alone.

Lauren and Gia slip into the room from the opposite side.

"Not interrupting anything, are we?" Lauren asks coolly, flicking a glance over at me in a way that feels like an accusation.

She's always been overprotective of Garrett. Possessive. It boggles my mind how someone as gorgeous as her can be so insecure. Even motherhood hasn't given her the confidence to stop seeing every woman in her vicinity as competition. Garrett is a good-looking man, but I've never once looked at him that way. He's been with Lauren for as long as I've known him, and I'm not attracted to other women's men. Even in the face of her thinly veiled hostility, I can't help but feel a little sympathy for her. It must be draining to always be so on guard. Love should bring comfort, not constant anxiety.

"Iris ran into Uncle Nolan last night," Garrett tells her.

Gia is clearly not interested. She barely glances up from her phone, her thumbs flying across the screen as the smile on her face widens. Whoever she's texting has her full attention. Probably one of her benefactors.

Lauren keeps her eyes on me, waiting to hear the rest of the story, and I wish Garrett had just kept this issue between us.

I part my lips to continue, but Violet pops into the room, and I lose my train of thought.

"Where are the glasses?" she asks no one in particular. "I'm making vodka cranberries."

"Bottom cabinet on the left," I say.

She frowns, her brows furrowing. "Weird."

"I know."

Violet bounces back out of the room, her interruption relieving the tension in the room only briefly. I turn my attention back to Garrett.

"I didn't run into him," I say, feeling my neck start to perspire now that we have an audience. "I saw him digging a hole out back."

"A . . . hole?"

I nod. "Looked like a . . ." I swallow. "A grave."

Lauren frowns and exchanges a skeptical glance with Garrett. "A grave for what?"

"I don't know," I say, feeling myself losing steam. "I know it sounds weird, but I was looking right at him."

"Boat's ready," Roman calls out as he ducks in from the front door behind me. His eyes meet mine. "Looking right at who?"

I start to explain, but Lauren beats me to it. "Iris thinks Uncle Nolan was here last night burying a dead body in the back."

It looks like she wants to laugh.

"Wait, what?" Gia says, finally looking up from her phone.

I've always thought Garrett and Roman look more like brothers than cousins. Now their perplexed expressions mirror one another's so perfectly that in the right lighting, it would be easy to confuse them.

"I came down for a glass of water to take my pills, and he—"

"Pills? Like you were high?" Gia scoffed.

"I don't see them," Violet announces with a hint of frustration, stepping back into the room. "Just highballs." Violet bartends at a Michelin-starred sushi restaurant in the most gentrified part of Brooklyn, and even when she's off duty, she's a perfectionist.

"I swear," I say, hopping on Garrett's heels as he steers Violet into the kitchen and toward the right cabinet. "It was late. I came down for some water and saw him digging a hole back there. He just kept going. It had to be a grave for something."

Violet starts pulling out glasses, but everyone else is frozen in befuddlement. I can tell by the glances traded between them that they're still doubting everything I've said.

"It takes a long time to dig a grave. You know that, right?" Roman asks, his husky voice breaking the silence. "And alone? Would've taken hours."

I know he's just pointing out a fact, but he sounds as skeptical as the rest of them. A part of me was hoping out of everyone, he would be the one on my side. I blink a few times to recalibrate my thoughts.

Gia cocks her head and squints. "Don't those pills mess with your memory?"

Violet nods and samples the vodka. "This one time, I popped some street shit that had me tripping the hell out for like two days straight."

"It's a prescription," I snap, losing patience. "And I've never had hallucinations on them. I saw him digging."

Garrett tips his head at Roman. "Did you see anything weird out there?"

He shakes his head. "Nah, I—"

"He wasn't looking," I say, unsure of when he even went out to the back. Seems like he's been preoccupied with the boat.

"I don't think it would be that hard to miss a *grave* someone dug up in the dark," Lauren says, backing up her man. She eases closer to him, his dedicated shadow.

"And aren't you, like, blind without your glasses?" Gia asks. My chest tightens at the bite in her words.

It stings. Not the truth of it. Her indifference. Like it's a small thing, something as simple as a missing accessory, not a vulnerability that I carry with me every day. My glasses are a tether, an anchor to something whole. The world blurs when I'm without them. Things slip out of focus in a way that makes me feel small, incomplete, like I'm only half present in my own life. But Gia doesn't know that. She doesn't know the frustration of feeling out of sync with the world, of having to second-guess every step, every movement. She doesn't see it as a wound. To her, it's a joke. And I hate how much it cuts. That casual dismissal, the way she makes something so integral to my world feel so insignificant.

I only have my mother to blame. In fourth grade, my math teacher pulled me aside after class and told me I needed glasses. She'd seen through my ruse, knew by my dismal test scores that my eagerness to sit in the front row wasn't due to my enthusiasm for fractions and decimals, but was out of necessity. When I got home and relayed the message to my mother, she waved her hand dismissively and said there was nothing wrong with me—everyone in her bloodline had perfect eyesight. I asked a second time, in sixth grade, and she held up a hand and asked me how many she was holding up. I said three, and she rolled her eyes and went back to watching *Judge Judy*. I begged and begged her for months after that, but she would never take me to the doctor. By the time I was old enough to go on my own, my eyesight had already deteriorated beyond repair, my optometrist citing it as the "worst case of neglect I've ever seen" as he shone a ludicrously bright light in my eyeballs.

"Yeah, babe. Your eyes could've been playing tricks on you," Violet says, agreeing with her, and it feels like a betrayal, like they're all turning against me.

I shake my head. "They weren't. I know what I—"

"It was late. You were high and couldn't see straight," Garrett reminds me. "Come on, Uncle Nolan was probably just out there having a smoke before getting on the road, like he always does."

"But I could've sworn he . . ." I close my eyes, trying to replay what I saw in my mind. "It looked like there was blood all over his jacket. Like he was *covered* in blood."

Garrett sighs, turning to me. "Look, think about it. If Uncle Nolan murdered someone here and then cleaned up all the evidence, the whole place would reek of bleach and antiseptic."

My eyes drop down to his chest, then flick back up. "What, you've killed someone before?"

"Chill," Lauren says, cutting in. "The ID channel is basically our lullaby once we get the two-year-old terrorist to bed."

I feel all of their eyes on me as I pace away, trying to figure out where to go from here. I should have never given in and taken those pills. My memories would be clearer. They wouldn't be able to dismiss me so easily.

"Babe, maybe you took one pill too many," Violet says, starting on the cocktails.

"I only took two, like I always do." I start to say more, but suddenly my words feel futile.

When I was little, my mother would leave me at home by myself for hours and hours, sometimes days at a time while she went on drinking binges, got high, chased after strange men for drug money or spent nights in jail for stealing or indecent exposure. I had all the responsibilities of an adult by the time I turned twelve. I knew how to cook three go-to meals and which groceries I would need and how many and where to clip coupons from. All the kids whispered that I was weird. I barely ever had friends and kept to myself. And now, I feel exactly like I did back then: alone. Neglected. Ignored. I wish Eli was here to back me up.

Lauren's patience has worn thin. "Well, I'm tired of being cooped up in here. Let's get out onto the water."

She struts out of the room, lifting up her shirt and revealing a tiny black bikini top with white trim underneath. Garrett follows behind her, his eyes glued to her body as she strips. Gia and Violet trail them, catching up quickly. Roman gives me a sympathetic look, then shrugs before joining them.

chapter
six

My shower is economical. I don't want to keep the others waiting, but the patch of dry dirt I saw earlier keeps flashing in my mind. It might not have been a grave; it was way too small to fit an entire body inside. But there's definitely something buried out there. The water rushes over my face as I contemplate what Nolan could have been trying to make sure no one ever finds. Just as I turn around to rinse off, I hear something.

I whip my head toward the door and strain to hear over the shower. Nothing. I swallow and take a deliberate breath. My fingers curl around the edge of the shower curtain. I suck my stomach tight to my spine before I snatch the curtain back.

The room is empty except for my things cluttered on the countertop. I shut off the water, listening again just to make sure. But I hear nothing except the faint voices and laughter coming from downstairs. I release a breath and grab a clean towel as I step out from behind the curtain. After slathering

SPF all over my body, I part my damp hair in half with my fingers and start on two cornrows. When I get to the end of the first one, I secure it with a hair tie, but when I finish the second, the edge of the sink is empty.

There were two. Before I stepped in the water, before that weird sound. I distinctly remember bringing two in with me.

"Did someone come into the bathroom while I was in the shower?" I ask, stepping into the kitchen. Four heads turn in my direction in unison. They take me in wearing nothing but one of the bath towels, but no one responds. "I can't find my hair tie."

They're all in swim trunks and itty-bitty cheeky bikinis, rubbing sunscreen all over their limbs, grabbing snacks, getting ready to spend the day in the sun. Collectively, they look like an old-school Gucci swimwear ad. Everyone bronzed and rippled with their flat stomachs and ideal proportions. I feel juvenile at the thought of my tame black one-piece upstairs.

Lauren checks her sebum levels with the mirror in her compact, a blotting paper in hand. "I have a bunch in my bag upstairs. The Louis, not the Dior. Inside pocket. Help yourself."

"No, that's not the point," I explain. "I put two on the sink before I got in the shower, and one of them was gone when I got out."

Gia scoffs, a confused sort of shock on her face. "Are you legit saying one of us stole your hair tie?"

A chorus of laughter fills the room, the mockery coming from all angles.

"Hey," Garrett calls, poking his head back inside the house. "What's the holdup?"

Gia shoots me a snide glance. "Now Iris thinks one of us stole her precious elastic band."

Violet ambles my way, fluffing her hair, emphasizing that it's hair tie–free. "It's not me, babe. But if you want to strip-search me for contraband, go for it. Cavities and all."

She laughs, but I roll my eyes, unamused. I heard something. One of them came in while I was in the shower. I know it.

"You want to check our wrists too?" Gia asks, jutting her slim arms toward me. She doesn't wait for a response, just grabs her oversized sunglasses and follows Garrett and Lauren outside.

Roman catches my eye before stepping out after Violet. "Maybe you only brought one in with you. I do that all the time."

"Oh, yeah? You're a fan of pigtails?"

He laughs, then grabs his bucket hat from the counter and heads outside too. I follow him with my eyes until he reaches the boat. Garrett hops on first, then holds out a hand to steady Gia as she steps on board. Lauren watches him closely to make sure he doesn't touch her anywhere she doesn't approve of, and I feel slightly better knowing it's not just me she sees as a threat.

I head upstairs to finish my hair, but really, I just want to go home. I call Eli, but he doesn't pick up.

"Garrett's ready to leave without you."

I startle at the sound of Lauren's voice. My phone drops into the sink, and I see her in the mirror under the doorframe, her arms folded across her chest.

"You can skip this one if you need to," she says. "No one's judging."

"I'm fine. Be down in a sec."

I watch her in the mirror until she disappears down the hall, a surge of defiance swelling inside me as I shift my gaze to my own reflection. I stare at my angles, my shadows, searching for any sign of weakness, any clue that might have given me away. *No one's judging.* In my head, I replay everything since they all arrived, dissecting each word, each awkward gesture. Was it something in my tone? Did my voice crack when I tried to sound casual? Did she notice how I barely made eye contact or the dark circles under my eyes? Am I slipping? I lean in closer, scrutinizing my lips. Did she notice how tight my smile was? How hard I was trying to seem normal, to hide how close I am to falling apart? I feel a tightness in my chest, doubt creeping in like a black shadow.

I shake my head, trying to snap myself out of it. I drop my towel and turn to grab my suit hanging from the towel rack. Before my fingers even brush the fabric, I jump back, a sharp gasp escaping my throat. Lauren. She's back. Standing at the threshold like she never left. Like she was always there, watching me.

"Is this because of the whole 'your mother died' thing?" she asks before I can get a word out.

I cover up with the towel again. "Is that what it is? A *thing*?"

"I'm worried about you. You just lost it over an elastic band," Lauren says, and when she puts it like that, it does seem ridiculous. She steps a little closer and softens her voice to a whisper. "Are you still having them? Eli told me. The nightma—"

"I'm just . . ." Not going to talk to her about this. Eli shouldn't have in the first place. "Kinda tired. That's all."

"Well, don't ruin the vibe. This week is my only time away from my kid in six months. I want to enjoy my husband before I have to go back to chasing that mini-terrorist around. He reached into his diaper yesterday and smeared it all over the walls. Took our maid an hour to clean it up. Cool?"

I nod and tell her I'll be down in two minutes. After she's gone, I glance at myself in the mirror again, but I can only see my mother's reflection in the glass.

It was just the two of us against the world until it wasn't, until I started school and saw how other people lived, how mothers could be soft and steady instead of sharp-edged and unpredictable. Most days were fine, which is why I let myself believe she had it under control. That the vodka and coke were habits, not lifelines. That there wasn't a storm inside her she was trying to drown, an immense trauma she swallowed down with every lie she told, every dollar she stole, every person she framed, conned or used. There was one man she shot. She never said why, only, with bored disdain, that the bullet missed every vital artery.

The morning she pressed that cold barrel into her mouth, I had left her a letter, three pages, handwritten, every word chosen with meticulous care, begging her to get help. I thought I was doing the right thing. I thought she'd understand. But no, she read it and raged, her fury so palpable it left me trembling. My legs palsied. I was rooted to the floor like an ancient sequoia as she grabbed the gun. The sound was terrible, not just the shot but the heavy, final thud of her body hitting the ground, like a felled tree, loud and unstoppable. And the blood; god, the blood, so dark it didn't look real, didn't look like something that could come from her.

She didn't just end her life that day. She took something else with her, something fragile and fleeting, something I'd been clinging to without even realizing it—the hope that she might get better. But maybe that's not fair. Maybe it was never hers to take. Because hope doesn't belong to anyone. It's a figment, isn't it? A shared hallucination we all hold on to, imagining futures that may never come.

chapter
seven

I inhale the faint pine scent in the air as I soak in the beautiful view, the sunlight dancing on the surface of the water. It looks like there are thousands of microscopic ballerinas flitting on it. I let my eyes squeeze shut, the heavy sun sealing them. Just as a sense of calm washes over me, the boat bucks. I jerk a glance to Garrett, who's at the helm, his hand too heavy on the throttle. The serenity of the landscape slips away as we speed away from the shore recklessly, the engine revving at full force. I grip the railing, the boat swaying violently, but no one else seems to notice or care.

The boat hums beneath us, the bass from the speakers reverberating through its frame, through my chest. I sit tucked in the back corner, watching as the others lose themselves in the moment. Lauren holds up a bottle of Stella Artois to Garrett's mouth, her arm steady despite the boat's subtle rocking. He takes a swig, but the beer spills anyway, dripping down the side of his neck, gleaming in the sunlight. They both laugh it off and then, all at once, they're kissing, the kind of kiss that makes the rest of the world feel smaller. Roman sways to the music, Gia close by, grinding against him playfully. Violet tips back the bottle of vodka and takes a swig straight from the mouth. The boat jerks again, sharper this time, and she stumbles, her weight carrying her closer to me, her eyes fluttering in the sun as she takes in the look on my face. She tilts her head, a small gesture, but it feels heavier than it should, like she's looking straight through me. She raises the bottle, presses the cold glass to my lips without a word. I don't move. I just let her.

"Open your mouth," she says, ready to tip the burning liquid down my throat, but I can't shake the feeling of being adrift, detached from the wild energy that's supposed to be exhilarating. I've never been a drinker. Lately I don't even like to politely sip anymore, not after I started taking the downers. I shake my head and she shrugs, then takes a gulp so large, I cringe on her behalf.

I turn to gaze out at the water, losing myself in the delicate patterns of light and shadow, the tranquil blue hue mesmerizing. A loud shriek of joy jolts me back into reality. I look over the edge and find Violet flapping in the water like the happiest fish returned to her natural habitat.

"What are you doing?" I call out to her, but she only laughs harder as the boat moves away from her, treading the water so effortlessly.

I get Garrett's attention, and when he sees her, he slows us down, letting the boat idle while Violet catches up with us.

"Is it nice?" I ask, taken by how peaceful she looks in the water.

I used to love swimming, though it's been years since I've actually been in the water. My mother taught me at a neighbor's pool. She told me the owner was a friend, that he'd said I could swim whenever I liked. I believed her, of course. I was seven and didn't realize she only took me there when no cars were in the driveway. It was the one thing we both loved. I used to watch her, so graceful in the water, cutting through it like she belonged there, like it knew her. She was a natural, better at swimming than anything else I'd ever seen her do. Violet reminds me of her in that way, moving through the lake like it's her second skin.

Of course, there was the time I almost drowned because she got high and passed out. I was left alone for hours. But when I think back to those days, before the owner came home and caught me in my strawberry one-piece, my memories of that time are mostly pleasant.

Violet laughs, making circles with her arms. "Gotta jump in to find out."

I hesitate, my hands gripping the edge. Then I force myself to let go. Tucking my legs, I leap into the lake, my arms high in the air. The water is cool and silky against my skin. It feels so nostalgic, therapeutic, nearly cathartic once I'm fully plunged. When I come up for air, Violet has made her way over to me already. But then the boat starts to move out of reach. We both shout for Garrett to stop. Finally he does, half a football field away.

"Whoever gets back to the boat first gets to throttle her up," Garrett yells.

I glance over at Violet, and she takes off without warning. She looks like a swan, buoyant and perfectly photogenic, her long neck extended as she slices through the water, her body so unafraid to take up space. I take off behind her and try to gain as much momentum as quickly as I can. I hate to lose at anything. So does Violet.

I stroke as hard as I can, and it feels good to be out of my own head for once and just focus on something physical. No anxiety. No dissonant thoughts. Just my body and a challenge. I don't even think about Violet anymore, just keep my gaze on my end point until the boat is within reach. When I look up, Roman is there, holding out his hand. I grip it and pull myself up.

"I'm impressed," he says, handing me a towel. "You just crushed Ms. Swim Champ."

I do my best to catch my breath, a smile tugging at the corner of my mouth, feeling a tad silly for how accomplished this makes me feel. My body is spent, but I love it—the sharpness in my chest, the slight tingle in my limbs. It feels like old times. Immediately, I want to do it again. I glance back over my shoulder to help Violet up, shocked it isn't her helping me, but she's not behind me. I squint into the distance, but there's no break in the surface.

"Where'd she go?" I ask, still looking for her.

"I don't know," Roman says. He shouts her name, and I follow suit.

The only answer we get is a stifling silence, as if the air itself is holding its breath.

chapter
eight

"Maybe one of you should go in," I say to Garrett and Roman, expecting their egos to take over and spark a competition to see who will play the hero. I brace myself for the chest-puffing and macho posturing these two have practically carved their sense of masculinity out of, anticipating the insults that will fly as they debate who's the better swimmer.

But instead, they just exchange a look, neither one of them volunteering.

"She's just messing with us," Garrett says after a moment.

I step over to the opposite side of the boat, checking to see if she's made it back yet. The water is too calm. No ripples. No splashes. Nothing.

"I still don't see her."

"There's a shocker," Gia says, tossing back a swig of her peach schnapps, her long, bouncy curls blowing in the soft breeze.

I ignore her and keep looking.

"Would you relax," Lauren says, adjusting her aviators. "She's the Little Fucking Mermaid. She's *fine*."

"She would've come up by now," I insist, using my hand to shield my eyes from the glare of sun.

Nobody moves.

Panic barrels through me as I scan the spot where we were last together, desperate for any sign of her. I search for anything that she could have hit her head on or gotten stuck inside, but nothing stands out.

"*Violet*," I scream, my voice cracking.

Time stretches out. Every second feels like hours. The water remains completely undisturbed, its surface ominously still. My hand twitches at my side, dread settling over me. She could have hit her head. What if she doesn't come up?

I call her name again, louder this time, and Garrett looks over at me. "Iris, don't—"

He reaches for me, trying to hold me back, but I'm already in the water. I dive straight in this time, staying under the surface as long as I can. The water is clear, but I don't see anything. No sign of Violet at all.

My mind reels as I continue to call out for her, my arms and legs moving frantically under the water. I can't go through this again. I can't watch another person die right in front of me. I have to find her. I go under one last time, then push my head through the surface.

"She's not here," I shout to everyone else once I swim back to the stairs, the sun beaming down on my back so hard, it feels like a giant hand. "I couldn't find her. I think she might've . . ."

My words trail off and disappear under the sound of laughter breaking out on the deck of the boat. Everyone joins in except Roman. I scan all of their faces, unsure of what I'm missing, and then Violet struts out from behind Garrett, a playful glint in her eyes. A wave of relief rushes through me, but it's quickly eclipsed by the rush of fury that replaces it.

She's fine. This whole time, she's been fine.

Roman offers to help me up again, but I refuse his hand even though he doesn't seem like he had a part in any of this. I use all the strength left in my arms to hoist myself up and brush past Violet. She follows me, water dripping from her lean body like she's some Greek warrior goddess. She's still laughing, waiting for me to join in.

"That wasn't funny," I snap at her, my shoulder brushing against hers again. But this time she grabs my forearm.

"Come on," she says, pulling me back. "I go Houdini on your ass and you're not even gonna crack a smile?"

I snatch my arm from her grasp, then my towel from my seat in the corner. I wrap it around my shoulders. My leg bounces as I try to calm myself down.

"Iris, don't be mad. I—"

"I was scared," I say, my voice shaking. "Do you get it? *I was scared*."

Violet flinches at my words as if she's just been hit. I stop myself from saying more, feeling tears well up in my eyes, catching in my throat. She staggers off without another word, joining the rest of the group. I sway a little, then dig my heels into the floor as the boat picks up speed. Violet is clutching a bottle in her hand when she meets my eyes again from across the deck. I look away, the embarrassment still stinging.

When I glance down, I realize my legs are still trembling—not just from the adrenaline, but from something deeper. The anniversary of my mother's death is only ten days away. The day we leave this lake is the day she left my world. I close my eyes against the harsh rays, so many complicated emotions battling inside me at once. For a moment I allow myself to feel the pain, the grief, the unbearable agony of her selfishness. Not her decision, but her final words. She made me watch her brains splatter against the wall, a final token of her rabid disdain. After a lifetime of weaponizing her own self-pity, she turned her death into a weapon and used it to hurt me one last time.

In some ways I'm glad she's gone. From my earliest memories, she hated being alive, almost as much as she hated the burden of keeping me alive. I always thought I could be the exception, her cure, the one who would save her. I didn't know the truth, or accept it, until that last moment of her life—that I had been the cause.

chapter
nine

I sit alone in my room as the sun slips from the sky. Music blares from somewhere in the house, probably the rec room. I've been debating going downstairs for a snack for the better part of an hour, but I don't want to bump into any of them. I close my book, unable to focus on the words, and decide to risk it. The soft hum of the refrigerator fills the kitchen when I pull the door open and scan my options. Pre-cut watermelon slices, Greek yogurt with honey, baby carrots, celery sticks, two types of hummus, red and green grapes, green olives—everything clean and healthy. I'm about to give up until I see a block of cheese, extra-sharp white cheddar. I open a few cabinets until I find a fresh pack of crackers, grab a handful, then turn to leave. I pause at the edge of the room when I hear someone say my name.

"That was just a joke," Violet says, and I slip behind the wall into the next room as she pads into the kitchen from the back.

"You think?" Roman asks, his voice low and harder to hear over the thumping trap beat. "To someone who has nightmares from watching someone die in front of them?"

It should feel good, knowing that he's taking up for me even when I'm not in the room, but it only makes me sick to my stomach, the fact that they're talking about me behind my back. I peek from behind the wall to see if anyone else is with them, but it's just those two. Roman shuffles around for something in the fridge.

"You know she still has a man, right?" Violet says. "You don't have to simp so hard. You have just as much a chance of pulling her as I do."

"I feel kinda bad for you, you know," Roman says, meeting her where she is. "It's gotta be painful playing roomie with her. So close yet so far away."

Once they're gone, I pull a knife out of the butcher block, then head across the room with my cheese and crackers. I pause at the glass doors and watch Garrett and Lauren half dipped in the hot tub outside. He rests his head back on the edge, watching Lauren like a lazy king as she strips off her last piece of clothing and slides inside the bubbling water with him. He bends over and buries his face in her breasts. She laughs and throws her head back, but her expression stills when he puts one of them in his mouth. They are beautiful under the moonlight. Just as passionate, obsessed and hungry for each other as they were when we all lived in minuscule dorm rooms and made terrible decisions because of our raging hormones.

I watch them for a moment and can't help but think that could've been us out there, me and Eli. I close my eyes, my cheese forgotten, craving him. I want to smell his hair, feel the friction of his warm skin against mine, taste his salty-sweet sweat.

A couple of drunken screams break me from my trance, and I shift away from the doors. More come from the opposite side of the deck, the one with the fire pit and view of the water. I move through the hall, heading back upstairs since both sides of the deck are occupied. Smoke drifts in through the windows from outside, the smell of barbecue turning the air intoxicating. I figure Roman is manning the grill, and for a second I'm tempted to go out and request a kabob, but when I pass a door I've only just now noticed and see there's a dark staircase on the other side, food is no longer on my mind.

I set down my cheese and crackers on the top step, but keep my grip on the knife as I carefully descend the stairs. I leave the door open behind me, wishing I had my phone with me, and feel around for a switch, a string, anything at the bottom of the stairs. There's nothing, but my curiosity pulls me into the depths of the darkness. I don't know what I'm looking for, but maybe there will be something down here that can explain what I saw last night.

A few strides in, I realize there's not much to the space. It's unfinished and completely dark, a faint musty scent filling the damp air. A black hole with piles of junk and old furniture strewn about. I keep one hand on the wall, the one with the knife stretched out in front of me, feeling for anything that might trip me up.

I pass by a few boxes filled with old books and random stacks of papers. I can't make out what any of it is in the dark, so I step away and feel along the wall. Something made of wood falls to the floor, just missing the tip of my nose. I can tell by the clatter of its landing that it's a handle. I crouch down and fumble blindly until my hand brushes against cold steel. Not a broom, not a mop. I feel along its length, searching for the wooden handle to grip it. I lean it back against the wall, but pause when I feel a peculiar gritty texture. I lift it to my eyeline, but can't make out what it is—something coarse and grainy, but sticky enough to cling to my skin. I lift my fingers closer and inhale gently in case the smell is putrid. It's not what I expected. It's almost pleasant. The pungent scent of raw earth grips me, and I realize what I've just touched.

The blade of the shovel Nolan used last night to bury something in the rain.

I straighten to my feet, and my heart knocks against my chest so hard I almost answer it. I wasn't imagining anything last night. I saw what I saw.

I stumble back a step, the darkness swallowing me whole, closing me in, and something hard crashes into my spine. I flip around and feel for it. A knob.

There's another door.

chapter
ten

A shudder moves through me, and then I push it open. Behind the door, there's more blackness, only this blackness is more potent without the sliver of light coming in from the hall to dilute it. I steady myself by holding on to the wall and groping blindly along it, but there's no light switch anywhere. I drift from the security of the wall and feel like I'm floating. I take careful, measured steps toward the center of the room and stop when a hard metal edge digs into my leg. I feel a few inches ahead of me, and there's some kind of heavy-duty box on what feels like a wooden stool. Next to it I feel something cylindrical with a decent weight to it. There's a switch. My heart thumps faster.

I think of the flashlight I saw Nolan with last night and flip the switch. It provides a decent beam of light, but my gaze narrows in on what's right in front of me. The box is actually a trunk. I lift the top, and the hinges seem like they're barely holding it together. Inside is an arsenal of antique tools, all sharp edges and pointy tips. I shine the light on them one by one: First a hammer, cracked on the side. A long knife, heavy and sturdy in my hand. Some kind of carving knife, the tip thick and curved, ridges like teeth. Then a small, sharper blade with a worn handle. A chill jolts down my spine, my mind spiraling.

I drop the flashlight and bolt out of the basement. After shutting the door behind me, I press my back against it, taking a moment to collect my thoughts. A few moments later, I turn out of the hall. Instead of heading straight upstairs, I continue checking out the parts of the house I haven't explored yet. I need to know everything about this man. I need to know if we're safe here.

I move as quietly as I can even though I don't think anyone can hear me over the music. Coming out of a turn, I jump when I see a glint of metal down by my side, then relax when I realize I'm the one holding it. I remember the cheese, the crackers. I left them both on the top step leading down into the basement. I open up every door I pass. Most are closets. None yield anything remotely interesting until I come across the photo sitting on top of a desk in the spare room off the kitchen.

I push into the study and lift the frame. The man in the photo is middle-aged, maybe fifty, and smiling. I swallow when I recognize it. The jacket. It's the same tactical jacket I saw the man wearing last night as he dug that hole. In the photo, he's holding up an enormous trout, proud of his conquest. It looks like the lake is behind him.

I set the photo back down, my hand shaking. Slowly, I open one of the drawers.

"What are we looking for?"

I jump, my hand flying up to cover my heart as I turn around to see Garrett's smile. He untucks his hands from his pockets and inches closer when he doesn't get the reaction he expected.

"Hey, you okay?" His eyes search mine, but I avert them. "That was just a little payback for earlier."

It takes a moment, but then I remember what he's talking about—when I surprised him on the stairs.

But that was an accident.

"I'm fine. I saw . . ." I take a breath, force myself to swallow. "I was in the basement, and . . ."

Garrett shifts his weight to both legs, standing at his full height. "What happened?"

I start to explain, then figure it's best if I just show him. I lead him down into the basement. He pulls his phone from his pocket and lights up the way to the door. He knows exactly where it is. Once we slip inside, he taps the phone light off.

"No, we need—"

Click.

Garrett releases the string suspended from the ceiling, which powers a single light bulb. I glance around the room as the bare bulb flickers to life. There's a lot more stuff in here than I thought, and there isn't any order to it, but something about the placement makes it seem like it's intentional, and not just a storage room. There's a blanket of sawdust and wood shavings covering the cement floor. A handsaw hangs from a peg on the wall, along with a bunch of other tools. Glass jars filled with loose nails and screwdrivers line metal shelves on the wall. I creep toward the trunk and peer down at the sharp tools inside. In the light, I see that they're all clean. No dirt, no blood. Just dust.

"Uncle Nolan's workshop," Garrett says, adjusting the edge of a blade so it's tucked out of harm's way. "He hasn't been down here in a while, though. He can't lift like he used to. Old military back injury."

I nod, feeling foolish. As I glance around, I see there are even more tools cluttering the space. I linger on a huge saw leaning against one of the walls as Garrett lifts what looks like a half-built table. There's nothing nefarious about anything in here. I rub both of my eyes with my fingertips, feeling a headache coming on. I need to get some sleep. I chant this inside my head until I remember the dirt on the shovel. I smelled it. I felt it.

Nolan might not have used any tools in here last night, but he definitely buried something.

"Hey. Sure you're okay?" Garrett asks, his voice low with concern.

I avoid his eyes and force a smile. "Yeah. I'm good, I just . . . I think I'm just a little tired. Gonna head upstairs."

I don't wait for him to reply. I rush out of the basement and shut the door behind me when I get back to my bedroom. Knowing it's the only way I'll actually get a decent night of sleep tonight, I swallow down two more pills. When I climb into bed, I think of Eli again, craving him now even more. Not just sex, but to be held. I check my phone for any missed calls or messages from him, but there aren't any. I send him a quick text, telling him I hope his grandmother is doing okay and asking him to give me an update whenever he gets a chance.

chapter
eleven

I roll over in bed and check my phone first thing in the morning. There's only one notification from Eli, a thumbs-up on the last text I sent before I fell asleep. Everything comes back to me in flashes while I'm standing under the shower. I want to head out back and inspect that patch again. I want to know what's hidden there before I share anything with the group again.

It's quiet as I towel off, but when I crack the door open to let out some of the steam, I hear the rumblings of breakfast downstairs. I put fresh braids in my hair, fill in my brows and swipe on a coat of mascara. When I turn into the kitchen, everyone has already started eating. They're congregated in one room, spread out on the stools, around the table, Roman flipping something at the stove. The table is loaded with food—an epic stack of pancakes, a jug of maple syrup, a bowl of mixed berries, a carton of orange juice. I see waffles too, and an obscene mountain of eggs in the frying pan, and then I remember what it takes to feed two former football players simultaneously.

They're all chipper and generally happy to be up early, so I pretend to also be in a good mood. I greet everyone and take the empty seat at the table next to Violet, who is hunched over eating a bowl of Frosted Flakes. Roman turns to me, a plaid bistro apron tied at his hips, and asks if I want eggs. When I say no, he asks if I prefer pancakes or waffles. I tell him I'm not that hungry and grab a banana just to have something to do with my hands. Across the table, Gia's plucking the blueberries from her pancakes, which makes sense, being that she's the kind of person who goes to a sushi restaurant and asks if the fish tastes "fishy." Lauren is saddled in Garrett's lap, their faces close as they share a stack of pancakes. He carves away the crispy edges, leaving the fluffy middles for her, just the way she likes them.

Eli and I used to be the same way in the beginning, completely inseparable, absolutely sickening. We ordered in every Friday night and gave each other half of each other's order, then left our dirty dishes in the sink until the morning. On Saturday nights he wined and dined me, white tablecloths, candlelight, the whole thing. We held hands and laughed and read books to each other at night. We cuddled together in bed on Sundays, him teaching me about finance, and me teasing him to cover how much I liked it. Back then, I melted when he lectured me through soft, breathy rumbles, the way he'd pontificate; his knowledge seemed infinite, his mind beautiful and brilliant, and I was happy just to have a piece of it.

We met sophomore year at an off-campus pajama party near Princeton. I'd seized the opportunity like every other girl there and used it as an excuse to show up half naked. Eli wore a white T-shirt and a pair of gray sweatpants that hung low on his hips. I found it almost impossible to not notice how magnificent he was from across the room, how everyone crowded around him. He looked both tempting and like a cautionary tale. My pull toward him felt like more than just attraction, something deeper than that, a force more powerful than magnetic. Gravitational. I didn't realize I'd still been checking him out until he smiled my way. I wish I could be at the hospital with him now, holding his hand, talking him through his complicated emotions, the way he was there for me this past year.

I peel the banana and force myself to nibble on it, my appetite a lone, distant thing. My anxiety feels like flames in the pit of my stomach. I rub my eyes in a futile attempt to relieve the fatigue weighing me down. Though I slept the whole night through, this is the kind of exhaustion that will take weeks to sleep off. I'm never consistent enough with the pills to fully recover, a vicious cycle that I both loathe and perpetuate.

"You coming, Iris?" Garrett asks, taking a swig of his orange juice, and I have no idea what he's talking about.

"Coming where?" I ask, wondering if someone texted or emailed some kind of itinerary and I missed it.

"We're blasting cans of spray paint," he says, popping a strawberry into his mouth, then slipping one between Lauren's lips.

"What?"

Violet looks over the edge of her bowl, which she has up to her mouth as she gulps down the leftover milk. "You know, like target shooting."

"Target shooting?"

"You don't remember when we drove up to Yonkers and blasted cans of Diet Coke?" Violet asks, and of course I remember. I'm just confused as to why they'd ask me to come.

It was at some point during winter break. I don't even remember why I tagged along, but it was probably because Lauren and Gia were going and I figured it couldn't be that bad if they agreed to it. Even before my mother sent that bullet through her skull, I hated guns. I've always hated guns.

I remember them shaking up cans of Diet Coke and shooting at them mid-air. They hooted and hollered when they'd explode, but I was somewhere behind a tree holding my ears. Eli was a decent shot, but not as consistent as Roman, and nobody was touching Garrett. He hit every single target, which shouldn't have been shocking because he's good at everything he does. As much as I hated all the noise, I did love seeing my man flexing his arms and concentrating in that sexy way. Garrett would stand behind Lauren to make sure she was holding the shotgun right. Then they'd shoot together and hit most of the targets. On her own she was a terrible shot, but as a team they were formidable. Gia was determined to get at least one on her own, but even after Roman coached her, she missed every single shot. Eli convinced me to try one target. I hated the recoil. I thought shooting guns would make me feel powerful, but really it just reminded me that all it took was one tiny motion to end it all.

"This time we're firing at cans of spray paint," Garrett says, exchanging an excited glance with Roman. "They burst when you hit them and do this zigzag through the air."

Just the thought sends an electric current through my entire body. I don't want to be anywhere near anyone who has a gun. I try to push them down, but the memories force their way to the surface. The sound of the gunshot, the way my mother's lifeless body slumped and bled and went cold. The sound of my own scream reverberating.

Lauren and Gia don't look particularly enthused, but they join in as they all hype themselves up for what's to come. I hate feeling the odd one out again as I choke down another bite of banana, but then I realize the beauty of them leaving me here alone. The dirt. I can check the patch of dirt in the back.

"I'm gonna stay here." They all look at me. "I'll clean this mess up."

Violet sets her empty bowl down. "You're still mad about yesterday?"

"I'm still *drunk* from yesterday," Gia mumbles.

"I just don't want to go," I tell Violet, and leave it at that, getting up to toss my peel.

"Do I need to repeat the rules again?" Garrett asks as Lauren reaches over to adjust a clump of stray hair on his head. His tone is playful, but I'm not in the mood.

Roman turns off the burner and scrapes the last batch of eggs onto a plate. "Bro, chill. Maybe gunshots are triggering for her."

I glance at him. He gives me a soft look, his eyes questioning if that was okay to say. I nod, grateful for him again, the only one in this room who seems to understand what I'm going through, or at least tries to empathize. He took up for me in private and now again in front of everybody.

"Oh shit," Garrett says, and his expression sobers instantly. "My bad, Iris."

I don't respond, just dump my trash and slip out of the kitchen, needing a moment to myself and some space to sit with my thoughts. Though I appreciate Roman sticking up for me, I wish he never said anything. Now I feel exposed as if all my armor has been stripped away. Now everyone can see it: that I'm struggling, that I'm in pain. That I'm weak, incapable of coping with something so basic, something as natural as death.

As I make my way toward the stairs, I hear footsteps behind me. I flip around and see Garrett, his shoulders slumped, eyes heavy with regret. Before I can say anything, he starts to apologize. I try to stop him, the pity in his voice unbearable, but he refuses once he gets going, saying he's truly sorry, that he was wrong and insensitive, and normally he's not this much of an asshole. I know he isn't and understand he genuinely didn't mean anything by what he said. I tell him it's not a big deal and to have fun today.

I crack open my book and force myself to focus on the words until the engine of the Jeep comes alive. I listen as everyone loads into the car, the clamor of the doors slamming closed one after the other a comforting sound. The house goes quiet almost in an instant.

I get to my feet so fast I lose my balance when turning out into the hall. I feel a little ridiculous; I'm sure they'll be gone for hours, but if I don't check now, it'll gnaw at me.

When I make it into the basement, I grab the shovel, and I head back up the stairs and out the sliding doors. Outside, the sun is bright and warm on my face. The dirt has dried out, and now the color looks even as far as I can see. I climb back up to the deck for a better vantage point and eyeball the spot I remember him digging up, but nothing stands out. My stomach twists. Maybe I did imagine it. I shake my head. I know what I saw. I grip the handle of the shovel again, head to where I know I saw him, and hurl out the dirt as fast as I can. Sweat drips down my neck, my spine, forming a slippery second skin under the blazing sun. It's pointless, I tell myself. There's nothing. There's—

Just as the heat starts to become too much to bear, I hit something solid. A tremble ripples through my entire body, my breath catching in my throat. I slow down, carefully clearing out the last layer of dirt. I have to squint to make out what's buried underneath, and when I recognize what it is, I lurch back. My jaw goes slack. I try to speak, but no words come out. The sound I make isn't quite a scream. It's more primal than that, a scraping ground as it leaves my mouth.

But there's no one around to hear.

No one to come running over and see the arm sticking out of the ground.

chapter
twelve

A wave of nausea rips through me so strong it bends me in half, a cyclone across longitudes. I fall to my hands and knees, but I don't feel the ground, only the turbulence tearing through my insides. My throat burns as vomit spews onto the soil, splattering the soft earth. I gasp for air between heaves, but my body convulses again. It feels like my organs are being wrung out. Another wave rises, hot and vile, sending foul-smelling bile splashing on the ground, dripping down my arms.

Somehow I make it up to the bathroom on my shaky legs and stagger inside. I head for the sink, but drop beside the tub instead, another wave attacking me, my stomach heaving viciously. When it finally subsides, the sting of tears burn my cheeks as the rancid stench of bile coats the air, choking me all over again.

After a few minutes, I push myself off the floor and turn on the faucet to rinse the tub. I try to catch my breath as I watch the sour remnants swirling down the drain. At the sink,

I splash water over my face, rinse the bile from my hands. The shock of the cold stings my skin and rouses something raw inside me. I grip the counter to steady myself, but another wave hits me, pulling from somewhere deep inside me, and for a second, I swear I feel something moving beneath my skin, clawing its way out. I lurch toward the toilet, my throat tightening, but nothing comes. Just saliva. Just the bitter taste of my own helplessness.

The truth of it slams into me. Nolan was here last night. Burying someone. It was dark, it was late, and I didn't have my glasses and was too drugged to think straight. But I wasn't seeing or imagining anything. Now I have proof.

I stumble into the bedroom, my equilibrium still off, and hold on to the wall as I find my bag. I slip on a clean shirt, then look for my phone. I nearly tear the room apart only to glance down and realize it's already in my hand.

Garrett doesn't answer when I call. I hold my stomach, trying not to get sick again, and call him right back, pacing hard and fast. I try three times, the call going to voicemail after five rings each time. Then I try Roman.

"Hey," he answers on the third ring, and I hear Lauren and Gia laughing in the background. "What's up?"

"You guys have to come back," I say, my voice breathy and panicked even to my own ears.

"What?" He sounds distracted. "What are you talking about?"

"Now. You have to . . ." The image of the arm floods my mind—pallid, cold, a dirt-encrusted elbow stark against the turned earth—and the words catch in my throat. "There's . . ."

"Iris, what's wrong?" Roman's tone is sharp and serious now, cutting through the static of my fear as if my terror has bled through the phone and seeped into his bones.

"I can't . . ." I wheeze, struggling to draw in air as if a pair of metal claws is clamped around my lungs, squeezing tight.

"Hey, hey. Calm down. Take a breath." I hear some rustling like he's moving to a quieter area. Then he comes back on the line, his voice clearer now. "What's going on?"

I draw in another deep breath and close, then open my eyes. "There's a body."

"A what?"

"Well, an arm," I say, my voice still shaking. "There's an arm. An elbow."

"What do you mean, 'There's an arm?'"

"In the back. It's buried in the back." I pace the room, my head shaking over and over. "I told you. Somebody was here the other night. I saw him. There might be more back there. Maybe there's a whole body. I couldn't look. I got sick."

"Wait, wait. You're saying there's an actual—"

"You have to get back here," I plead, desperate. "We have to call the police."

A moment passes, the silence so loud. Then Roman speaks again, his voice with new resolve. "Okay, hang tight. We'll come back right now. Just don't panic."

I hang up and try to do as he says. I shut my eyes and chant my way through the breathing technique my therapist taught me. I suck in a deep breath, hold it and draw in an even deeper breath, then release all the air in a long, drawn-out exhalation. I do this over and over, but it doesn't work. I can't stay still. I pace faster, feeling like I'm suffocating. My hands won't stop trembling.

Someone's body is spread across the property. I try to place where the rest of the body could be, the legs, the torso, the head. God, the *head*.

THE HOUSE GUESTS

Twenty minutes later, the Jeep finally pulls up on the gravel. I hurry downstairs, meeting everyone in the main room as they pile in, one by one.

"We need to call the cops and get out of here," I say as soon as Garrett slips inside the door.

"No way." Lauren scoffs, a step behind him, looking tipsy already. "I've got six more days of peace before I'm going back home."

"There's a body back there. A *corpse*." I lock eyes with Garrett, hoping he'll be more reasonable. "Right where I saw your uncle digging last night."

Garrett stands frozen, his face twisting. I can't tell if it's shock or disbelief, but he doesn't jump in to deny me, and for a fleeting moment, his silence feels like a small victory.

Roman catches my eye. His expression softens with quiet concern, his eyes searching mine as if trying to unspool the tangles of my brain. "Are you sure it wasn't something else?"

"I know an elbow when I see one."

"I get that, but—"

"I just saw it in broad daylight."

"Yeah, without your glasses," Gia points out, and I clench my teeth to keep myself from going off on her.

My eyes might be bad, but it was an arm. It had to be.

"Well, one of you go check it out," Violet says, looking between Roman and Garrett, who exchange a hesitant glance. "Forget it, I'll go," she says, breaking off from the huddle. "It's probably nothing anyway."

Garrett is quick to stop her, grabbing her by the arm. "Whoa, whoa. If there's really something out there, one of the men will go."

"So go," she says, her patience wearing thin.

"I'll go." Roman exhales sharply and crosses the room, his back straight, shoulders squared. "Stay here and look after the women," he says, catching his cousin's eye, a faint smirk tugging at his mouth like he still thinks this is all some kind of joke.

"I got you," Garrett replies, saluting him with mock solemnity.

I want to follow Roman as he cuts through to the back, but I stay put, relief creeping in as he slips out the door.

"So was it just an elbow, or a full arm?" Gia asks, sidling up to me, and though I know she's being facetious, I answer her question in earnest.

"I don't know. I didn't finish . . ." I falter, her scathing stare corrupting the words as they form on my tongue. "I only saw part of it."

I stop when I see Violet and Lauren's equally skeptical expressions, the weight of their collective doubt sinking into me, unraveling whatever resolve I have left. The rest of the body could be in there, but the hole doesn't seem big enough. Did I see wrong? Was it really an elbow, or just a pale stone in the dirt or something?

Violet inches closer to me, taking this all seriously now, a cloud of horror in her eyes. "So the body is like . . . all chopped up?"

Lauren visibly gags at the thought. "Gross."

"Hey," Violet says, rubbing my back. "You're okay. We're here, alright?"

I nod, then slump into the couch, but my body refuses to settle. I can't sit. My nerves are a live wire, thrumming with each passing second. Somehow Lauren and Gia are glued to their phones, but Violet looks just as on edge as me. The air feels suffocating. The silence is thick, time stretching out as we wait.

Finally, Roman ducks back in the room. The second I hear his footfall, I shuffle toward him, my heart hammering in my chest, skin buzzing with the raw, jagged edges of panic.

"Attached or not attached?" Garrett asks, barely containing his laughter.

Roman meets my eyes. It's not quite an apology, but it's something raw, something unspoken, a silent acknowledgment of the weight of what I've seen, of the truth he can no longer deny.

"Attached," he says softly, and the earth tips off its axis.

My stomach roils. Never in my life had I so desperately wanted to be wrong. I hoped it was just my mind playing tricks on me, a fevered hallucination or the remnants of a dream that refused to fade when I woke. But now, with the cold reality seeping in, I can't escape the truth. I was right. And that fact, sharp and undeniable, sinks its claws into my very soul.

For the first time, Gia doesn't have anything snide to say. The air in the room is different now. Noxious. Lauren glances at me, then back at Roman, then to Garrett, and the fear in her eyes goes from distant to palpable. Violet is frozen from the waist up. Her right leg bounces furiously, the only sign she's still with us.

"So, there's really . . ." Gia shakes her head in disbelief. "A dead body?"

"You guys should come see for yourself," Roman says, and with that, he turns to head back outside.

I catch a flicker of shame in Violet's eyes when she glances at me before getting up to follow Roman. Lauren and Gia hold hands, nervous, their faces squeamish as they move behind Garrett across the deck, down to the edge of the property. I trail a few steps behind them. I don't want to get too close again.

I hold my breath as the huddle forms around the hole. It's quiet for a few moments, except for the distant call of a crow, everyone leaning in to see the body. One by one, they all burst into histrionics. Lauren covers her mouth, and Violet does the same. Then someone snorts, and I realize these are sounds of laughter, not horror.

I push my way through the barricade of bodies, baffled as to how anything about this could possibly be funny. We could be in danger. We are staying in the home of a murderer.

Garrett squats down and lifts something out of the dirt, then turns to me. I scream and lurch backward, but the laughter only crescendos. I glance down at what's in his hands. It's not an arm. Or an elbow. Or human.

I gawk at the vintage baby doll, its head almost completely turned around like an owl's, its thick, brittle plastic skin a pale, unnatural shade, slightly yellowed with age. One of its eyes winks, the other one frozen and staring right through me.

chapter
thirteen

"You made us rush back for a *doll?*" Lauren snaps, her laughter finally subsiding.

"No." I can do nothing but shake my head in disbelief. "I . . ."

But I don't know what to say. That is a doll in Garrett's hand. My eyes drop down to the ground, but somehow it feels like I'm floating away. I scrutinize the shallow hole while they play hot potato with the plastic baby. There's nothing left but dirt and a few scattered rocks. Maybe it's the wrong spot. Maybe it's somewhere else around here. I could have gotten it wrong.

"I'm all for a good stunt," Violet starts, and I wish she wouldn't finish. "But haven't we all outgrown petty pranks?"

"You mean like the one you played on *me* while we were out on the water?"

She tilts her head as if putting a final piece in a puzzle. "Is that what this is? Payback?"

"Come on, Iris," Lauren says, rolling her eyes. "My toddler is more mature, and that's saying a lot because he's an asshole."

Garrett admonishes her with a look, but she doesn't back down or apologize.

"It's not a prank," I say, trying to keep my cool but failing miserably. "There was an arm in the ground when I came out here earlier."

Gia catches the doll, the first time I've ever seen her catch something without flinching at the thought of her manicure being ruined. She leans in close to my face like I'm some kind of marred exhibit to gawk at. "Oh, my god. You really are having hallucinations."

"I'm not having hallucinations. That's not what—"

"Sounds like it's time for a nap, hon," Lauren says, brushing past me with her shoulder, hard enough to make me stumble back a step. I watch as she heads inside, Garrett right on her heels.

"What is this, some weird cry for attention?" Gia asks. She waits for me to respond, but I can't find the words. Everything I think to say sounds too wild, too far-fetched. She won't believe me anyway.

She tosses the doll my way and peels away. I look down at it, trying to convince myself that this is what I saw. But it doesn't work. I saw an elbow, not a plastic relic with joints that barely function properly.

Violet watches me for a beat. When she speaks, her voice is unlike Gia's or Lauren's. She's sincere, and somehow her tenderness stings even more. "Look, me jumping off the boat was just a joke. You don't have to—"

"I don't care about what happened on the boat," I snap before she can finish. "It was here. I saw it."

She nods like she's genuinely trying to understand. "An arm."

"Yes."

"A *human* arm?"

I run a hand over my braids and sigh heavily. "I guess I didn't really look that close. I was freaking out."

Violet searches my face again, inching a step closer. "Do you need to talk?"

"I need you to *believe me*," I say, shoving the doll in her arms, my voice suddenly fierce again.

My tone offends her, and she drops the doll to the ground. She takes off, heading inside with the others. I wait for Roman to say something, to patronize me like I'm some clueless child. But he doesn't.

"Guess you think I'm lying too."

"No one's saying you're lying," he says, a little resigned, and I look up at him, his big body towering over mine.

"Well, I prefer *liar* to *crazy*," I say, squatting down to examine the dirt closer, my hand brushing across the surface in disbelief.

There are plenty of words designed to belittle and demean women—*slut*, *bitch*, *whore*. But the most cutting ones are *c* words. *Catty*, *cow*, *cunt*, *crazy*. Centuries ago we were *witches*. Then we were *hysterical* when really we just had something to say. It was nothing more than an attempt to strip us of our autonomy so men could maintain their authority. Now we're *crazy*.

"I don't think you're crazy," Roman says, crouching down so that he can meet my eyes. "Maybe you're just tired."

I shake my head. "I slept last night."

"With the benzos?"

"Seven hours," I say with a nod, and I catch the sheen of worry veil his face. "It was my regular dose. I'm not hallucinating."

"So what happened? The arm reattached itself to its torso, found its legs and hid somewhere?"

I know how malleable memory can be. I've read about the experiments that have been done on the Mandela effect. I know about hindsight bias, that eyewitness testimony is often unreliable, how people often fill in the blanks subconsciously because the brain likes completed circles. But this isn't a malfunction of memory. I *saw* that arm. Somebody had to move it. I wonder if he's still around. Uncle Nolan. He must have seen me find it and moved it while I was upstairs.

I start to share this theory with Roman, but he stands up too and leaves me all alone. I look at the doll and think this ugly little thing is something my mother would have brought home for me after pulling it out of a dumpster, thinking I would love it, or hoping it would keep me occupied long enough so she could get high.

chapter
fourteen

The rest of the morning moves past me in a thick fog. I keep to myself by the lake, swimming laps and soaking in the sun. Someone calls for me to come in for lunch, but I pass. In my solitude, I think of my mother. She was perpetually alone, but at least she chose her loneliness. Embracing it was the first form of rebellion she dabbled in, her first taste of perversity. It was all she'd known—not mattering to anyone. Since no one wanted her, she wanted no one. She had no interest in living, just did whatever she had to in order to survive another torturous day. She made a lot of people hate her, and then she got pregnant.

Maybe I'm destined to be alone just like her. Like mother, like daughter.

As I finish a chapter in my book, the clouds suddenly darken. I stare out at the clear blue water as it turns a somber gray, mirroring the brooding sky. A distant rumble of thunder breaks the serenity, a prelude. First there's a gentle patter of rain falling softly on the surface. Then it quickly escalates into a steady downpour. I inhale a deep breath, reveling in the soothing petrichor scent, the sound. I toss my book inside the empty cooler someone left behind and stretch out beneath the gentle downpour as if it can baptize me, as if I will be born anew.

The rain picks up, hammering the roof like a warning, and I slip back into the house. The air feels heavier now, pressing down on my shoulders as I make my way toward the stairs. When I pass the basement door, my steps falter. Something about it draws me, a gnawing feeling I can't shake.

I hesitate, glancing around first, then step closer. Maybe I missed something earlier. A detail. My hand hovers over the knob, heart racing in my chest. Footsteps echo from the hallway. Garrett rounds the corner, his easy smile breaking the tension. I force one of my own, shaky and thin, and shift my weight like I was just passing through.

"Snack run," I lie, motioning toward the kitchen.

He nods, completely oblivious, but I can feel the blood pulsing in my ears as I edge away.

I grab a banana and sit in the front room for a while, watching the rain, flipping through channels on the TV. Before I find something I'm interested in, the rain has already cleared up and the sun is beaming again, the weather here as mercurial as my mother. Almost immediately, everyone flocks downstairs dressed in their swimsuits, making a beeline for the dock. I head upstairs to change, but before I can pull up the straps of my swimsuit, the boat's engine roars alive. I sprint outside, shouting for them to wait as the boat peels away from the shore, but Garrett just picks up speed.

They don't get back until four hours later, when the sun is starting its kaleidoscopic daily descent. When I confront Garrett about no one giving me a heads-up, he says he didn't know I wanted to come, swears he would have waited if he had, but behind him Gia and Lauren are smothering laughter. They didn't want me to come. They think I'm bringing down the vibe, ruining the fun for everyone.

As the sky glows in sorbet oranges and pinks, the sun casting a golden hue across the lake, Garrett and Roman light up a bonfire. I watch from the window upstairs. It takes a while, and the girls cheer when it finally starts to burn, drinks in hand. Garrett leans into Lauren and they kiss by the fire, her arms wrapped around his neck. I make my way downstairs, telling myself to enjoy this, but I can't stop thinking of how much better this would all be if Eli was here.

He would believe me. He would stick by my side.

As I make my way over to the fire, I pass Roman heading into the woods. I'm tempted to follow him. I want to ask him about the photo I saw, but before I can, Gia sidles up to me, a small burning log in her hand.

"Want me to cast out your inner demons?" she asks. "You know, exorcize the dark spirits that are making you see things?"

I step around her, jaw tight. "I'll pass."

"You sure?"

"There's no such thing as dark spirits," I say and move away from her.

She follows me to a spot near the fire. "Yeah, there is. My stepdad's a reverend. He taught me a little something."

"There was an arm in that dirt," I tell her through clenched teeth. "Not a doll. A *person's* arm."

She laughs and rolls her eyes. "Weird hill to die on."

After that, she leaves me alone, and I watch the fire for a moment, lulled by the crackles and pops. I think of all it carries with it, ancient secrets that must rival the ocean's, and wonder how something so soothing can have such a vicious hunger. It's a guardian against the cold and the dark yet can scorch and consume, turn life into ashes in seconds.

"You do realize we *all* saw the doll."

I look at Lauren, annoyed that she's pulled me from my trance.

"You're the only one who saw a corpse," she says, waiting for me to react.

Gia turns back around, taking another sip of her drink. I say nothing, hoping they'll just leave me with the fire. I'd rather take my chance with the flames than their company.

"I don't know," Gia says, her tone laced with mock sincerity. "Might be time for a higher dose."

They both laugh, drunk, Gia looking so very satisfied with herself. Before I can respond, Violet tells them to chill. But I'm done enduring their casual cruelty. I slam the front door shut behind me and pace the unlit space, debating whether or not I should just pack my stuff and call Eli to come get me. I don't want to be intrusive, or clingy, or make this week all about me. But I don't know how much more of this I can take.

"You okay?"

I spin around at the voice and see Roman standing in the dark, tall and broad and brooding. I shut my mouth and breathe a sigh of relief as he eases closer.

"God, stop sneaking up on me," I mutter, folding my arms.

His smile is slow and easy. "Not trying, I promise."

"I know," I concede with a sigh. "I'm just a little jumpy after . . ."

I stop myself, and it seems like we both know why. Just saying the words feels foolish now since no one believes me. There *was* a doll. I can't deny that. But there was an arm too.

And arms don't just disappear. Could it really have been just a delusion? A hallucination?

Roman stops a few feet away, his expression soft, and I already appreciate his company more than I thought I would. "Sure you're okay?" he asks again, more emphatically this time.

"Yeah, I . . ." My head shakes. "Maybe I'm hungry?"

He laughs. "Hungry?"

"Only thing I had today was a banana," I say, then think about it. "But I threw it up like ten minutes later."

"Are you serious?"

"I was sick earlier, and I guess I just forgot."

"Well, I'm about to fire up the grill. I just got more cherrywood."

My smile is genuine. "Sounds amazing."

"Can you wait that long? I think there's some leftovers in the fridge from last night."

"I can wait," I say, watching him for a moment before I continue. "Your mom died when you were young, right?"

"Yeah, but it was different. I was two. I don't think I remember her. I remember her from the pictures. And my dreams. Sometimes I think they're memories, but I'm pretty sure it's just my mind conjuring her out of the bits and scraps my dad told me about her, you know?"

I let out a breath. "Yeah."

"I miss her, though," he says, nodding to himself, his voice full of longing, and there's suddenly something vulnerable and innocent about him. "Is that even possible? Can you miss someone you can't remember?"

"Maybe," I whisper, thinking of my mother.

Roman might not have been traumatized by his mother's death the way I was, but we have something in common: We both miss someone we never got to know. All we have left is the hope that we'll get a chance to see them in our dreams at night, reunited in the fleeting space between sleep and waking, where time stands still and we can whisper the words we never got to say.

My eyes move over him, and he looks so different to me now. I wonder what it must have been like to grow up in a stable environment with a father who was always there and met all of his needs. My mother needed chaos in order to bear the days, her frequency unremitting. Unforgiving. I'm the same way—drawn to the tangles and the knots, and sometimes it feels like there's no way I could have ever been normal. It's like I was born this way, a capricious, feeble apparatus incapable of order and destined only for destruction, wreaking havoc just to stay calm.

Roman seems to sense my discomfort. "Hey."

I look up at him, and suddenly it feels like he's too close. Maybe it's the quiet, or the velvety darkness. But this feels too intimate.

"You'll be fine, alright?" Roman says. "I've got steaks, burgers and some chicken breasts marinating. Gonna make some kabobs."

"I love those," I say, forcing a smile.

"Don't worry, I got you. I'll get some meat in your belly, put you to bed. Then you can sleep off today, and we'll all start fresh tomorrow. Cool?"

I nod, but I can't help but feel like he's flirting with me. "Cool."

Roman smiles, still lingering, and just as I'm starting to feel awkward, Garrett calls out to him from the deck, waving a pack of buns in the air through the window. Roman slips into the kitchen, then jogs back out with the meat in an aluminum foil tray. He nods at me before slipping onto the other side of the glass.

When I make it upstairs, I shut myself in the bedroom and dial Eli's number, needing to hear the familiar timbre of his voice. He answers on the third ring. When the soft rumble of his voice comes through the line, it feels like we haven't talked in eons. I tell him about what happened—the hole, the shovel, the arm, the doll, everything—just to see what he thinks. He says he believes I saw something, but doesn't think it was actually there. He suggests it was a residual effect of the benzos. His honesty hits me hard. He knows me better than everyone here, so his opinion holds more weight.

I ask Eli about his grandmother, not wanting to talk about the arm anymore. I hope he'll say she's doing better, that he can drive out here tomorrow. But he says she's still in critical condition, and he's spending the night at the hospital by his mother's side.

After we hang up, I slink into the hall and knock before pushing into the master bedroom, the one Garrett and Lauren are staying in. I don't turn on the lights; I don't want anyone outside to know I'm in here. I flip through the rack in the closet, looking for the jacket I saw in that photo, the one Nolan was wearing. Aside from an alarming number of flannels, there's nothing but a few coats and a pair of snow boots tucked in the corner. I immediately recognize the faint menthol smell permeating the space. Unfiltered Camels. The same ones my mother used to smoke. She went through a pack a day when she could afford them, when she was still clean. I rummage through the drawers briefly, but they're only stuffed with thermal underwear, socks, sweats and T-shirts, all organized and shockingly neat, especially for a man who lives alone. I find a hamper in the attached bathroom, but it's empty, the jacket nowhere to be found.

On my way back out to the deck to check on the food, I stop in the spare room just off the kitchen, needing to see that photo of Nolan again. I squint down at the frame as I lift it closer. He's definitely wearing the jacket I saw the other night. He must still be wearing it.

Either that, or he got rid of it because of the blood.

chapter
fifteen

Outside, the temperature has dropped to a crisp, cool breeze, exactly how Eli likes it. The air carries the faint scent of pine, but the aroma wafting from the grill overpowers the smells of nature.

I sidle up next to Roman manning the grill with his apron tied at his hips, flipping over medium rare steaks, well-done burgers and juicy chicken breasts, charring bell peppers and perfectly blackened corn on the cob. It smells delicious. Smoky wood with hints of sizzling meat, the heat of the peppers adding a savoriness to the mix. It looks as good as it smells. My stomach rumbles. When he notices me, he hands me a burger he's already set aside, the juices oozing out from the sides, and points me to the table with the accoutrements, then lets me know he's firing up the kabobs in a few minutes.

As I layer on red onions, greens and a generous squirt of spicy Dijon, Violet is within reach but far away, her focus intense as she mixes drinks at the makeshift bar she's set up. Her brow furrows as she measures and stirs. She bites her lip as she pours a margarita into a salt-rimmed glass and adds a lime wedge before handing it to Gia.

I don't even sit; I lift my burger and scarf it down without taking a single breath between bites, and it's glorious. I don't care who sees me. I gorge like it's my last meal and let the crumbs fall down my shirt, not reaching for a napkin until it's gone. I'm always getting on Eli—how he demolishes his food in two minutes flat, no matter how oversized the portion is. A burger for him takes only three bites, but I practically get mine down in one and bounce right back over to Roman. He laughs, pleased as I lick mustard from my fingers. I watch him sear the kabobs, and then he watches me taste them. We both laugh when I burn my tongue, too eager. He blows on the kabob for me, and the next bite is just right.

I sit down on one of the lounge chairs to properly enjoy my second kabob and catch Lauren stepping out of the house, sipping a glass of water. My mouth opens in shock as she immediately spits it out, spraying Violet right in the face.

"What the hell!" Violet says, wiping the water from her eyes.

"That water is disgusting," Lauren says, gagging. "Tastes like something rotten. But, like, sweet, too."

"What?" Violet asks, as confused as me.

"I don't know," she says. "Just fucking *gross*."

"Where'd you get it?" Gia asks, leaning over to sniff it.

"The tap."

I pause mid-bite. The water was fine the other night when I drank some to wash down my pills. Actually, it tasted really good, crisp and fresh.

Roman reaches for the glass and takes a sip. He swallows, but his throat seems to hesitate, a slight gag rising in his chest. His eyes flicker with confusion. Then he blinks rapidly, trying to shake the aftertaste that lingers in his mouth.

Garrett leans over. "You should be drinking something stronger anyway," he says, lifting the bottle of tequila to Lauren's lips.

She takes a big gulp with a smile, but instead of swallowing, empties it into his mouth. He laughs, then turns to Violet. She opens her mouth wide, eager to continue the chain, which goes from her to Gia, who scurries over to empty what's left into Roman's mouth. Roman looks at me and I hesitate, feeling everyone's eyes land on my face at once.

"Don't stop the train, Iris," Violet says, egging me on.

The juice train is nothing new. We did it at almost every party in college, but Eli would always make sure I was his recipient. It feels too intimate to do it with anyone else, especially with Roman after the look he gave me after talking about his mother. But I'm the only one left. I shrug and angle my neck so he can fill my mouth, but there's only a drop left. He laughs and I do too, relieved I don't have to swallow everyone's backwash.

"Want a real drink?" Violet asks as everyone disperses, but she doesn't wait for a response. She steps off and comes back with a shot glass filled with an amber-hued liquid that I know will burn all the way down.

"I haven't really eaten much yet," I say, hoping she'll back off.

"Roman is making plenty of food." She holds out the shot glass, wiggling it in front of my face. "Come on, just one? For me? You're so much more fun when you loosen up."

I stare at the tiny glass. The liquid inside catches the firelight, warm and inviting. I take the shot and toss it back. The tequila hits the back of my throat with an ugly, thick burn, spreading over my chest, warming my body from the inside out.

"No cringe," Violet says, flashing almost all of her teeth. "And here I thought you were a softie. Okay, hold on. I'll get you some of the good shit. You down?"

I nod reluctantly, and Violet shuffles over to her station. I look out at the water until she's back, handing me a cocktail. Pink and bright with sugar on the rim.

"What is it?"

Violet smirks. "Would you ask a magician to reveal his tricks?"

I take the glass and down it as fast as I can just to get it over with. For the next hour or so, Violet keeps a glass in my hand. I normally hate the feeling of alcohol in my body, but tonight, the buzz feels more like a tingle, and it feels good. For the first time since I've gotten here, I don't think about the hole. The shovel. The jacket. The photo. The arm. The doll. My mother's brains. The blood. The gun. The empty pews. The needles. The baggies.

I don't think at all.

I watch Lauren and Gia give Roman a very tame lap dance, their bodies swaying slightly out of rhythm. They must be as drunk as me. Garrett and Violet cheer them on, and Roman is drunk enough to enjoy it. When Lauren gets bored, she moves over to Garrett. She grinds her hips into his, then turns around and bounces her ass in his face, her moves serious now. Turning around again, she slowly slides Garrett's shirt up and over his shoulders, then tosses it off the edge of the deck for show. He reaches up, moving his hands over her body, pulling her onto his lap and grinding back like they're going to make that second baby Lauren doesn't want right here in front of everyone.

I wobble to my feet, needing to walk off some of this drunkenness. My head is starting to whirl. I only make it a few steps toward the house before I stumble and crash into the table. Something shatters.

Violet grabs my arm and helps me up to my feet. "You okay? Watch out for the glass."

I clutch onto her as I struggle to regain my balance. Everything spins, everyone becoming figurines on a grotesque carousel. I blink deliberately a few times, but the dizziness won't subside.

"Think I had too much . . ." I take a breath, hoping a surge of oxygen in my blood will help. "Gonna go lay down."

I peel away from her, holding my arms out for balance as I stumble toward the house, my head pounding. I expect the cool embrace of the air-conditioned entryway, but instead, my head slams into the glass door. It looked so clear. My world flashes for a moment, and then I feel hands on me, ushering me inside the door, the pain reverberating in the center of my skull. It's Roman. I smell him, the grill, the meat, the smoke. He asks if I'm okay.

"Thought it was open," I mutter, holding my head where it hurts, the ache spreading like smoke after a fire.

Violet is nearby too. I hear her. She takes over for Roman and guides me over to the couch, then says she'll be right back. I ask where she's going. She says I need ice for my head. I wave her off, insisting that I'm fine, just a little dizzy. She tells me to lie down, then disappears. I shut my eyes, a heavy drowsiness washing over me in waves.

"How's the head?"

My eyes flutter open. I have to blink a few times to make out Garrett's face.

"I'm fine," I say, though I can't even feel my face anymore. I can barely feel any of my limbs. "I just had too much to drink."

"We were all going pretty hard." Garrett bends over and lifts my arm. "Come on. I'll get you upstairs."

He's still shirtless, so it feels strange to grab onto his bare shoulders, but I don't really have another option. He lets me lean my weight into him as we make our way up the stairs and into my room. He leaves the light off and guides me down onto the bed carefully, handling me the way I suspect he handles his son. I try to pull off my shoes but give up halfway.

"I got you," Garrett says, dropping down to his knees.

I want to thank him, but somehow even trying to speak seems to hurt. Slumping back onto the bed, I close my eyes, and they immediately feel sewn shut. Garrett pulls off my shoes one at a time. He calls my name, and I try to answer, but nothing comes out. I feel him lean over me, asking me something, but I can't make out the words. I try to peel open my eyes, but they feel weighed down by anchors.

And then I hear another voice. A familiar voice. My favorite voice.

Eli? How can it be Eli?

I force my eyes open, my vision blurry, and see him through the haze. He's here. I fight to stay awake, but sleep pulls me in completely, drowning me in its darkness.

chapter
sixteen

My head pounds as I sit on top of the toilet seat, needing a break after hopping out of the shower. A haze clings to my mind, clouding my thoughts. The room is too bright. Faint sounds from downstairs reverberate against my skull like an African drum.

I ease in front of the mirror, a towel secured around my body. As I stare at my reflection, my stomach churns as if I might vomit. I take a deep breath, pushing the queasiness down, and try to remember last night. My mind goes blank. Everything blurs together in one big blob of nothingness. I undo my braids, then lean in once I see the swollen knot on my forehead. It's tender and red. I try to place it, but nothing comes.

I pad into the bedroom, each step heavy and deliberate as I concentrate on not falling. I reach for my bag on the floor, then stop short. My glasses. I blink in disbelief and stare at them on the nightstand. When I slide them on, the relief is instant.

For a moment, I wonder if they've been here this whole time and I'm actually losing my mind. Then I release a breath, remembering that Eli showed up last night. I remember hearing his voice, seeing him standing under the threshold. He must have brought them. I want to run into his arms and bury my nose in his neck. It's my favorite part of his body. I always feel safe there. At home.

I forget about the pain and throw on clothes as fast as I can. As I slip on my shoes, I spot my baggie of pills on the floor. I dump them into the toilet, then pause with my hand on the handle. I count the pills swirling in the water, then again to make sure. Three pills are missing. I shake my head. Maybe I dropped some in the room. I don't waste time checking. I flush the toilet and hurry down the stairs to see Eli.

When I turn into the kitchen, everyone has already begun eating without me, as usual, but I'm surprised to see that Eli has too. He doesn't see me come into the room, his back to me as I walk in. He grabs a muffin from the massive spread on the table, turning it over in his hand as he inspects it. I smile, just to myself, so relieved to see him. The last few days have been demoralizing.

"Do these have nuts in them?" he asks, looking at Roman.

"Nah, bro," Roman says, flipping a pancake with his spatula. "You're good."

Eli takes a huge bite out of the muffin, and I meet his eyes as I cross the room.

"Look who finally decided to grace us with her presence," Gia says, standing at Roman's side, whisking more eggs for him to scramble. She's wearing two tiny strips of clothing—a miniskirt that resembles a Post-it more than a garment, and semi-sheer crop top.

"Sorry, I . . ." I rub my temples. "I'm not feeling good. I can barely remember last night."

Lauren scoffs. "I mean, you only guzzled a gallon of tequila and walked face-first into a glass door."

And now it makes sense. The bump on my head.

Violet grabs an orange and slips out of the room.

I ease closer to Eli as he takes another bite of his muffin. "Hey."

He looks up, just as I hook my hand around his neck and lean down for a kiss. He turns at the last second, forcing my lips to graze his ear.

"Thanks for bringing my glasses," I say softly.

He doesn't reply, just keeps chewing with the utmost focus. I study his face, but he won't meet my eyes. When I start to speak again, I pause, realizing something's wrong. It's all over him.

"What happened?" I ask so only he can hear.

"Nothing."

My mind jumps to the worst-case scenario. "Is it your grandma? Did something happen?"

"She's good," he says, his voice strangely void of emotion. "She's stable."

I wait, expecting him to go on, but he just stuffs the rest of the muffin in his mouth.

"That's it?" I ask, wishing we were alone, because clearly there's something he's not telling me.

"What else is there?" Eli finally looks up at me, showing me his eyes, and I don't like the look in them. Just like his voice, there's nothing in his expression that shows me he's happy to see me.

"Why didn't you tell me you were coming up here?" I ask, taking the empty chair next to him. "Didn't expect to see you until I got back."

"Wanted to surprise you." Eli shrugs and takes a sip of his coffee. "But I'm the one who got surprised, huh?"

I can't recall a time he's ever been like this with me, so short and petulant. "What?"

"Forget it."

"No, tell me," I insist, pulling his arm gently. "I don't remember."

He snorts. "You don't remember."

"I had too much to drink," I say, keeping my voice low, but I can already feel everyone's eyes sneaking glances at us.

Muscles work in Eli's jaw before he turns to face me. "Well, why don't you ask Garrett? He knows what you did."

As if pulled by an invisible thread, everyone turns to Garrett.

"What?" he asks, looking just as confused as I am.

I feel Lauren's eyes on me like a laser beam of heat, but I pretend not to.

"I said you know what she did last night," Eli says, his eyes square on Garrett. "You were there, weren't you?"

"Bro, I told you nothing happened," he says, and it's the first time I've heard Garrett raise his voice.

"I saw you with my own eyes," Eli says, refusing to let this go.

"Saw what?" Lauren asks, her gaze locked on Garrett.

I stare at him too, just as curious as she is. What could Eli have possibly seen?

Garrett shrugs and drizzles maple syrup over his waffles. "I don't know what he's talking about."

Lauren shifts her gaze over to Eli. So do I.

"What'd you see?" she asks, her voice low and controlled.

Eli starts to respond, but Garrett cuts him off, his eyes on his wife. "Baby, nothing happened."

Lauren glares at me from across the table, her blue eyes sharp and narrow. Just when I think she's going to leap over and strangle me, she stuffs her mouth with a piece of Garrett's waffle. The table falls quiet. I don't even bother to fill my plate. My appetite has been obliterated. When I came down here, I saw this all going so differently. I thought Eli would be as happy to see me as I am him.

I slide my hand onto his strong leg and speak close to his ear. "Can we go somewhere else?"

"Whatever you want to say to me," he starts, using his full voice, "you can say in front of my friends."

His friends.

With those few words, he casts me away on a deserted island. The world around me shrinks, collapsing into a suffocating silence. I can't look at him anymore. I want to bolt out of here, but it would only draw even more attention to myself. I force myself to stay, feeling exposed, made so vulnerable by the person who's supposed to be on my side.

"Hey, we like you *too*," Gia says, her voice slicing through the tension like a machete. "Which says a lot, because you're no fun and kinda psychotic."

Roman glances back over his shoulder. "Can you chill for five seconds? She's obviously going through something."

"I'm not *going through* anything," I snap, and when Roman meets my eyes, he looks hurt.

I instantly regret my tone. He's been so nice and supportive, but I'm tired of this. Being here, being told I'm lying, blind, insane—it's all getting to me. I should have bailed when I had the chance.

"There was an arm buried out there whether you assholes believe me or not," I say, the words ripping from me before I can stop them. "And somebody took my hair tie."

I jump up from the table, anger coursing through my veins, and actually, it feels good to feel something so intensely. I snatch a knife from the butcher block on the counter, then grab a grapefruit from the fridge and slice it in half with more force than necessary as I feel everyone turn to stare. I don't even like grapefruit, the acidity and sourness grossly unappealing, but something about it calls my name.

"Hey, Roman." Eli waits until he has his undivided attention. "Last I checked, Iris doesn't need you to speak for her."

Roman starts to respond, but I beat him to it. "At least he's willing to say something."

Eli refuses to look in my direction. "Oh, I see what's going on. You want next, huh?"

I hold my breath as he rises to his feet and walks up behind Roman at the stove. Roman looks to me for an explanation, but all I can offer is a shrug.

"What are you doing?" Gia asks Eli, her voice low and tight.

Eli glances at her, then continues glaring at Roman. "Garrett hit last night, so now you think you got a chance?"

Roman and I both stare at him, stunned and confused.

Garrett stands up too. "Bro, you want to let the rest of us know what the hell you're talking about? The suspense is killing us."

"I saw you," Eli says just over his breath. "I saw you in her room last night."

Everyone's eyes come to me. I squeeze the handle of the knife, the grapefruit forgotten.

chapter
seventeen

At first it doesn't even register, what Eli is accusing me and Garrett of. It's so preposterous it seems like a poorly timed joke. But the punchline never comes.

Lauren turns to Garrett, her eyes on fire. "You were in her room last night?"

"Look, man, whatever you think you saw, you didn't see, okay?" Garrett says, breaking eye contact with Eli midway through.

It makes blood rush up into my ears. Maybe he's lying. But if he's not telling the truth, then what was he really doing in my room? I remember Violet giving me a pretty pink drink, and I know I hit my head. I see a flash of Eli in my bedroom, and everything else is black.

"What did he see?" Lauren demands to know, and I wait with as little patience as she does.

Garrett hesitates.

"Someone please tell us," Gia says. "The suspense is making my scalp itch."

"I was helping her into bed," Garrett says in a dismissive tone, like this is the last he plans on explaining this. "That's it."

But Eli doesn't back down. "You were taking her clothes off."

"Just her jacket so she—"

Lauren jumps between them. "Why were you even in her room?"

"She was out of it downstairs. She hit her head. Hard. I was just making sure she got to bed okay." Garrett turns to Lauren, reaching for her hand, but she steps just out of reach. "Nothing happened, baby. You know I would never do that to you."

But she isn't completely convinced. "I don't understand why you were in her room in the first place."

"I just told you, I . . ." Garrett stops, quickly switching gears. "Baby, we made love last night, didn't we?"

I don't think I've ever seen Lauren go shy, but by the way she tucks her head, it's obvious she would have preferred Garrett to not speak about this in front of everyone. Gia and Roman exchange a glance, then promptly filter out of the room. This is none of their business, and I wish I could say the same. I wish Eli would take me by the hand and drag me out of here. I want to go back to the city, back to our world, our life.

"Why would I go to her when I have you? Come on, baby," Garrett pulls her close and waits until she looks up into his eyes. "You know nothing happened."

Lauren nods, almost imperceptibly, her eyes already softening as his arms slink around her waist. He kisses her softly on the lips, and Lauren kisses him back with her eyes closed.

I let out a sigh of relief, thinking it's over. But Eli mumbles something under his breath and charges out of the room. I jump to my feet and call after him, but he turns down the hall. Garrett goes after him, leaving me alone with Lauren.

There's a sneer in her eyes when they meet mine. "You couldn't get in bed yourself?"

"I didn't ask him to help me," I say, resenting that I even have to defend myself. "I don't even remember anything."

"Oh, right. You blacked out, and now your mind's conveniently wiped, right?"

I stare at her, incredulous. "He *just* told you nothing happened."

"You don't drink," Lauren says with an indignant shrug, her expression calm as she narrows the gap between us, but I can smell the fury simmering just beneath the surface. "Maybe you can't handle your liquor and the real you came out."

"I have a man," I say, holding her gaze.

"You sure? Because your man clearly saw something he didn't like."

"It's a misunderstanding. Nothing happened."

Lauren cocks her head. "You just said you don't remember anything. Which one is it? You don't remember? Or nothing happened?"

"Why don't you take it up with him? He's the one who was in *my* room."

I turn my back on her, refusing to give her any more of my energy, and continue slicing my grapefruit.

"Well, who let him in?" Lauren asks from behind me.

I don't look at her. "I didn't let anyone in."

"You're saying he forced his way into your room?"

"No, I . . ."

I whip around, and Lauren is standing right behind me. She lurches back, and I follow her horrified eyes to the knife still in my grasp. I must have missed her by an inch or two.

"What the hell," Lauren shrieks. "Watch that thing."

"Sorry. I'm just . . ." Shaking, I toss the knife back onto the table and wipe my hands on my shorts. "Over this."

Lauren scoffs. "*You're* over this?"

I ignore her and storm out of the kitchen.

I need to find Eli. I need him to believe me.

I sweep the first level of the house, then drift outside, but I don't find him on the front deck either. I peer down at the lake and scan the shoreline. It feels like there's a tight band wrapped around my skull, squeezing with each pulse, but at least with my glasses everything looks sharper. The water is bluer. The clouds are puffier. I can see the delicate ripples on the lake's surface, shimmering like silver threads. I can make out the small waves lapping against the rocks. Even the mountains are clearer now, their outlines sharp against the bright blue, and I can just make out a hawk circling high above.

But no Eli.

I circle around to the back deck. Somebody left a bottle floating in the hot tub, but other than that, it's empty too. I cut through the house, calling for him, but get no answer. When I go down to the gravel and peer inside both cars, no one's inside. Violet calls out to me from the deck. She's standing with Roman, who says he saw Eli and Garrett go into the woods.

I hesitate, contemplating going in after them, and peer into the forest. The sunlight filters through the canopy, casting intricate patterns of shadow and light on the ground. It looks inviting, serene. But my sense of direction is hopeless. Without the geometric grid of New York City—the predictable corners, the graciously numbered avenues—there's no way I'd not get lost. The woods are a maze with no clear exit. Everything from every angle looks the same, trees upon trees upon trees stretching out endlessly, no landmarks to guide me.

Upstairs in my room, I grab my duffel. I want to be ready when Eli gets back. This whole thing was a mistake from the beginning. I should never have let him talk me into coming here by myself. I should have been right there by his side while he held his grandmother's hand in the hospital.

I dart around the room in a blur, hurling everything in my bag as quickly as I can. Clothes, shoes, my laptop. Just as I spin around to head into the bathroom for my toothbrush and toiletries, I freeze mid-step.

A pair of dead eyes stares blankly at me. I jump back, a startled scream escaping my lips.

Tucked neatly into the sheets as if tucked into a coffin, the doll that was buried outside taunts me, its face molded into an eerie, unnatural smile. Like it knows something I don't. Like it's mocking me.

My skin prickles. The air feels thick, heavy. My breath catches in my throat.

I release the handle of my bag. It thunks to my feet.

Slowly, I inch closer to the bed until the doll is within arm's reach, then lift it from the bed. Immediately I recoil and drop it in shock.

Crude black lines are drawn on its body. Someone has given it two black eyes, hairy nipples, and a thatch of pubic hair.

chapter
eighteen

Rage surges through me, hot and vicious. I snatch up the doll, my nails scraping against the yellowed plastic. Someone in this house is fucking with me. Whoever did this took my hair tie while I showered. I *know* there were two.

I grit my teeth, trying to make sense of it, but my head pounds. I turn for the door, then stop short.

I stare at Gia, stunned, wondering how I didn't hear her come into the room behind me, how long she's been standing here. Watching me.

"What is *up* with you?" she asks, her eyes crawling down my body, then back up.

"Nothing," I say, swallowing, trying to shake off my uneasiness. "You just . . . you just scared me."

Gia cocks her head and stares at me for a while. "I literally called your name like three times."

I study her, trying to see if she's lying or not. Nothing in her expression breaks. She steps deeper into the room, her eyes narrowing on the doll in my hand.

"Okay, I heard you have trouble sleeping, and I get that, but if that ugly little shit is the kind of thing that helps . . . you're worse off than I thought."

"I didn't . . ." I look down at it, gripping it so hard my fingers tremble. "I don't even know how this got in here."

I hold it up, and she notices the crass modifications.

"Nice drawing," she says, smuggling a laugh. "Didn't know you were so artistically inclined."

"I didn't do this."

She frowns with one side of her face. "Then who did?"

"I don't know."

Gia scoffs, shaking her head with pity. "Yeah, I'm just gonna go. I've heard it's not kind to speak poorly of the mentally ill."

My teeth grind together as she backs out of the room. It takes everything in me to not lunge at her.

I stand there, seething, the fury like lava in my blood now. When I finally blink, my bag comes into focus. A couple of things have toppled out. I crouch down to slip everything back in, but as I drop the doll to the floor, I realize I still don't know why Gia was even in my room. She had no reason to be here, not unless she wanted to see my reaction to finding the doll.

I jump back to my feet and bolt out the door. My footsteps pound down the hall as I race after her, my breaths coming in sharp, angry bursts.

"What did you want?" I call out from the top of the landing.

Gia pauses halfway down the stairs and peers back at me over her shoulder. "What?"

"You came up here for something," I say, but she only parts her lips, her eyes wide with surprise. "You put that doll in my bed, didn't you?"

"No."

"You think this is funny?"

"I think you're seriously losing it," she says, and starts back down the stairs.

"Wait."

She ignores me. I run after her and grab her arm at the bottom of the steps.

"Why are you messing with me?"

"Nobody is messing with you." She breaks her arm free. "I was just gonna give you shit for messing around with Lauren's man, but you've clearly got enough problems. You need to get a grip."

"Yeah, and you need to grow up."

I stomp back up the stairs and hear her laugh behind my back. It only adds more fuel to my fury. I storm into the bedroom, ignore my bag and grab the doll. When I push out onto the front deck, I burst through like a hurricane into the bright sunlight. Whoever did this wanted a reaction, and they're going to get one.

"Which one of you did this?" I shout, my voice full and raw, holding up the doll so everyone can get a good look at the markings.

There is a moment of perfect silence as they collectively take in what has been done to the doll. Then laughter erupts. It begins with a few snickers, then builds until everyone is doubled over, their mouths opened wide in hysterical, braying laughter. I stand there shaking with rage, the defiled doll dangling from my hand, and catch Gia leaning against the railing, an infuriating smirk curling the edges of her lips. My face flushes hot. My skin prickles with humiliation. It feels like I'm shrinking, like the ground is swallowing me up as my anger morphs into raw, stinging mortification.

"What the hell is that?" Eli asks between laughs.

"The dead body Iris saw buried in the back," Lauren says before I can speak, unable to control her laughter.

I want to rip out her pretty pink tongue and strangle her with it.

I try again to get someone to own up to it, but no one admits to planting the doll in my room or marking it up. I stalk through the house and toss the doll in one of the trash cans in the back. When I make it upstairs, I scoop my toothbrush and toiletries into my arms. As I slip into the bedroom, I see Violet turning off the landing but ignore her.

"What are you doing?" she asks moments later, easing in the room behind me as I try to get the zipper of my bag shut.

"What does it look like?"

"You can't leave. We have the house for four more days."

"I don't want to be here."

"Babe—"

"There was a dead body out back," I snap, shrugging her hand away as she tries to touch my arm. "My boyfriend thinks I cheated on him, which I didn't, and everybody thinks I'm crazy. I don't need this. I'm going home."

I know what I saw. And the longer I sit with it, the more I realize I need to trust my own instincts.

"Don't be dramatic. You—"

"Name one good reason I should stay."

Violet shrugs. "You don't actually have a choice? We all came in one car."

"Eli dropped me off. He can take me home."

"No offense, but I don't think you're Eli's favorite person right now," she says, and shuffles around in a drawer for something.

I sit on the edge of the bed, wondering how things devolved so quickly. As much as I hate it, she's right. I want to leave right now, but it's probably better to let Eli cool off before I ask him to drive me home.

I've never seen Eli this angry before except on the field, back when he would charge a defender with the ferocity of a bull, leaving bodies sprawling in the dirt. I remember one game where he stiff-armed a cornerback so hard, the guy went flying through the air like a Frisbee.

Off the field he's always been a beacon of composure. It's something I've always admired, the stark juxtaposition of the way he'd pulverize industrial-sized men, yet would come home and be all restrained and coolheaded with me. When he's in uniform, it's like a switch flips. All that quiet strength turns into raw, uncontainable power. Seeing a flash of it when he stormed out of the room has me a little uneasy. His absolute refusal to look me in the eyes makes me feel like something deeper is going on inside. It must be his trepidation about his grandmother, all that angst and fear coming out the wrong way. It has to be.

chapter
nineteen

When I stir awake, everything feels hazy. I stretch, groaning as my body protests. There's still a lingering dull ache in my head from where I bumped it last night. I glance over at my packed bag on the floor and try to remember how I dozed off. The last thing I recall is trying to think of a way to ask Eli to take me home.

I reach for my phone and glance at the time. I've been out for three hours. I sit up too quickly, my legs stiff and aching. My body is sluggish, my mind just as foggy as before, and I brace myself for the rest of last night to catch up to me.

After searching all the upstairs rooms for Eli, I head downstairs. Stepping into the living room, I find Roman and Violet huddled around Lauren, who's drawing something on Garrett's shoulder with a black marker. He carefully replicates her doodle onto the sheet of paper that Roman's holding against the wall. They finish up, and Roman and Violet burst into fits of laughter. Garrett has drawn a heart with an arrow through it while Lauren has drawn an erect penis. I pause, staring at the marker in her hand. The one Garrett's using has red ink. But hers is black, just like the marker that desecrated that doll. It doesn't seem like Lauren's brand of humor, but maybe it was Garrett's idea.

The front deck is empty, so I cut through the house and head straight to the back, where I find Eli coming up the stairs to the rear deck, a bottle of peach schnapps in his hand. I've never seen him drink schnapps.

"I want to leave tonight," I say, shutting the sliding glass door behind me.

"What?"

I start to explain, but pause when I see Gia coming up the stairs behind him in her tiny white bikini. She all but rolls her eyes when she sees me, taking a swig from her matching bottle as she passes by.

"I need to speak to Eli," I tell her, assuming she'll take the hint and go inside.

But she shrugs and drifts over to the hot tub and slides in, still within earshot.

I look up at him. "Hey."

"Hey," he mumbles back, taking a swig.

Gia sinks deeper into the bubbling water with a loud sigh and Eli flicks a quick glance toward her.

"Let's go inside," I say, taking his wrist and pulling him toward the doors.

I'm stunned when he pulls out of my grip.

"I'm cool out here," he says, and walks away.

He spreads out on one of the lounge chairs, and I move closer to him, lowering my voice just enough so Gia can't hear me, but it's still loud enough to cut through the music. "Don't you think we should talk?"

"Free country." He takes another swig, his eyes averted away from mine, jaw visibly tense. "You want to talk, go ahead. Talk."

"No, I mean really talk. About what happened. Not in front of your friends or yelling at each other over Drake. We should go home and talk about this."

"I just got here," he says, his tone clipped as if just talking to me is enough to test his patience.

"Well, I already packed my stuff."

He looks up at me, but barely. "You what?"

"I want to leave. Now. We can talk on the drive home. I'll wait in the car for you."

I don't wait for him to object again. I head for the sliding door.

"I'm not going back to the city tonight," Eli says from behind me, his voice resolute. "I just drove all the way down here. Gonna stay until Sunday like we planned."

"I don't want to be here, Eli," I say, hating how my voice shakes. I don't want him to think I'm being too emotional. I want him to see that I'm thinking clearly and rationally and capable of making a basic decision.

"Then why'd you come?"

I stare at him, confused at how he can even ask me that. "Because you made me."

He frowns. "I *made* you? All I did was suggest you come up here so you could relax and finally get some sleep. But then I catch you in bed with one of my best friends, so really the joke's on me, right?"

On his feet now, Eli abandons his schnapps and turns his back to me, facing the forest. I stare at him for a moment, wondering what happened to the sweet, caring guy I fell in love with, the one who would never look at me or talk to me this way. The one who trusted me. This isn't him. I've never given him any reason to think I would ever cheat on him. I barely even *know* Garrett.

"Do you really believe that?" I ask, standing next to him by the railing.

A moment passes. "I believe what I saw."

"Just because you saw something doesn't mean anything happened."

"Oh, you mean like the dead body you saw in the back?"

"There was an arm," I say in a small, decrepit voice.

"Yeah, a hollow plastic one." Eli shakes his head and scoffs. "Gia was just telling me how weird you've been acting."

I cut my eyes over to her. She's bobbing in and out of the water, her body slick and toned and glistening. She shoots me a small smile. I nearly flinch in shock, but then see Eli returning the subtle gesture.

It wasn't for me.

"I haven't been 'acting' weird," I say, folding my arms across my chest. "Something weird is going on."

Eli shakes his head without glancing at me, unconvinced. "She made it sound like you've been acting unhinged."

"Of course she would say that. She's the main one who's been terrorizing me." Eli rolls his eyes at that, but I don't let him dismiss me so easily. "You made me feel guilty for not wanting to come, yet ever since I've been here, they've been horrible to me. All of them. Snide comments. Playing tricks on me. Leaving me behind on purpose. And I'm pretty sure somebody drugged me last night."

It's a strong accusation, and I see a flash of the man I love when Eli looks at me in surprise. I don't have the energy to explain my missing pills, the throbbing headache, the black spots in my memory. I just want him to whisk me out of here and enjoy the ride back to the city. Or we could go up to Boston and sit with his grandmother. Anything but stay here.

"You're right," I say, hoping it earns me some grace. "They're *your* friends. And when you're not around, they make sure I know it."

Eli frowns. "Since when?"

"Since always," I say, and it's like a weight lifted off my shoulders, finally being honest about this with him. "But especially this week. It's like they were hoping I wouldn't come since you had to go to see your grandma."

I respect Eli and love his love for his friends. I've never fit in with them, but I've also made efforts not to come in between them. I've honored his friendships and tried all these years to play nice, to ignore, to push through what has now become thinly veiled bullying. We all have our limits. This is mine.

"It's all in your head," Eli says, because of course he believes his tribe over me; they were there first. "Everybody likes you."

"No, they don't. They just tolerate me because I'm with you."

Eli shakes his head in genuine disbelief, then looks me over. "What, am I supposed to feel bad? You mess around with my best friend, and *you're* the victim?"

I clamp my eyes shut and take a beat to gather myself. I don't want to shout at him. Not here. Not in front of Gia.

"I just want to go home," I say, hoping he'll look at me, but he stares out at the trees, deliberately avoiding eye contact.

After a moment, he gives in and glances my way. "How do you think it felt to drive up here to surprise you and end up walking in on that? Everything I'm already dealing with, and I have to see you in bed with another man? A couple days ago I thought I was gonna have to bury my grandmother. I thought we lost her. I've been stressed out, worried about my mom, trying to hold it together for her, and you—"

"I wasn't 'in bed' with him. He was helping me—"

"Helping you what?"

"Nothing happened. I passed out. I told you, somebody drugged me."

Eli shifts his eyes back to the view of the forest, and I see it now. There's a hawk that's caught his attention. "I've never even seen you drink, but you get drunk with him and—"

"I didn't get drunk 'with him.' Violet made me a few drinks, and I only went with it because everybody was on my neck, pressuring me. They were so mean to me, I just thought . . ." I stop myself, feeling tears welling in my eyes. I try to blink them back, but they fall anyway. I wipe my cheeks with the back of my hand, not wanting Eli to see me break down right now.

"I know it's a lot with the anniversary coming up," he says. "But acting out for attention isn't—"

"I'm not acting out."

"Being drunk isn't an excuse for—"

"It's not an excuse. I . . ." My words fade as Eli steps off. "Where are you going?"

"I don't know. For a walk. Need to clear my head."

Another tear falls onto my cheek. I swipe it away. "Will you just talk to Garrett?"

"I don't care what Garrett has to say," Eli retorts. "Garrett doesn't sleep in my bed."

I call after him a couple times, but he slides the door open and shuts himself inside. I watch him until he vanishes inside the house, the embers of my anger flaring back to roaring flames. This has nothing to do with my mental state or my mother's death. I haven't been seeking attention or comfort from another man. This is all wrong.

"So," Gia says, adjusting the top of her bikini. "Guess you guys are staying."

chapter **twenty**

I don't sleep. I can't. When I drag myself out of bed in the morning, I instinctively look around for Eli, but he's nowhere to be found. Violet is still asleep in her bed; last night he chose to room with Roman instead of switching with her. His rejection felt like sharp nails clawing at all of my vital organs, piercing them slowly and all at once.

Seeing Eli now, walking a few steps ahead of me with the rest of the group as we head toward the ATV trail a few miles out from the lake, the pain still hasn't subsided. I push it down—the sinking feeling in my gut, the sobs threatening to rise from my chest—and try to stay positive. Maybe doing something physical together, me holding tight onto his waist while he drives, will soften him up, and I can convince him to hear me out once we get back to the house.

Lauren slides onto the back of an ATV with Garrett. He checks to make sure she's fastened her helmet properly as she straddles the rear, and when he turns back around to pull his own on, I can't help but feel a sting in my gut. It's like there's no tension between them at all, but there's an entire continent between me and Eli. Roman hops onto the back of Violet's ATV after she insists on driving first, leaving Eli to pick from two left. He chooses the larger one, running a hand over the gear bag as if testing its sturdiness. I crouch down to tie my laces, and when I straighten out, Gia is already swinging her leg over the seat behind him.

I glare at her, my mouth falling open in disbelief. "What are you doing?"

Gia flicks a glance at Eli.

"She doesn't know how to drive one," he says, lifting his helmet and sliding it on.

"And?"

"You do," Gia says with an eye roll as if it should have been obvious to me that she'd be clinging to my man while the rough terrain jolts and jerks their bodies into one another. "So *I'm* riding with Eli. Common sense."

I look at Eli, waiting for him to revoke this. He doesn't, and my blood turns hot.

"She's not riding with you," I tell him firmly, my indignation unmistakable.

"Controlling *and* psychotic?" Gia gasps in mock horror. "That's borderline serial killer territory."

I step closer to her, my footsteps heavy and loud on the gravel. "Gia, I promise, you do not want the smoke with me."

"Hmm. I think I'm supposed to be scared . . . but, like, I'm not?"

Garrett and Violet both make their engines roar a bit, clearly ready to go, but I refuse to let this one go. I fold my arms across my chest and glare at Eli, his passiveness infuriating.

"You're *not* riding with her," I say again.

Eli lets out a sigh. "Iris."

"I'm serious."

"Oh, my god, he was just trying to be nice," Gia says. "He doesn't want to ride with you."

My bottom lip trembles as I try to process her words. I search Eli's face, wait for him to tell her she's wrong, but he says nothing. His silence blares louder than anything he could have said, and it's like being attacked from the inside. Like a thousand straight pins impaling every pore on every inch of my body.

"Iris, you alright?" Roman calls out to me, lifting his helmet.

"I'm fine," I call back, and I see Eli's head snap my way out the corner of my eye. "Thanks."

Eli climbs down off his ATV, his eyes on Roman. "You guys go ahead. The three of us will catch up."

Garrett and Violet take off with Lauren and Roman in tow. Once the rumble of their engines dissipates, I grab Eli's arm, dragging him out of Gia's earshot.

He mumbles some kind of objection, but I talk over him. "Why are you doing this? Is this to get back at me? Are you seriously—"

"It's just a ride, Iris."

"With her? If she doesn't know how to drive an ATV, she should have stayed back at the house."

Eli takes a breath, then rolls his neck to crack it. "Are you really going to make this big a deal out of this?"

"You didn't even defend me back there."

"Back where?"

"What she said about me." It feels humiliating to have to say, "She said I was *psychotic*, and you just stood there and let her."

"She didn't mean it *literally*."

I study him for a moment, and for the first time since we've met, he feels like a stranger.

"Can we please go?" Gia calls out from behind him, her voice a petulant whine. "This sun is roasting me in this spot."

I shoot her a hard look, then look up at Eli again. "I don't want you going with her."

"I didn't want you alone in a dark bedroom with Garrett the other night either."

"This is different."

"Yeah, because this is nothing. I'm driving her, not fucking her. But you can't say the same thing, can you?"

Before I can respond, he steps off and heads back over to Gia. I grab his arm, holding him back.

"If you want to ride with her, go ahead," I say, my voice one second away from breaking. "But if you do, we're done."

My own words shock me. I don't know if they're true, or why I even said them. I think I meant them only as a threat, a Hail Mary, but as Eli peels away, a part of me knows it's more than that. All I can do is watch, my feet rooted to the ground, paralyzed by a wall of shock and humiliation as he joins her on the ATV.

"Go easy on me, okay?" Gia says, wrapping her arms around Eli's waist. "It's my first time."

He revs the engine, and Gia glances back at me, a smirk in her eyes.

I don't bother putting on my helmet. I straddle the last vehicle left, pull off my glasses and let my tears fall. It's over. After everything we've been through, after everything I've given him, it's over.

chapter
twenty-one

The ATV ride was unbearable. Every bump and jolt left me feeling more rattled, more out of place. The others thrived in the chaos, their laughter ricocheting through the trees like a hymn to joy. Back at the house, they spill onto the deck, flushed and ravenous, as Roman fires up the grill. I can't bring myself to eat. There's a sourness at the back of my throat that no food could chase away.

After I change into my swimsuit and cutoffs, the house feels momentarily quiet, everyone dispersed to their own corners. I start to pass through the living room, then stop short. Garrett and Lauren are tangled together against the wall, completely oblivious to my presence. They kiss each other, languid, deliberate. His hand cradles the small of her back, and hers cups his face. They move like a slow dance, unhurried and unashamed.

Envy coils tight in my chest, hot and acidic. I clear my throat. They pull apart, not startled, but smiling. Soft, unabashed. They look almost grateful for my interruption, as if inviting me to witness their affection and marvel at its purity.

"Who has the key to the boat?" I ask, my voice too clipped, betraying my simmering agitation.

Garrett blinks, still caught in the haze of their moment. "Roman has it. Why?"

"I want to take it out."

Lauren tilts her head, incredulous. "On the water?"

"By yourself?" Garrett asks, his brow furrowed.

I shrug, aiming for nonchalance, though I know I miss the mark. It comes off brittle, defensive. "Eli showed me how to drive one once."

What I don't mention is that it was years ago, and he wasn't exactly thorough. He only taught me a few tidbits because I grabbed the wheel and teased him, mimicking the way he handled the boat, then asked if I looked sexy doing it. He laughed and indulged me. He adjusted my hand on the throttle, his palms over mine, then abandoned the lesson halfway through to take pictures of me in my bikini. It was never about teaching me per se; it was about us just enjoying the moment.

But I have a good memory—I'll figure it out. I just need to get out of this house. Away from them. Away from him.

I step through the sliding door and onto the deck. The water stretches out before me, vast and calm, a sheet of molten silver under the gentle sun. It looks steady. Inviting.

Gia's shrieking laughter slices through the air, sharp as a guillotine. She's standing too close to Eli, her arm grazing his as they wait for Roman to finish the burgers. Eli catches me looking. I quickly avert my eyes, the bitterness rising in my chest making it impossible to face him again.

But that glance is all the fuel I need. I won't back out now, not with them watching. I steel myself and head toward Roman. The heat of the grill wafts around him, smoke curling lazily in the warm air.

"Hey."

He glances up, the sunlight catching his easy grin. "Well-done double cheeseburger coming right up."

"No," I say quickly, shaking my head. "Can I have the key to the boat?"

He pauses, the spatula hovering over the sizzling meat. "Oh." He sets it down, then reaches into his back pocket, pulling out the key. There's a flicker of confusion on his face as he hands it over. "All yours."

I take it and glance at the dock where the boat sits waiting, sturdy and glimmering. Without a word, I start toward it.

"Iris."

I pause mid-step on the stairs and glance over my shoulder. Garrett steps out of the house, and the sight of him alone unsettles me. I can feel the weight of Lauren's eyes watching from inside.

"You want some company?" he asks, his voice low, tentative.

"No," I say, avoiding his eyes. "I really just want to be alone." I need solitude. I need to think, to scream, to cry.

Garrett hesitates, raking a hand through his hair. "I don't think you should go out there by yourself."

"I'll be fine."

He looks like he wants to protest, his mouth opening, then closing with a sigh. "Fine. Let me at least get the cover off for you."

Relieved, I nod, handing him the key. "Okay."

"Hang here," he says, already heading past me on the steps. "Be back in a couple minutes."

I nod again, watching him go. But the reprieve is short-lived.

"Go out where?" Eli asks, walking up behind me.

I roll my eyes and step farther down the stairs. Eli follows me, and I can feel Gia's gaze burning into us, her presence heavy even from a distance.

"Go out where?" he repeats, his tone now demanding an answer.

I sigh and glance toward Garrett, who's busy untethering the boat, his back to us.

"Out on the water," I say finally, my voice robotic, hoping the answer will pacify him enough to leave me alone.

"You're going on the boat?" Eli laughs, the sound full of derision. When he catches the glare I shoot at him, he stops abruptly. "You're serious? Alone?"

"Yes, *alone*." My voice sharpens. "I can ride an ATV alone, can't I? What makes you think I can't drive a boat?"

"*That's* what this is about? You're doing all of this just to make a point because of what happened ear—"

"This isn't about you, Eli. It's about me."

"You can barely drive a car," he says, his words like a needle to my pride.

I hate that he's right. But I hate him more for saying it. I start to push past him, but he grabs my arm, stopping me.

"Fine," he says, his grip firm but not painful. "I'll drive you."

I whip around to face him, my eyes narrowing. "I asked you to drive me earlier."

"That was different." He shakes his head, frustration flaring in his eyes. "She didn't know how to drive an ATV. You don't know how to drive a boat."

"You showed me in Whistler."

"Yeah, and you were all over the place."

His admission stings. Maybe that's true, but there's no way he can think it's that simple. He didn't just drive her because she didn't know how. He chose her over me. He wanted to hurt me.

"Come on." His voice softens into a plea. "Don't be stubborn. Let me—"

"You made your choice." I snap, my gaze cutting to Gia, then back to him. "Let go of me."

He lets go of my arm, but it feels like more than a physical release. It feels like every shared moment, every whispered promise, every memory we built slips away with that single gesture.

I storm off toward the dock, my chest tight. The anger I don't mind, but I hate the disappointment that washes over me. I wanted him to fight for me.

The sight of the water is grounding. Its blue expanse stretches out for at least half a mile, shimmering under the midday sun. Garrett is waiting for me at the edge.

"All set," he says, stepping aside as I approach. "You sure you got this?"

"Yeah, thanks."

Garrett extends a hand and helps me climb aboard. The boat rocks gently beneath my weight, the water shifting like liquid glass.

He points out each control, walking through them one by one. The throttle, the steering wheel, the trim controls, the kill switch. His voice is calm and low, and as he explains, I practice in my head, envisioning how each piece moves under my hands.

"What's the first thing you do if the engine stalls?" Garrett asks, a paternal edge to his voice.

"I don't need a test," I reply, brushing past him toward the driver's seat.

He steps in front of me, blocking my way, his expression suddenly stern. "I get that you don't want to be around Eli right now, but if something happened out there, it would be on me."

I think of last night, of the missing spots in my memory, and meet his gaze. "I don't think Lauren would appreciate you being alone with me."

"You're probably right." A faint smile tugs at his mouth, but it doesn't reach his eyes. "I'll get Roman. That cool?"

I hesitate, my gaze drifting to the open water. It looks so calm and inviting, but even I know better than to let pride steer me into danger. With a reluctant nod, I relent.

Roman appears at the dock moments later, his easy grin already in place. He hops aboard and cranks the engine into gear, his movements practiced and sure.

I sink into the passenger seat, strapping a life jacket on as the boat peels away from the dock. True to his word, Roman stays quiet, giving me room to breathe when it's my turn to steer. He watches from the corner of his eye while I man the wheel, but he doesn't hover.

Then the boat lurches. My hands falter on the controls. Roman is by my side in an instant, steadying the wheel with his firm grip.

"Like this," he murmurs as he guides my hands back into position.

We stay like this for a moment, side by side, looking out over the water. It stretches endlessly before us as if it holds all the answers I'm too afraid to ask. Then a sharp, acrid scent pierces the air, catching me mid-breath. I stiffen, my gaze darting toward Roman. He smells it too.

He crouches near the engine hatch, flipping it open with force. The smell intensifies, thick and metallic, curling in my nose and settling in the back of my throat. Roman leans closer, inspecting the compartment, then glances at me with a bewildered expression.

"It's the fuel line," he says.

"Is that bad?" My voice comes out smaller than I'd like.

"Could be." His face is calm as he wipes his hands on his shorts, but his eyes flick to the engine with unease.

I fumble for my phone, dialing Garrett's number. It rings and rings, but he doesn't answer. When I look up, Roman is already pointing at something near the base of the fuel tank.

I peer inside, and a shiver rolls through me. A dark, oily sheen pools beneath the engine, much more than I expected.

"Shit," Roman mutters, running both hands through his hair. "This is worse than I thought. Get back."

The air thickens with a hum, a premonition, and I stand frozen, caught between disbelief and the suffocating weight of impending disaster. Roman's hand grips my arm, yanking me back just before the air tears with a searing roar. A blaze rips through the silence, the world splitting in two.

We're hurled backward, a searing wave of heat swallowing everything in its path. My body crashes into the water, and I lose sight of Roman. My ears ring. My lungs scream for air. I break the surface first, my vest still tight around my chest. I cough and gasp, my limbs thrashing until I find Roman's hand. He struggles to keep his body above the surface, the aftermath churning the water in chaotic surges. I strap his arm around my back as he continues to struggle for air, his face pale, blood trailing from a cut on his temple.

We push through the water together, every stroke an effort, every breath a battle. The land feels miles away. I keep my eyes on it, refusing to look away.

Everyone runs for the shore before we even reach the shallows. All I hear are shouts and screams, a cacophony. I drag myself through the dirt, the cool earth biting at my back as I hold a hand to my chest, coughing up water, too weak to move. Roman collapses beside me, his chest rising and falling with shallow, uneven breaths. Then he stills, his neck rolling to the side. I call him, pushing up to my knees, but he doesn't answer.

The others crowd around, frantic, their voices panicked. Gia's hands cover Roman's chest, shaking him, urging him to wake up. Violet sobs, her cries sharp and jagged. Lauren shouts for Garrett to call 911 while Eli crouches beside me, his face tight with fear, like he's afraid to touch me.

Roman finally stirs, his eyes popping open just before the sirens peal through the air. Garrett props Roman up as he heaves, coughing up water. A fire truck screeches to a halt, an ambulance right on its heels. The men file out quickly, their boots pounding the earth as they head toward the wreckage on the water. A pair of paramedics rushes over to Roman and crouches beside him, speaking in low, calming voices.

He's okay, I keep thinking. *He's going to be okay.*

The rest is a blur. Voices overlap. Men run in and out. And then the paramedic stands, patting Roman on the back and wishing him well. The chaos dissolves into a murmur. The firemen pack up their hoses and head back onto the truck. All that's left of the boat when they leave is a blackened skeleton bobbing in the water. The house settles into an eerie stillness, the hum of the trucks fading as the last wisps of smoke unravel into the sky. We all crowd around in the front room for what feels like hours. No one speaks. The silence swells, thick and oppressive, heavy with thousands of what-ifs. Roman is the one to shatter it.

"This is your fault, you know," he says, his voice sharp, his gaze pinned on Garrett.

It's not what anyone expected to break the quiet.

Garrett stares at him, a flicker of incredulity darkening his features. "You think I *planned* for the engine to blow? You heard them. They said it could have been a spark from the engine. A leak in the fuel line that could've happened over time—"

"Over time?" Roman moves to his feet abruptly, the chair legs scraping harshly against the floor. His tone bites, every word carrying an accusation. "You're supposed to check that stuff."

"I'm sorry, were you the one who volunteered to help me do maintenance last year? I'm the only one who ever takes care of that boat."

Roman's nostrils flare. "We could have died out there and all you—"

"Hey, chill." Eli, slouched in the corner, straightens to his feet, his tone low but urgent as his gaze flicks between the two of them. "It's over."

But Eli's attempt at peace only stokes the fire. Roman's stance tightens, fists curling at his sides. Garrett leans forward slightly, his shoulders squaring, his jaw taut. On the couch, Lauren, Violet and Gia shift uneasily, the tension in their bodies palpable. Gia glances down, crossing her arms tightly, her foot bouncing against the floor. Violet's shoulders slump, but her gaze remains fixed, flickering between the two men like she's waiting for another explosion.

"Will you both please just stop?" Lauren's voice cuts through the tension swelling in the room as she steps between them, in full mom mode. "God, what is wrong with you two? We're all in one piece. That's all that matters."

Am I? Am I still in one piece? Is all of me still here?

For a moment, everything is still again, the calm a heavy blanket over the turmoil beneath.

I take a breath and swallow hard. "What if it wasn't an accident?"

Everyone turns to me.

"What do you mean?" Violet asks, looking as confused and exasperated as everyone else.

"What if somebody blew it up? On purpose," I clarify, but the words come out fragile and unsure, like a castle made out of sugar.

"Who?"

I'm not even sure who asks it. It's like they all do at once.

I know it's a bit of a leap, but I also know there's only one person who would've had access to the boat besides us. One person who could have moved that arm and put that doll in that hole in the back instead. One person who knows the property like the back of their hand.

But before the name forms on my tongue, the aggressive doubt on all their faces holds it captive.

"Never mind," I mumble, the exhaustion of the day pulling at my bones.

It's easier to let it go, to hold my silence than to fight for the truth they refuse to hear.

chapter
twenty-two

Everyone quietly abandons their plans for tonight. Since the explosion, Eli hasn't once checked on me. He's been hovering over Gia all evening, leaning in to whisper in her ear, sitting so close to her their knees touch. At one point he brushes hair from her face. I wonder if it's all just a performance, a game he's playing, trying to provoke something in me, make me jealous, make me unravel, make me scream. Or if he does this when I'm not in the room to witness it.

I pass by the kitchen, the large rooms, high ceilings and endless hallways. It all feels suffocating now. I slip out unnoticed and make my way down to the dock. The old boards creak beneath me as I walk toward the water. The tang of burnt wood lingers in the air from the flames. I refuse to replay any of it in my mind and force myself to focus on the pearlescent moonlight dancing on the surface of the water. I want to dive in and baptize myself.

As I peer out at the water, I can't help but resent it, despite its beauty—or maybe in spite of it. If it wasn't for this lake, if neither of us had ever come here, Eli and I would still be together. My bottom lip trembles as I try to process his decision.

Over the years, Eli has become my rock. In the months after my mother's death, when the weight of grief was suffocating and the world felt hollow and cruel, Eli stood beside me. He was there in the quiet hours, in the loud ones too, holding me up when I could barely stand, when grief made a ruin of my body, when even lifting my head felt impossible. He never left, not once, always ready to piece me back together, no matter how jagged the edges, no matter how many times I splintered again. And now I can't make sense of it, can't reconcile that we are here, that this is how it ends, that everything I believe about him, about us, is so staggeringly wrong.

Because how could I be so blind? How could I not see how little I matter to him, how all this time I have only ever been a shadow of what he means to me? We have survived something unthinkable together, and I thought that surviving meant we could endure anything, thought he would fight for us, or at the very least listen. Hear me out. But instead, I am left turning over every moment, every conversation, every small and inconsequential thing, searching for the signs I must have missed. They have to be there, don't they? Some quiet signal, some warning in the way he spoke or didn't speak, some proof that this was inevitable, that I was always going to lose him. Or maybe I am just inventing these signs now, building them out of scraps of memory to make sense of the incomprehensible. Maybe there is never anything to see, nothing beneath the surface but the emptiness I feel now.

What I can't bear most of all is the injustice of it, the way he's thrown it all away without giving me the chance to defend myself. As if I am some stranger, as if my love doesn't matter, as if *I* don't matter. To be accused of something I didn't do, and to be silenced before I can speak. It's like trying to scream underwater. How can he not try to understand? How can he say he loves me and still choose to believe the worst about me without question? It feels like a betrayal of everything we are, everything I thought we were, and now all I have left are the questions, circling like vultures, and no one to answer them but myself. In the quiet, in the wreckage, I turn it over and over in my mind, wondering if I'll ever understand, if understanding even matters now, or if this is simply the price of loving someone too much.

"Not hungry?"

Violet's quiet footsteps pad across the wooden planks, and then her small, narrow feet appear beside mine. I shake my head, food far from my mind, even though I can't remember eating more than a few crackers today. She stands next to me for a moment, taking in the view, then sits down, her legs swinging over the edge, just like mine.

"You okay?" Violet asks, her voice now a whisper. "Haven't seen you since we got back from the trail."

I don't turn to look at her. "I'm fine."

"Wanna go for a swim?"

The evening air is balmy, still warm and humid, but the thought of getting in the water churns something inside me. Its quiet surface is now only a reminder of the explosion, the power that roared and split the sky. I just want to be alone.

"I'll pass," I say, hoping she'll leave with the rejection, but she lingers, her legs swinging as she stares out at the water.

Even though Violet says nothing, I can sense her gaze drifting my way more than a few times. I deliberately meet her eyes and am struck by her gentle expression. There's a warmth in her gaze, a shimmer that could be compassion or pity. At this moment, I'd welcome either.

"Do you think I'm losing it too?" I ask her, but I instantly regret it, not sure I want her honest answer.

She considers her words before speaking, and I brace myself. "I think that doll is creepy as hell, but it's not an arm."

"You don't have to believe me about the arm, okay? Or that Nolan was burying something in the back that night. But my hair tie going missing when I know I had it, that doll just showing up in my bed like that . . ." I take a breath, knowing how silly this all sounds. "That happened. And somebody drugged me last night."

Violet's eyes widen. "Somebody *drugged* you?"

"I blacked out. It wasn't just alcohol. It had to be something else."

"Babe, you're just not used to it. And you went pretty hard. Knocked a couple down back-to-back . . ."

I shake my head, stopping her from going on uselessly. "A few of my pills are missing."

She opens and closes her mouth a couple times, then eyes me cautiously. "You sure?"

I nod. "And I didn't do anything with Garrett."

Violet nods back. "I believe you."

Her words feel like a salve, easing the sting of a raw wound. I watch her for a moment. "You do?"

"Lauren believes you too. Well, she believes Garrett, so by default, she believes you."

Ever since I got here, I've been dismissed as if my reality is nothing more than an elaborate illusion. I've been feeling so isolated, desperate for someone to confide in, for someone to believe me. It's a moment of grace, a fleeting but profound acknowledgment that maybe I'm not as alone as I've felt for so long. I cling to it, this tiny thing, and savor it, allow it to mend the pieces of my fractured trust.

"I could never," I say, feeling compelled to explain myself. "They're married. They have a baby."

"I know."

"I would never destroy a family. How could Eli even think—"

I stop. I don't want to think about him right now or I'll break down again.

We lapse into silence. Violet doesn't try to fill it, and I'm grateful for it.

"Eli won't even hear me out," I say, breaking it gently after a few moments.

Violet reaches over and rubs my back. "You can talk to me."

I nod, but something about her offering me that, like a door slowly creaking open, has me retreating inside myself, small and unsure. Her touch lingers, and when I look at her, everything between us suddenly shifts.

Before I can even grasp what's happening, she leans into me. Her lips brush against mine. Soft, tentative, like a question. My heart jolts, my body frozen. I pull back instinctively, startled, disoriented. I want to say something, to explain, to reassure her that I didn't mean to make this more than it was, but the words stay lodged in my throat, suffocated by my own embarrassment. I don't know what happened, or what it means. I just know it's not what I expected. Not at all.

"I can help you forget about him," Violet whispers, her voice a cross between a purr and a hum.

"You're drunk," I tell her, peering out at the lake again.

"No, babe. I'm not."

The air between us thickens with a tension that feels sharp and volatile, like a storm about to break. Violet pushes up to her feet and turns her back to me. I watch her. She slides off her curved-hem shorts, revealing her thong bikini bottoms. Without hesitation, she dives off the edge of the deck, a swift arc that slices the surface of the water in one seamless motion. The moonlight catches her limbs, flashes off her skin as she disappears beneath the surface, moving through the water as though her legs have transformed into fins, her body a part of the water itself.

I watch her glide deeper, the water swallowing her whole. We've spent years locked in this dance. Teasing each other, sometimes crossing lines with a laugh, a wink, a comment that could be read as flirtation. I thought it was just for fun, that she never took any of it seriously.

Complicated thoughts follow me as I step away, my bare feet quiet on the wood. A line has been crossed, an invisible barrier broken. I thought we had something not quite solid, but safe. I can't help but feel betrayed. It's like she's been waiting for an opening this whole time and used my heartbreak as a chance to fulfill some secret agenda. She didn't come out to comfort me. She came to seize an opportunity.

Eli was right. These are all his friends. I feel like a fool to have ever thought otherwise.

When I'm halfway to the front door, Violet's scream sends shivers up my spine. My heart jumps. I stop, turn back, my eyes straining to find her in the dark. I spot her, struggling against the water, her form wild and uncoordinated.

I call out to her. "What's wrong?"

"There's something in there." Her voice shakes frantically as she claws her way to the surface.

I just stand there, watching her in the dark. I don't have the patience for any more of her stunts.

"I'm serious, Iris," Violet says, her voice trembling slightly, and it's the tremor that makes me stop short. Violet doesn't tremble. Not when she's angry, not when she's scared. Not ever.

I take a few steps toward her, my arms folded across my chest. "You're messing with me."

She shakes her head, rivulets of water tracing the angles of her face. I catch her eyes, wide and unsteady, and for a moment, I feel the smallest crack in my armor.

"I'm not, I swear," she says, climbing onto the dock with a quick, desperate motion. She shivers, droplets of water pooling at her feet. "There's something down there."

I don't give her any reaction. "I'm going inside."

"Iris," she snaps, and the sharpness of her voice brings my eyes back to hers. "I felt something. Under the water."

"You're serious?"

She nods, her breathing uneven. "It . . . it felt like a skull."

The word hangs in the air, heavy and strange, and for a moment, all I can do is stare at her. I wait for the smirk, the roll of her eyes, the inevitable punchline. But it doesn't come.

"Come in. Please," Violet insists, stepping closer, her hand reaching out to grab my wrist. "Just check for yourself."

I pull my arm back, staring at her. "Violet . . ."

"Please," she says again, softer this time, and there's something vulnerable in her voice that unnerves me.

Against my better judgment, I follow her to the edge of the dock. She points to a spot just a few feet out where the water ripples slightly.

"It was right there," she says, her voice tight.

I slide off my shoes and slip into the water, the chill biting against my skin. Violet watches, her arms wrapped around herself as I drift toward the spot. The water is murky. I hesitate, then reach down, my fingers brushing against rough stones, slimy algae, the occasional stray twig.

"There's nothing here," I call out, still feeling around.

Violet's voice cuts back, sharper now. "Go deeper."

I grit my teeth and plunge my hands lower. My fingers scrape against something hard and smooth, and my breath catches. My mind races, and I force myself to pull it up.

A rock. It's just a rock.

I hold it up, water dripping down my arm. Violet hesitates, staring at the rock like it might morph into something sinister. Then she exhales shakily, rubbing her eyes.

"Sorry," she whispers.

"It's fine," I say, then grab my shoes and head back to the house.

I stop in the kitchen for a glass of water when I make it back inside, but as I hold the cup under the tap, I catch it out of the corner of my eye.

My escape.

chapter
twenty-three

I reach into the right pocket of Eli's jacket and grab his car keys. I clutch them tight as I run upstairs for my phone and my bag. I have no idea what my plan is, how Eli will react when he notices I've taken his car. He'll figure it out. He'll have to figure it out.

Adrenaline surging, I fumble with the key, jamming it into the ignition with a shaky hand, then take one last look at the house. For a moment, I almost talk myself into staying. But then the image of Eli walking away from me and onto that ATV with Gia flashes in my head. I push through the guilt and force myself to move.

I reach for the gearshift, but when I draw it back, it resists. I jerk it harder. Nothing. I glance down to see what the problem is, and it's staring at me in the face. Numbers instead of letters. I forgot Eli drives a manual transmission. I'm not thinking straight. I need to calm down and pull it together, but when I look at it again, I want to wail in frustration. The gearshift might as well be a Rubik's Cube. He's tried to teach me multiple times how to drive a stick, but it's a useless skill in the city when the subway gets you to your destination twice as fast, so I've never paid much attention. Now I wish I had.

I slam my foot onto the clutch, praying this works. The engine roars to life, but shifting into first feels like trying to move a boulder. I press the gas, then release the clutch. The car lurches, then stalls. I slam the clutch back in, and the engine sputters. Cursing under my breath, I twist the ignition again, desperate now. The engine grumbles. I try again, my hands shaking. Gas, clutch, gas. The car doesn't move, just jerks forward, then dies again.

I take a few deep breaths, willing myself to calm down. Defeated, I slump forward. The moment my forehead hits the steering wheel, the horn blares, slicing through the stillness like a knife. I jolt upright, my heart pounding. My eyes flick to the side mirror, the rearview, the windshield.

Then I see him. Garrett.

He ducks down enough so he can meet my eyes. I stare at him and feel my escape slipping between my fingers. He's saying something, but it's all muffled.

"You need to release the clutch slowly while giving it more gas," he says as I roll the window down on his side so I can hear him better. "Jerking it just stalls the engine."

I nod, forcing a small smile though it feels more like a grimace, the humiliation pressing down on me like a weight. Of course I can't even drive off properly. *Of course.*

"Where you headed?" Garrett wants to know.

"I wasn't . . ." I struggle to find my voice as I straighten out. "I just needed someplace quiet. My head hurts."

His eyes shift to my duffel on the passenger seat. "Ah. Packed bags help with migraines these days?"

I see it in his eyes; I've been caught. I lean my head back against the headrest, letting my eyes shut for a moment. I glance down at the gearshift again, but I know it's over. Even if I figured it out, Garrett would only tell Eli, and they'd jump in his Jeep and catch up to me.

I hear Garrett asking if I'm okay and let him talk until I've accepted that I won't be leaving tonight.

"What happened last night?" I ask, preparing myself for the answer I've avoided all day. "What did Eli see?"

"Nothing."

"No, just tell me. Please. I think I was . . ." I hesitate, my words getting caught in my throat, unsure if I should confide in him. "I had too much to drink."

"Yeah. Me too, but nothing happened." I see nothing but sincerity in the calm blue of his eyes. "I helped get you in bed. That's it."

"Then why is he icing me out?"

"I don't know." He shrugs. "Maybe he's projecting."

"What?" I ask, my heart skipping a beat.

"I don't know anything for sure," he says, pausing for a moment before tucking himself in the passenger seat and shutting us in together. "But it sounds like he's guilty."

"Why do you say that?"

"I don't know. He won't even hear me out."

"Me either," I say, the weight of all this sinking down on me. It's reassuring, though, that Garrett is finding Eli's behavior abnormal too.

"He's being irrational about this whole thing," Garrett says.

I nod. "It's almost like he wants it to be true."

"Yeah," he says, his voice low, unsure. "It's so weird."

He's right. Eli usually is a very methodical thinker. I try to imagine him sneaking around behind my back, but it's like trying to picture a ghost in broad daylight—nothing fits, nothing makes sense. He's never given me any reason to suspect him. He's always so attentive, so caring, a constant in a world that too often feels chaotic. I can barely consider that the person who has always been so reliably present could be hiding something. The idea feels foreign and uncomfortable. So desperately I want to hold on to the clear, uncomplicated image I've had of him all these years, but he's already let me go.

Garrett gestures at the key in the ignition with his chin, breaking me away from my thoughts. "Why are you trying to bail?"

"I just want to go home."

His smile is faint. "Not having fun, huh?"

"How'd you guess?"

Garrett watches me for a beat. "Eli will come around. Come back inside. Try to enjoy the rest of the week."

I don't even know if that's possible, but I'm too drained to do anything but heed. Moments later, we head up the steps together, and Garrett pulls the front door open for me.

I hesitate, glancing inside the house, then back into his eyes. "That arm was there."

"What?

"Before you guys got back, I ran upstairs because I was sick," I tell him. "There was plenty of time for it to be moved."

But he shakes his head. "No one else is here, Iris. It's just us."

"How do you know that?"

"Have you looked around? There's no other property for miles."

I let his words sink in, but then I think of that photo, of his uncle. Nolan. His truck was here that night.

He was in the back, digging.

His jacket covered in blood. "Something happened back there," I say, stepping inside. "I'm gonna figure out what."

chapter
twenty-four

Violet isn't in our room when I push in. The quiet greets me with a gentle sigh, and I sigh back, grateful for a few stolen moments of solitude. I sink onto the bed and open my book. The spine cracks under my touch, a sharp sound that sparks a small, fleeting pleasure. But the words blur, unsteady. I read the same page four times and still can't tell what it says. My thoughts scatter like leaves in a restless wind.

I close the book and reach for my laptop. The glow of the screen cuts through the dark as my fingers hover above the keys. A pause. A breath. Then I type *missing persons* and the name of this county.

Because the arm was real.

I know it was.

The memory of glimpsing it feels like a splinter lodged under my skin—impossible to ignore. Let Gia call me crazy. Let Lauren laugh. Let Eli defend their cruelty. I don't care. I saw what I saw, and I'll prove it to them. If not for them, for me.

I scroll down the first page of results, skim articles with intriguing headlines, but I don't find what I'm looking for until I come across a link to the New York State Police. The page shows a list of names with thumbnails and *last seen* dates. I grab a pen off the nightstand and flip to a blank page at the beginning of my book. I scribble down the first ten names with the most recent dates next to them, then put the most recent person's full name and search *missing persons case*.

Just as I hit Enter on my keyboard, the sound of footsteps approaching draws my attention. They pause right outside the door, which I left ajar. I close the book and snap my laptop shut, staring at the door, waiting for Violet or Eli to step in. I hope it's him, ready to take me into his arms and apologize. I wait a few seconds, but the door never swings in.

I quietly cross the room, then push the door open with no warning, hoping to startle whoever's on the other side. But the hallway is empty. I lean out of the doorframe and glance both ways but still see no one.

I shut the door and make sure to lock it this time. Violet can knock. I curl up in bed with my laptop and go back to my search. I pause on an article that reports on human remains discovered buried in the woods. The location mentioned catches my eye, triggering something in my memory. It sounds eerily familiar. I put it in Google Maps and realize it's near the area everyone went shooting the other day. Only ten minutes away from the property.

The details are hard to stomach, laid bare with such clinical precision, the brutality and suffering stark on the page. I think it's sick how Lauren and Garrett watch all those true crime documentaries. Consuming endless content about bloody crime scenes, dismembered bodies, interviews with sobbing family members, the clinical recounting of brutal assaults, graphic autopsies, police footage of crime scenes—it feels wrong, almost voyeuristic. I can't understand how they do it, letting all that horror seep into their subconscious just before they close their eyes. I can't imagine inviting more monsters inside my head. It's like they don't realize how real it all is, how it's not just a story someone made up to entertain them. Even reading about this case, I feel a twinge of guilt, like I'm intruding somehow. I hate this feeling that I'm consuming someone else's trauma for my own ends. But I push through it. I have to know if this case correlates to the arm I saw. The proximity is promising.

And horrifying.

I swallow and keep reading. The article says the medical examiner couldn't identify the victim because all of her teeth were extracted before her body was dumped in a ravine. Only limbs have ever been recovered, which were too badly decomposed to yield any successful DNA results.

My heart pounds. The body was found dismembered, just like the corpse I saw in the back. I can't say for sure if the elbow I saw was from a male or female. I didn't get a good enough look at it, not even to see if the arm was covered in hair. What if it was one of them, these women? I speed-read the article again, but then I realize it can't be the same person. The report states that two arms were found.

I type out the second name on my list, my fingers trembling, and watch as the search engine churns out results. I skim past the clutter, the irrelevant links, until one catches my eye. I click, and there she is. Her face stares back at me, a photo clipped from some better moment, before her name became a headline. Her smile is small, hesitant, but the eyes feel familiar. Too familiar.

She's different from the first but somehow the same. Not identical, no. But close enough for it to feel deliberate. The slope of their noses, the arch of their brows, the way their hair falls just so. The details blur into sameness. A pattern.

If I tilt my head a certain way, if I imagine the shadows falling differently, it's there. That sharp, uncanny resemblance. My hand rises to my face, grazing my cheekbone. The more I stare, the more the edges between us dissolve. It's as though I'm looking at my reflection in shattered glass, distorted and rearranged. It could be me. My photo could be the next one, pasted onto flyers and websites, tagged with pleas for answers.

I shake my head, squeeze my eyes shut, but the feeling doesn't leave. I can't tell if I truly look like them or if my mind is twisting the truth, projecting my own fears onto their faces. It could be any woman.

I move on to the next girl, desperate to see if she matches the pattern. The page doesn't load. I hit Enter again, and an error message covers the screen: no Wi-Fi connection. I reload five times, but it won't connect.

I search the room for my phone, trying to recall the last time I saw it. It's not here. Then I remember I had it in Eli's car. I must have left it there. I slip on my shoes and head downstairs in the dark. Violet, Lauren and Roman are all hanging out in the front room, drinking and bumping to the music, but there's no sign of Eli and Gia.

"Hey, did you know that the Wi-Fi is out?" I say to no one in particular.

"Obviously," Lauren says. "A fuse blew."

I glance around the room. No wonder all the lights are out.

Roman turns to me. "Garrett's downstairs checking the circuit breaker."

"No, he's not."

We all turn to see him ducking into the room behind me. Lauren playfully punches him for sneaking up on us, then lifts to the tips of her toes for a quick kiss that turns into them drunkenly sucking each other's faces.

"Did you see what the problem was?" I ask Garrett, and he finally pulls away for some air.

"I don't know what happened. Everything looked fine. Power's out. Water's still running. Don't ask me how, though."

Violet jumps to her feet. "Sounds like it's time for a manhunt. Let's go out in the back."

Apparently this is a great idea, because everyone heads to the back of the house, Violet leading the way.

Lauren slips on her sandals. "What are the rules again?" she asks, and then they're all gone.

I don't follow them outside. I have no desire to play this childish game ever again. We played on campus a few times, and I was never found. They would all just move on.

Instead, I make my way down into the basement. I need to get the power back on so I can finish my research. I want something concrete to present to Eli in the morning. Even if he doesn't want to be together, doesn't want to fight for us, he can still convince the others I'm not insane, and he can get us out of here.

I try to remember where I put that flashlight I found, but I can't recall where I set it down. I take the stairs one by one, my fingers brushing along the cool wall as I try to find my way to the circuit breaker . . . I hope. I think I've found it, but then realize what I'm actually feeling. Another door. This one has a padlock wrapped around the handle.

My pulse quickens as I yank on it, hoping it's rusty enough to pop. I turn around and head toward the trunk with the tools in the other room. One of those miniature axes should do the trick. My glasses don't really help in the dark. I fumble my way toward it, but it's impossible to navigate without my phone. I can barely make out the outline of my own body in the shadows.

My foot snags on something solid, and my body propels forward, slamming onto the cold floor. A jolt of pain shoots through my wrist, up my arm. I let out a whimper, rocking myself to ease the ache. Before I steady myself on my feet again, I hear the softest click.

My eyes dart toward the stairs. "I'm down here."

My words echo in the dark, but I don't get a response. I repeat myself, but the door doesn't open. I head back toward the stairs, take them two at a time. When I twist the knob, it won't turn. I jerk it back and forth, pulling and wrenching to no avail.

With both fists, I pound on the door. "I'm down here! Open the door!"

Nothing. No footsteps. Just suffocating silence. It only takes a couple seconds for the dark to feel claustrophobic. I bang my fists into the thick wood until my hands hurt. I ram my shoulder into the door, then my hip. I kick and scream and grunt until my body gives out on me. My back to the door, I melt to the hard concrete like burning candle wax.

Once I catch my breath, I recalibrate, then grip the doorknob with both hands, yanking as hard as I can. I pull harder, and it gives way with a sudden snap. I stumble backward in shock, the broken doorknob still clutched in my hand, and tumble down the stairs.

chapter
twenty-five

I curl up at the base of the stairs, my body folded into itself. The walls seem closer than they were before, and the darkness presses in, heavy and unforgiving. It feels like I'm falling into some kind of void, and the silence is the loudest I've ever heard.

Then, suddenly, I hear something: the creak and groan of pipes, followed by a strange hissing sound. It's probably just air leaks or pressure shifts in the plumbing, but the longer I lie here, the more it seems like it could be something else—something more ominous.

I close my eyes, and the image of that hole out back comes to life. Nolan was out there. He must have been the one who moved the arm I saw poking out of the dirt. I think about the articles I read about the women who went missing, about the jacket in that photo, all the weird shit that's been happening since my first night here. Something isn't adding up, and no one can convince me otherwise.

I try to push away the dark, nihilistic thoughts that threaten to take over my mind, but down here they seem to smother me, creeping up faster than I can swat them away. I'm stuck in this house for a few more days, and as sick as it makes me feel to be trapped here, somehow the idea of going back home seems even more horrifying. Without Eli, I don't even know what home *is*. Over the years, home has evolved from simply being a place. It's the way Eli looks at me from across a crowded room. The way his hand always seems to find mine in the dark. We've shared every aspect of our lives for so long. Without him, our apartment will just be a box filled with pointless walls.

Time draws out, and then I hear another noise. Footsteps. They get louder and louder. I push myself up to my feet and jog up the stairs as fast as I can. Balling both hands into fists, I pound on the door as hard as I can and scream to be let out. The footsteps stop. I pound harder. A beat of silence, and then the door opens an inch. I shove my way out of the pitch-blackness.

Violet stumbles into the wall, her drink slipping from her hands and crashing to the ground. "What the hell?"

She steps around the broken glass and stares at me like I've assaulted her. I take a beat to catch my breath. Her gaze settles on mine, and I feel our last conversation still lingering in the air. I push through the awkwardness, just glad to be out of the basement.

"I went down to see if I could get the circuit breaker working, and somebody locked me in," I tell her, brushing dust off my arms with my hands.

She narrows her eyes at me. "Nobody locked you in."

"I was stuck down there this whole time," I insist, but she steps off, heading down the hall. I hop on her heels. "You think I locked myself in the basement? It was creepy as hell down there."

Violet stops and scrutinizes me over her shoulder, as if she's trying to gauge whether or not to take me seriously. "Iris, you weren't locked in."

She takes off again, and so do I. "Whoever is messing with me is—"

"Nobody is messing with you," Violet snaps, stopping again to grab me by the arm.

She drags me back to the basement door, opens it, and then motions to the latch on the door. I glance down at it, not understanding her point until I notice that it locks from the inside. Like any other interior door. I stare at it, my mind reeling. This can't be right. I tried everything to open that door. I twisted, I pulled, I jerked, I rattled, I rammed—nothing would open it.

"But . . ." I shake my head, none of this making sense. "No, I swear, I couldn't get it open. That's why the knob broke off."

I open the door to show her that it's missing. But that still doesn't explain why I couldn't get the door open in the first place.

I swallow, and I wonder if I'm just being paranoid now. If I just freaked out over nothing. I wonder if the dark got to me, if it's the exhaustion still deep in my bones or the narcotic that is heartache that caused me to spiral. When I blink, I see Violet staring at me, a cross between disbelief and pity in her eyes.

"Maybe the lock just jammed or . . ." Doubt chokes the conviction out of my voice. "Or something."

"I changed my mind," she says, her voice flat. "You really *are* losing it."

"I'm not—"

"I thought this shit was funny at first, but you need some help."

"What's that supposed to mean?"

"I get it. Lauren can be a bitch, Gia is annoying as hell, and Eli's being an asshole. But all of these stunts are getting just a little pathetic."

A knot tightens in the pit of my stomach. "They're not *stunts*. I—"

"None of us has any reason to lock you in the basement, Iris." Her words slam into me, sending a tremble down my spine. "No offense, but no one's even thinking about you that much."

Violet steps around me and walks off.

"Then who did it?" I shout at her back. "No one else is . . ."

My words trail off as a disturbing thought grips me. Garrett said the same thing to me. *No one else is here.* But what about Nolan? He has the key. He knows his way around the property better than anyone. He could easily be hiding somewhere, sneaking in and out whenever he chooses. But as much as I rack my brain, I can't figure out why Nolan would play stupid little tricks on me. Why would he taunt me with a doll and lock me in a basement and steal my hair tie? The more I think about it, the more it seems like something Gia would do. Lauren is too busy fooling around with Garrett, and Roman would never do something like this to me. It has to be Gia.

"Maybe it's a ghost," Violet says, and I can tell by the tone of her voice that she's being facetious.

"Forget it," I tell her, and brush past her.

"Serious," Violet says, following behind me now. "Maybe it's your mother's spirit haunting you, messing with your head. She blamed you, didn't she?"

I stop short, her words slicing into my back like a knife.

Only Eli and my therapist know about my mother's hurtful last words. I had no idea he told his friends that part. I confided in him. I trusted him. It hurts knowing he shared that with these people who don't even trust my judgment, who mock the remnants of my trauma every chance they get.

My mother's words still sting. Not so much the sentiment, but the intention behind them. She ended her life but couldn't let me go. She had to make it so that she would be with me every day for the rest of my life, her presence ubiquitous even as her body turns to dust. It wasn't my fault. I know that now. I was a good daughter. I loved my mother more than my mother ever loved herself.

"What about the skull?" I say, turning around, the thought coming to me just before I start to leave again.

Violet hesitates, and I hold my breath, hoping for a communion. A moment where we commiserate over the unease that has been gnawing at me since I've been at this lake.

"There was no skull," she says flatly, her denial cutting deeper than it should.

"We don't know that. I've been looking up some—"

"There. Was. No. Skull." She doesn't raise her voice, but the words land heavy, deliberate, one after the other like heavy stones dropped into water. "It was just a rock. I was tipsy when I went in the water. That's all."

I stare at her, and her eyes flicker away, a brief betrayal of her own discomfort. I search her face, looking for a crack in her composure, but all I find is an impenetrable wall.

My jaw tightens as I force myself to turn away from her. I wait for Violet to stop me before I leave, but she never does.

chapter
twenty-six

I stop in the kitchen for a glass of water, feeling a headache coming on from all the screaming and banging. Gia, Eli and Lauren are in the back playing hopscotch on the deck with glow-in-the-dark chalk. I'm not even drunk like they clearly are, but a part of me wants just a tiny taste of childhood. I'm tempted to join them, but only for a split second. In the kitchen, I feel around the cabinet for a glass in the dark. I look over my shoulder when Garrett stumbles in behind me.

"You coming out?" he asks, leaning his arm against the threshold.

I force a smile. "Maybe later."

"Cool. I just need another one of these," he says, grabbing a bottle of vodka from the island. "And I'm out."

He returns my smile as he leaves, sliding the door shut behind him. I head across the room to the fridge, but as I take another step, something sharp pierces my bare foot, crunching loudly as it breaks my skin. My breath catches as the pain spreads from my sole through to my shin, shooting all the way up to my knee. I stumble back, stunned, and another brittle snap steals my next breath. Warmth spreads under my foot, sticky and unmistakable.

I hobble around the peninsula, lift my foot and squint through the dark. A large piece of glass from Violet's shattered drink is lodged into my sole. Eli always warns me about walking around our apartment barefoot. I lean against the wall so I can pull out the shard of glass, but pause when a shadow covers the room.

I look up, relieved to see Roman ducking inside. I tell him what happened, and he lifts his phone from his pocket, shining the light on my foot. I look away, scared to look at it in the light. He takes one of my arms and wraps it around his neck, then helps me up the stairs and into the bathroom.

Roman sits me down onto the edge of the bathtub and rummages around inside one of the cabinets for something. He uses the light from his phone to find some gauze and hydrogen peroxide. I bite my lip, trying not to cry out as he shuffles around, the pain sharp and burning. "You okay?"

"Yeah."

Roman quickly washes his hands with soap, then kneels down on the floor in front of me. He hands me his phone, and I angle the light so he can see what he's doing. I turn away, the blood already making my stomach churn. He tells me to hold my breath just before he pulls the biggest piece of glass out of my foot, then quickly covers the wound with a folded paper towel. The pain flashes white behind my eyes, but I hold back a cry. He pushes the wad against my foot with enough force for the blood flow to slow. It soaks through almost immediately, and he grabs another towel. This time it stops bleeding completely.

"Okay, hold it there," he says, concentrating, and I take over, applying pressure to the wound. "Tight. More pressure."

I press harder, squirming, and Roman's hand presses down on top of mine, intensifying the amount of compression. A small whimper escapes my lips.

"Sorry," he says, looking up into my eyes. "It's gonna hurt for a sec, okay? Just hold it tight for me."

I nod and stare at the ceiling, counting the seconds until he tells me to stop. "Why is there so much blood?"

"Your foot has a large blood supply." Roman stands and turns away for a second. "It's a good thing. It helps flush out dirt and bacteria. Keeps you from getting infected."

"So I'm not gonna die?"

He chuckles with his lips together. "No."

"Promise?"

"Promise."

Roman flashes me a smile, then drops back down onto his knees with the bottle of hydrogen peroxide in his hand. He twists off the top, and I squirm in anticipation. He places a hand over my calf, adjusting my leg so it's closer to his chest.

"Don't worry, I'll be gentle," he says, dabbing a wad of paper towel with the tip of the bottle.

Roman stays true to his word. He's tender and precise, but it's not enough to distract me from the sting. I curse through the pain, firing them off in such rapid succession, he laughs again. Soon I'm laughing too, and despite everything, this moment is nice.

Roman refocuses, finishes cleaning up my foot, then wraps it in gauze so carefully, I can tell he's trying hard not to hurt me. I hold my breath until he's done, and when I start to put my foot down, he holds it in place, tilting it to the side. He reangles the flashlight, and I catch what has his attention—another smaller piece of glass lodged in my heel.

"Hold on," Roman says, giving me a brief glance. "I need..."

He doesn't finish, just gets to his feet, taking the light with him to the medicine cabinet. He shuffles around and finds a pair of tweezers. I watch him as he sterilizes them with alcohol first, and I'm glad his father, a retired EMT, has clearly taught him all of this. My plan was just to slap on a humongous Band-Aid after pulling out the glass.

I squeeze my eyes tight as he pulls out a tiny shard of glass, but it doesn't hurt as much as I expect. I barely feel it.

"Sorry about that," Roman says, giving my foot a final inspection. "Think I got it all now."

I glance down and see the bottom of my foot is stained red. "Sure I don't need stitches?"

"The other one's pretty big, but it's shallow. You have a couple that are like really bad paper cuts, but you'll be fine."

Roman cleans the smaller cuts with the hydrogen peroxide, and I watch him.

And then a scream peals through the air, the shrill sound of pure terror.

chapter
twenty-seven

Roman whispers for me to hang back while he goes to find the source of the scream. My pulse pounding in my ears, I nod, my breath sharp in my throat.

"Look at all that blood," Gia shrieks, her voice piercing through the quiet as Roman turns into the hallway.

I hoist myself onto my good foot and hobble across the room. I lean out of the doorway just as he reaches the top landing, her phone the only beam of light in the dark.

"Hey, hey. It's me," Roman says.

"What are you doing?" Gia asks, her voice rattled and unsure.

"What the hell, man?" I can't see Eli, but his voice carries up to me. "You just got your period?"

"The blood isn't mine."

"Man, right now that's not a good thing."

Roman explains that I cut my foot and bled up the staircase on my way to the bathroom. I retreat back inside and lean my weight against the sink, not wanting to see either of them. Once they disperse, Roman offers to help me to my room, but I tell him I want to take a bath to clean myself up.

I shut the door and run the faucet in the tub. Steam rises into the air as scalding water gushes out. I don't temper it much. I want it to burn. I need the searing heat to drown out everything else. The sound of the water instantly soothes me. I undress, set my glasses on the edge of the tub, then climb inside once it's full, holding onto the wall so I don't slip. I sink down into the water until my shoulders are fully submerged, until it feels like I'm floating, my injured foot hanging over the edge. The weight of the world momentarily dissipates. But as soon as I shut my eyes and recede into the darkness, the cold, sharp ache of heartache gnaws at me from somewhere deep. The cruel weight of betrayal slams into me, crushes my bones, liquefies all the fat and muscle inside my body.

I can't move; I can barely breathe when I picture them in the dark. Together. On the stairs. He was following Gia upstairs, and I can't help but wonder what would have happened if that glass never impaled my skin. My blood stopped them, but what if I hadn't bled and she hadn't screamed? Would they have ended up in one of the bedrooms, covering her mouth with his hands so none of us heard them over the music? Were they holding hands before she noticed the blood? Did he make her laugh? Did he get her drunk? Did she get *him* drunk? Is this an act of rebellion, a way to get back at me, or does he really see something in her? I run through every interaction they've ever had in front of me, a discordant mélange, trying to find anything that I've missed. A hand on his leg, an unexplained absence, unspoken tension. But nothing sticks out. I can't decide if this is about me, or if this is about her.

It's overwhelming, the idea of us splitting, of returning home and packing, moving into another apartment with my cat but without my rock. There are times when it's hard to eat without him, as if my digestive tract is attuned to the beat of his pulse. Indigestion plagues me if we're apart too long, and though sleep often evades me these days, it's easier lying in the darkness with his arm around my waist. Even the loss of this, of him tightening his grip in his sleep, feels like a loss too profound to bear.

I sink deeper into the water, let it swallow me up to my chin. I want to go deeper, just to see what happens. Then—a flicker. A hum. The electricity surges back on with a violent shudder. The bathroom light blazes above me.

My eyes snap open. Water ripples around me. I squint beneath the bright light, cover my eyes for a moment, then open them again slowly. I reach for my glasses, and as my eyes readjust, a scream rips from my throat. Panic surges through my body as I peer down into the water. It's black, opaque, and littered with thick chunks floating on the surface.

I leap out of the tub, forgetting all about my injury, and when I put my full weight on it, pain shoots up my foot, sharp and blinding. I collapse onto the tiles, my knees bracing my fall and sending more white-hot pain throughout my leg. I grab onto the edge of the sink and try to pull myself up from the floor, groaning through the agony.

Someone knocks on the door, two pounds in quick succession.

"Iris?" Roman calls, knocking on the door again. "Are you—"

"I'm fine," I lie, my voice sharp but cracking at the edges. It feels like my knees might be bleeding, but I'm naked and wet. There's no way I'm going to let him in. I wish he was

Eli. I wish he would take me in his arms and carry me to the bed and read chapters from my book aloud until he falls asleep. Then I can watch him sleep and hold him, and in the morning we can go home. Together.

Roman relents, though he sounds skeptical when he tells me he won't be far, just across the hall. I grab the edge of the sink again, shifting my weight onto my good foot. I hold on for balance as I lean over the edge of the tub and peer down into the murky water, swirling with filth. I lift one of the small chunks. The smell hits me immediately, pungent and foul. I drop it back, and it splashes with a little *plunk*.

When I step out of the bathroom, a streak of blood glistens in the dark, leading to the stairs. My stomach twists as a metallic tang hits my tongue, a wave of nausea creeping up my throat as I follow the trail. It looks like there's been a massacre. It's hard to comprehend this all came from me, and so fast. I hobble down to the first level, and there's more on the stairs. Someone must have stepped in some, because there's a bloody half footprint on the first stair.

I find Garrett out on the front deck, smoking a cigarette. He motions to the box of Camels on the table when he sees me. I shake my head. I didn't know he still smoked. Garrett asks about my foot when he notices it dangling a couple of inches from the ground, and I downplay the severity of my injury. I don't want his pity.

I watch him pull on his cigarette as I work up the courage to ask what I came out here to ask. "You said your uncle dates younger women, right?"

I figure I'll ease into this slowly.

"Something like that." Garrett snorts a laugh. "Wouldn't exactly call it *dating*, if you know what I mean."

He doesn't say more, but he doesn't need to. I've heard about the men who kill young women not out of necessity or rage, but purely for the thrill of it. Nolan could be one of those predators, dismembering his victims' bodies, ripping out their teeth to ensure they leave no trace behind.

"Where is he staying while we're here?" I ask, leaning next to him on the railing. I keep a safe distance away, the gap between us deliberate.

He blows smoke from his nose, the blue of his eyes faint in the darkness. "Lake Como. He goes every year."

I nod, pretending to be entranced by the nighttime view of the deep blue-black water, the hum of the crickets, the chorus of frogs croaking. But my mind is racing. Garrett tosses the cigarette, the scent of soap clinging to his skin as he draws nearer, leaning over the edge to watch a little brown rabbit hop along the gravel.

"And you're sure he's gone?" I ask, trying to sound as aloof as I can.

Garrett opens his mouth to respond but stops as the door opens. I glance over my shoulder and see Lauren stepping out onto the deck in a white cotton dress.

"Well, don't let me interrupt," she says, her eyes cutting between the both of us.

She barrels down the stairs, never once looking back. Garrett gives me an apologetic shrug, then jogs down after her. They stop at the water's edge, spinning around to face each other like two storms colliding. They argue back and forth, Lauren shouting at him, but I still can't make out much. Just as I turn to head back inside, she grabs a fistful of his shirt as if she can no longer bear the distance between them. Garrett's hands reach up to clutch her face. The kiss is frantic, mostly air and teeth, their passion changing shape and form but not intensity. Within seconds, his shorts are in her hands. Her dress is a puff of fabric at her ankles, quickly being swallowed by the water. They make no effort to move out of view. It feels deliberate, a pointed message to me. *He wants me, not you.* But she has no idea how beautiful I think they are together.

I turn away when he grips her bikini bottoms to slide them off, a sinking feeling engulfing me. I wonder where Eli has snuck off to and squeeze my eyes shut, hoping he's not alone with Gia.

chapter
twenty-eight

The next morning, my eyes sting from tossing and turning all night. I sit on the edge of the dock, letting my bandaged foot dangle over the water. The sun beats down on me as I soak in the beautiful view. I try to enjoy it, to let it heal me and calm the noise in my mind, the intrusive thoughts that won't stop coming. I don't know what time it is. I have no idea where Eli is. Tilting my head back, I let the heat seal my eyelids shut, and just as I start to feel some peace, I hear laughter erupt, loud and obnoxious.

I look back over my shoulder to see who it is. Violet is doubled over, the water lapping at her calves. Garrett's shorts are pooled around his ankles, his face a mixture of shock and playful annoyance. Lauren's laughing just as hard. They must be drunk already. She grabs Violet's arm, and as they run deeper into the water, they peel out of their skimpy clothes. I expect them to strip down to their bikinis, but they're both naked underneath. Garrett steps out of his shorts and runs after them, determined to get revenge. He catches up to them fast and dunks both of their heads beneath the surface. They shriek and splash around in the water, their toned, tan bodies glistening under the sun, and I try to think of the last time I laughed that hard.

That girl I used to be before my mother died, I think she used to be able to have fun, to frolic, to galivant, to let go and exist only in the current moment. That girl seems like a stranger to me now, an illusion. I barely remember what it was like to move through the world in her skin. Before the nightmares. The dizzy spells. The restlessness and lapsed thoughts and sedatives.

Violet calls out my name. I turn, expecting the worst, but she waves a hand.

"Come swim with us!" The water is up to their chests now. "I won't drown this time, I promise."

But there's no way I'm skinny dipping with them in broad daylight. After that kiss, I don't feel comfortable being around Violet without clothes on, and absolutely not in front of Garrett with Lauren right beside him. It feels like a trap, this invitation, and I remind myself that none of them are my friends.

"My foot hurts," I tell her, flicking it in the air so she can see the bandage, glad I have an easy excuse.

"Oh, come on," Garrett says. "When's the last time you just said fuck it, and went with it?"

Never. Not like this. Not even my past self. My mother's instability was the perfect breeding ground to become a serial overthinker. I'm always running worst-case scenarios in my head, always anxious, constantly weighing every outcome of every decision as if my life depends on it. Never knowing what mood I'd come home to and always tiptoeing around the edges of her chaos, I've always had to be the sound, responsible one, the one who kept things from falling apart. Everything was always on my shoulders—the bills, the meals, the emotional fallout from her binges. I learned early on to expect the unexpected, to brace myself for impact, because someone had to. Someone had to be the adult. And now, I can't seem to turn it off, this constant state of vigilance.

"She told you she doesn't want to," Lauren says, her eyes on Garrett. "Why don't you just leave her alone?"

Garrett paddles in the water. "I'm just trying to—"

"You're such a liar," Lauren growls, pushing him in the chest. "You like her, don't you?"

Lauren glides away before Garrett can answer. He swims after her, catching up to her quickly, but she pushes him off again and wades out of the water. Garrett covers himself with his hands as they start tearing into each other again.

"Why don't you just go ahead and fuck her?" Lauren snaps back. "I'll watch. Maybe I can pick up some pointers, since apparently I don't do it for you anymore."

She marches out of the water, picks up her dress and snatches it down over her shoulders. The thin fabric clings to her skin like Saran wrap. Violet grabs her clothes and runs after her without stopping to put them on. I sigh, exhausted by her antics. They can barely keep their hands off each other one moment; the next, she wants blood.

In a way, I understand. Once a certain seed gets planted, it's hard to see through an unfiltered lens. Just like when Eli saw Garrett in my bedroom and immediately assumed we were sleeping together despite the many times we told him nothing was going on between us. Maybe I should just give Eli more time. Maybe Garrett is right that he'll come around eventually. His emotions are probably just raw and heightened because of dealing with his grandmother. He went from one high-stress situation to another. He's not thinking straight, letting his feelings rule and ruin. Maybe I just have to be patient.

Or maybe it's just part of being human, an inexplicable part of our evolution—our sense of preservation—to want even the things that harm us.

I stay out on the dock for what feels like forever. Two hours, maybe more. The lake breathes. The clouds shift above. Nolan never leaves my mind. I can't shake the image of him, his shadow crawling through the house. Watching. Waiting.

When I finally push myself up to my feet, my foot throbs like it's mocking me. I limp toward the house, gripping at anything that will hold my weight—the dock rail, the doorframe. Each step feels unsteady, like I might go down at any second.

Just as I reach the door, it swings open.

Garrett smiles but doesn't say anything. He takes one look at me and steps forward to help. His hand grips my arm, guiding me inside as if I might break if he lets go. He eases me into an armchair without a word, but I can feel his eyes on me the entire time.

"It's fine," I say, waving him off. "You don't have to."

"It's nothing."

Garrett pulls the ottoman closer and gently nudges it under my foot before turning to leave.

"Wait."

"Yeah?" he asks, spinning back around.

"Can you call him?"

He blinks, clearly confused. "What?"

"Can you call him? Your uncle."

Garrett freezes, his brow furrowing. "Why?"

"I just . . ." I hesitate, trying to think of a way to say this without sounding completely unhinged. "I'd feel a lot better if I knew where he was."

Garrett studies me, his expression wary now. "Is this about the arm thing?"

"No," I lie quickly, shaking my head. "No, I'm . . . I'm over that."

"You don't still think—"

"Can you please just . . ." I squeeze my eyes shut, biting back my frustration. "Just call him?"

His lips press into a thin line, and for a second, I think he's going to argue. But then he shrugs. "Fine."

He pulls his phone from his back pocket. I watch his thumb tap the screen as he finds his number, my pulse quickening. He lifts the phone to his ear and waits. A faint hum fills the silence.

Five rings, but Nolan doesn't answer.

"It's pretty late there. They're ahead five hours, I think," Garrett says, lowering the phone and looking me over. "If it's really bothering you, I'll call him back in the morning."

"Just try one more time." My voice is sharper now, a little too desperate.

He dials again, glancing at me like he's humoring a child. I hold my breath, but the result is the same.

"No answer," he says, sliding his phone back into his pocket with an air of finality.

But then he looks at me, his gaze steady, watching me as I keep my head down, unable to meet his eyes.

"Here." He pulls his phone back out and starts typing. "I'll text him."

When he's done, he holds the screen out to me, showing a short, straightforward message: *Where are you?*

I nod, swallowing the knot in my throat. "Thanks."

We both wait for it to buzz, but nothing comes. The minutes stretch on, and after a while, I tell Garrett he doesn't have to wait here, to just let me know when Nolan texts back. He walks off, leaving me alone with the uneasy silence.

About half an hour later, he strides back into the room, his phone in hand.

"Here," he says, flipping the screen toward me.

I lean forward to read the thread, the first time I think I've moved since he left. Beneath Garrett's question are a handful of photos. Clear skies, sparkling turquoise water, snow-capped peaks in the distance. A vacation paradise.

"He's . . ."

"Over four thousand miles away," he says, using his finger to scroll up and show me the rest of the exchange.

"Oh," I say, but somehow instead of relief, a wave of confusion washes over me.

I skim the conversation. He was out on a hike when Garrett called earlier. Dodgy reception, he claims.

I glance at the pictures again, and something about them feels wrong. They're too perfect, like something out of a brochure. I force myself to nod.

"Yeah," I say softly, my voice hollow. "Looks nice."

Fine. He's in Italy. I chant this to myself like an incantation. He didn't blow up the boat. He didn't leave the doll outside, or scribble those perverse drawings on it and put it in my bed. He isn't creeping around the house, waiting for the perfect moment to make himself known. Fine. But the thought doesn't settle in my chest the way it should. It doesn't soothe. Something is off. I can feel it.

Later, when the house has gone still, I glance over at Violet. She's in bed smelling like peaches, her damp hair leaving a dark streak on her pillow. When she's not looking, I slip out of the room. The floor groans beneath me. I grip the banister to steady myself as I hobble down the stairs. Every sound feels amplified. Every shadow stretches just a little too far.

The door to Nolan's study doesn't creak when I push it open, but the sound of the latch clicking as I shut it behind me sends a shiver up my spine. I check inside the desk first, not exactly sure what I'm looking for. The drawers are cluttered, but nothing sticks out as odd. Pens, receipts, a half-empty box of staples. The computer sits on the center of the desk, screen black, the faint smudge of a fingerprint in the corner. I tap the keyboard, and it flickers to life. A password box pops up. I put it back to sleep and move over to the filing cabinet. I sort through folders, papers that feel too crisp to hold anything useful. My movements are clumsy. Frantic. Like if I stop, even for a second, someone will pop in and catch me.

Then I hear it. A creak from the hallway.

My body stiffens like prey caught out in the open.

Someone's here.

I wait, my lips parted. The air feels charged, pressing against me, tightening around my lungs.

Another creak. Then nothing.

My ears strain to catch any other sound, but the silence is so loud it drowns out everything else. I swallow hard and keep going, my hands trembling now. I open the last drawer, tugging it hard when it jams. Folders neatly line the inside, but behind them, a stack of random papers spills out. I flip through them. Buried at the bottom, something small and deep blue catches my eye.

I pull it out, my breath hitching in my throat. Nolan's passport.

My hands fumble as I flip it open, the pages stiff and smooth beneath my fingers.

There he is. Nolan's face stares back at me, his name printed neatly under the photo.

He can't be in Italy without this.

He's here. I know he is.

And yet the truth feels slippery. Like it's moving farther and farther out of reach.

chapter
twenty-nine

The soft rhythm of Violet's light snores fills the room. I don't waste any energy trying to will myself to sleep. I see their faces, the girls from the missing persons reports. I hear their screams, their terror, their desperation, their pleas. I wonder if they died knowing it was the end or if he at least gave them the courtesy of killing them instantly. I imagine Nolan slitting their throats. I think of them bleeding out slowly, anticipating their last breaths, saying their goodbyes in their heads, calling out for their mothers. A soft creak from outside the door jolts me upright.

I reach onto the nightstand and feel around for my glasses, but they fall to the floor. I pull back the covers and crouch down to pick them up, but the bedroom door eases open. My entire body freezes from the inside out. The door only opens a crack.

I glance at Violet, still sleeping deeply, and quickly scan the room for something to use as a weapon. My shoes are within reach, my book too, but I grab the lamp on the nightstand, lifting it with both hands. Shaking, my arms are shaking, but I grip it tighter. Then I wait, in the dark, in the silence, until he creeps in over the threshold.

Eli.

Even in the dark, I can make out the outline of his body, his wide shoulders and narrow hips filling the doorway. I blow out a breath and release the lamp. He slips into the room wearing a white T-shirt and shorts. He creeps closer, trying to not wake Violet. I sit back on the bed. He stops in front of me, looming over me like a tree on a blazing-hot day.

"What are you doing?" I whisper, flicking a quick glance at Violet to make sure she's still asleep.

Eli presses a finger to his lips and crawls onto the bed with me. His frame takes up most of it; the only way we can both fit is if he's under me or on top of me. So he climbs aboard, mounting me slowly, careful not to bump my injured foot.

My heart pounds to a completely different rhythm now. I can barely meet his eyes. "Eli—"

"I talked to Garrett," he says, his words falling into my ear like drops of rain on the lake, making me shiver down to the tips of my toes. "I should've talked to you."

His words derail my thoughts. I want to tell him about Nolan, about the passport. But when his lips graze my ear, then my neck, my brain glitches. He kisses me softly, and I feel myself weakening against him, everything solid inside my body emulsifying. He draws back just enough to stare deep into my eyes, and I stare into his. This is home. This is all I needed this whole time. He tells me he's sorry, he's truly sorry, and I believe him. I have no idea who this mystery Eli is that's been here until now, but this is the Eli I fell for, the one I want to marry. Soft, tender, warm.

"I'm sorry, too," I say, my voice barely above a whisper. "I shouldn't have—"

Again, Eli hushes me, this time with a deep kiss, his weight crushing me in the way that makes me feel dainty and safe. I don't think about Nolan as I kiss him back. I don't think about the arm. Or that stupid doll. Or the weapons in the basement. Or the shovel. Or the bloody jacket.

Eli's hand slides down between my legs, and I gently stop him. "We can't," I whisper, turning to glance at her bed. "Violet . . ."

Eli kisses me again, and my eyes fall shut. Then he's moving down. My neck, my collarbone. Lower. I open my eyes to watch.

But Eli is gone.

No. He was never here.

I let out a scream, but the sound stays trapped in my throat as *Nolan* covers it with his massive hand. I try to push him off, but he climbs on the bed, straddling my body as he pins my arm down with his other hand. I kick and writhe, trying to break free from the crushing weight of his body, but he's too heavy, like dead weight pinning me down into the mattress. I thrash, but his grip only tightens. Air. I need *air*. I claw at his hands, my nails scraping his skin, but he doesn't flinch. Black dots dance behind my eyes. My chest burns. I try to kick, to push him off, but my strength is fading. My legs flail against the sheets in vain.

The lamp.

I stretch out my arm, but I can't reach it. I strain, fighting the darkness closing in on me. My vision blurs. Everything is slipping away.

But then, I grip it and swing with every ounce of strength I have left. I feel the base connect with a soft thud. It's not a good hit, not enough to knock him cold like I'd hoped, but he grunts, stunned for a moment, his grip loosening enough for me to turn to Violet and scream for her to help. But when I squint in the dark, her body is gone.

The bed is empty except for a gun.

A Beretta. Then next to it, a woman. Six feet tall. Rail-thin. She stares right into my eyes, her face gaunt.

My mother.

She's *alive*, sitting erect on the bed, her eyes wide, something haunted in them. I call out to her, but she's catatonic. She doesn't blink. Doesn't help me, her only daughter. She sees me, what he's doing to me. But she doesn't jump up and blow his brains out. She only watches.

"Mom! Help me! *Please* . . ."

I see his fist coming too late.

There's a flash of pain, white-hot and blinding. My head jerks to the side, teeth cutting into the inside of my cheek. I taste blood, metallic and warm. It fills my mouth, drips down my chin. My face throbs, skin burning where his knuckles struck. I choke on the blood, gasping, eyes watering. My skull feels like it's been split open, and for a moment, I can't see, can't think.

His shadow looms over me again, but my mind screams. Move, fight, *survive*. I spit blood, my lips split and trembling, and try to push myself up, but my limbs feel heavy, useless. This time Nolan clamps both hands around my neck, squeezing as tight as he can. His eyes are empty, cold. He squeezes harder, cutting off every last gasp. Sweat drips from his temple onto my cheek. Tears stream down my face. My mouth opens, but nothing comes out.

I reach out to my mother with my hand, but she still doesn't blink. I flail my arm, desperate, screaming with every breath left inside me. It's like she's a specter, still and ghostly. I think maybe she's only a figment of my imagination until there's movement in the corner of my eye.

She lifts her gun, the metal glinting with hope in the dark.

"Shoot him," I beg. "*Shoot him, Mom.*"

She angles the gun.

And slides it into her mouth.

"Mom, no!" I scream, my voice breaking. "*Don—*"

The gunshot echoes and I jerk up from the mattress, gasping for air. I touch my face. My neck. There's no blood. Just sweat.

I take deep breaths, trying to calm down as the remnants of the nightmare linger in my brain. I can barely breathe.

It felt so real. They *always* feel so real.

My eyes drift over to the other bed. My mother is gone. But so is Violet. The bed is empty. I'm alone.

I shut my eyes, and when I open them, my gaze settles on Eli, softly stepping into the room, his face twisted with concern.

"Heard you screaming," he says, shutting the door behind him.

I drop my eyes, feeling vulnerable, wondering who else heard. "I had another nightmare. It was . . ."

This isn't how I wanted him to come to me. I didn't want him to see me like this. Frazzled and breathless and sweaty.

Eli doesn't say anything else. He drifts further into the room, then takes an edge of the bed. The mattress groans with the addition of his two hundred pounds. He opens an arm, draping it around my shoulder, and I let out a breath, it seems, for the first time. I rest my head on his shoulder, and tears stream from my eyes. Eli holds me as I cry, his arm dropping to my back. Then he lifts my chin and stares deep into my eyes, whispering a soft apology. He kisses me, slow and deep. I try to speak, to tell him about Nolan, the white pickup truck that pulled up out front the other night, but he tells me to relax, his mouth pressing into mine, opening it softly.

I fall back onto the bed, and Eli pulls away his clothes. When he moves on top of me, he presses his face into my neck, takes a long inhale of my sweat. He hovers close and rocks slow, steady, the room silent except for his sighs and my soft cries. My eyes clamp shut as I grip the edge of the mattress, his voice a rasp in my ear when he tells me he's close, his legs quivering. I whisper his name, tell him to stay inside me, but he draws back, his eyes shut as he shudders hard.

Warmth splatters my chest, my neck, my face.

When I glance down, a scream rips straight from the core of me.

My body is covered in blood.

chapter **thirty**

I jerk awake, a scream lodged in my throat as my legs thrash, my hands clawing the sheets. A shriek echoes in the room, and it takes a moment for me to realize it was me.

"Babe, babe," a voice says, and I squint in the dark, Violet's face slowly coming into focus. "It's okay. It's okay."

She leans over me, her face my entire world for a few beats. Panting, I look myself over.

There's no blood.

Instead, my body is covered in sweat, my top soaked through, clinging to my skin.

No blood. No Eli.

Nolan isn't here. He was never here.

I push myself into an upright position, then close and open my eyes, willing myself to stay in the moment.

"I didn't know what to do," Violet says, her voice soft with concern. "Didn't want you waking everybody up."

"Sorry, sorry. I . . ." I suck in a breath to slow my heart rate. "You were right to wake me. Thank you."

I take a few more moments to calm myself down. Violet offers to get me a glass of water. I nod, just to get rid of her for a while. She slips out of the room in a pair of boxers and a tank top. I lie back down, afraid to close my eyes.

A knock at the door startles me. I wait a few moments, wondering if it's Violet. Then my body tenses. She wouldn't knock. She'd just come back in.

For a second, my mind goes to the worst, my heart pounding again. I think of Eli. Then Nolan. Distorted images from both dreams overlap in my head, and suddenly I'm frozen. I can't speak. I can't move.

"Everything okay in there?"

Garrett's voice cuts through the silence, and a cool wave of relief washes over me. I release a breath, preparing to tell him that I'm fine when I hear another voice. Violet. She explains what happened, then slips back into the room. I close my eyes at the last moment, pretending to have fallen back asleep.

But rest never comes. I watch the sun emerge from wherever it goes when it dips below the horizon. The fantasia of pinks and purples, then the blue, gentle and omnipresent. I head straight into the bathroom after I get out of bed.

I still haven't gotten Nolan out of my mind. I know he's lying about being in Italy. That means he could be anywhere. He could be here. He could be the one who locked me in the basement. The one who moved the arm from the hole.

He could be watching me right now.

Maybe there're cameras.

I shake the thought out of my head as I swish around a capful of mouthwash. Glancing in the mirror, I notice the knot on my head has started to go down. But then something catches my eyes. I spit out the mouthwash in shock, covering the glass in fizzy blue spatter.

Through the drizzle, my gaze settles on the doll. It's back.

I threw it out, but somehow it's back, perched on the shelf behind me, one eye staring at me. The other winks.

I whip around, seething, every ounce of blood pumping in my veins boiling, and slam the plastic doll against the sharp edge of the sink until one of its little arms pop off. It bounces into the tub, but I don't stop. I keep going, grunting with each swing, my rage multiplying each time it makes contact with the porcelain.

"What the hell are you doing?" Gia says from behind me. "Are you crazy? *Stop.*"

I slam the doll against the counter again, and gratification blooms in my chest as the head topples to the floor, dented. The sight of it only fuels my rage. A guttural scream rips from my throat with my next swing. The other arm snaps off, ricocheting against the wall, onto the floor. I keep going, knowing I won't be satisfied until it's in pieces. Unrecognizable.

Gia grabs my arm, and I snatch away. But she won't give up. She reaches for me again, and I shove her with enough force that she stumbles back into the wall.

It's not about the doll anymore. Every bit of pent-up rage at my mother erupts like a geyser. For the first time, I allow myself to fully feel my rage for what she did, for being so selfish, for leaving me the way she did, for making me watch, for poisoning her brain with drugs. And it feels so good to finally be able to admit it, that she was a terrible mother. I've tried, I've tried so hard, with everything in me, to make excuses for her neglect, her ugly moods, her lies, her broken promises.

A torrent of hot tears streams down my face as I say her name—Genevieve. I could never call her Mom. Or Momma. Or Mommy. She didn't want me to mistake her for being a maternal force in my life. She wanted a hard line between us.

Genevieve.

The memories rush back all at once. The times when she spit in my face. When she shoved me to the ground. When she forced food down my throat after I said I was full. When she gave the police my name after she was arrested on a possession charge. When she locked me in the utility closet in the basement of our apartment building and fell asleep. When she crushed a Percocet in my orange juice and didn't come back to the apartment for two weeks. When she sold my school uniform for a hit. When she made weapons out of broomsticks, lampshades, cassette decks, high heels, frying pans, cantaloupes, perfume bottles, textbooks, umbrellas.

Genevieve.

Now I see what Eli's always seen, what my therapist has been trying to get me to see. I see it in color, glaring hues and vivid clarity. No more excuses. Just the truth. I pull us apart, and I finally see what I could never let myself see. I come from her blood, her flesh, her bone, but I am not her. She is not me.

Genevieve.

Genevieve.

Genevieve.

I slam the doll into the sink until its little torso splits in half. I pull at the hard plastic with my hands until it cracks, the jagged edges digging into my skin.

I scream my mother's name as I fight against the pair of strong arms that grips me suddenly, pinning my arms to my side. I scream at her as if she'll hear me from the grave. My throat goes raw, but I keep screaming and writhing and crying.

"Iris, it's okay," Roman says, his voice low and close to my ear. "It's me, it's me."

I pant and blink the room into existence. The muscles in my arms and back tremble with exhaustion. I can't fight him anymore. My chest heaves as I struggle to catch my breath, Roman strong and solid behind me. Only a black pair of boxer briefs and my shorts separate us. He must have been sleeping when he heard me. I meet his eyes in the mirror.

"Let it go, Iris," he whispers, and somehow it feels like he understands. Like he isn't just speaking about the doll, but all the hurt, the anger, the regret festering inside me.

I tell *him* to let *me* go, but he holds on to me until I drop what's left of the doll to the floor. Finally, it's in pieces. Two arms, two legs, a head and torso. Just like the bodies Nolan chops up and buries.

I do what Roman says. I clamp my eyes shut and do my best to release it all. The anger ebbs, draining away, but the pain lingers like a scar.

"Thanks," I say, still looking at him through the mirror, and I mean it, though the words feel small.

Roman shifts, his voice low and steady. "You're good."

"Can I show you something?" I ask, turning around to face him. My voice comes out too soft, too fuzzy.

His brow lifts. "What's up?"

I hesitate. The words feel heavy in my throat. Roman waits, his body angled toward me as if he's bracing for something bad.

"It's about Nolan," I say finally, thinking of the passport.

He stiffens, his brow furrowing slightly, like this isn't the direction he expected me to take. Then he nods for me to go on.

"I was in his study last night," I tell him, my eyes darting toward the hall. "I just needed to see something. To check."

"Check what?"

I shake my head, trying to clear the panic building in my chest. Then I reach for his arm and pull him toward the door. "Come. I'll..."

My words falter as Eli steps into the doorway. His eyes sweep over me, my hand holding on to Roman.

He doesn't apologize like he did in my nightmare. He hasn't said a word to me since he went off to ride with Gia. I meet his eyes and hope it burns. It should have been him. He should have run to rescue me.

His bottom lip drops open as if he might speak, object.

But a scream pierces the air and drowns out his words.

chapter
thirty-one

Roman helps me down the stairs, and by the time we make it into the kitchen, Garrett is already there, hovering over Lauren. She leans against the counter, tears in her eyes. He looks up at all of us crowding around.

"Black widow," Garrett says, lifting her arm to inspect it.

Gia runs to her side and stares at it herself. "Oh, my god. Did it bite you?"

Lauren nods. "Little fucker."

I limp closer to see. It's faint, but visible, a small spot on her forearm, red and swelling. When I squint closer, I can make out two tiny puncture marks where the fangs sank into her flesh. Garrett cleans it with soap and water, which comes out of the tap clear, no chunks.

Roman slips out to get dressed. Garrett pulls ice out of the freezer and fills up a Ziploc bag. When he's done with the makeshift ice pack, he calls their family doctor. He ends the call and reassures everyone that Lauren should be fine. A collective sigh fills the room.

"It'll heal on its own," he adds. "As long as severe symptoms don't arise."

"Are you gonna be able to come on the trail with us later?" Violet asks, and Lauren says she's not up for it.

"You guys go," Garrett says, rubbing Lauren's back. "I'll stay back here with Lauren."

"No, babe, you've been talking about this trail for weeks," she says, running her hand through his hair. "Just go. I'll be fine, I promise."

"What if something happens while we're gone?" Gia asks, but she doesn't offer to stay back herself.

Violet turns to me and glances down at my foot, still bandaged and sore. "Iris, you're staying, right?"

"Actually," I say, my voice tighter than I mean it to be. This is the first I've heard anything about a hike, but I can't sit through this pretense any longer. "I saw something last night."

The room goes silent, all eyes shifting to me. I swallow, but it does nothing to loosen the knot in my throat.

"Your uncle," I say, looking straight at Garrett now. "He's not in Italy."

"What do you mean? I showed you the messages he sent." His voice is clipped, his jaw tightening. His irritation feels like a slap.

"I know." My pulse pounds in my chest, but I push through it. "But I found his—"

"Come on, Iris," Eli says, cutting me off like I'm embarrassing him by association. "You have to pull yourself together."

"I wasn't talking to you," I snap, the anger coming so fast it startles even me.

"Well, I'm speaking for everybody," Eli fires back. He gestures around the room as if daring someone to disagree. No one does. "This is getting ridiculous. You need to just chill."

"I need to *chill*?" I spit, my voice shaking. "I need to—"

"Listen," Garrett cuts in, stepping between us, his hands up like he's mediating a fight between toddlers. His eyes lock on mine. "I'm sorry whatever you think you saw freaked you out, but you need to let this go."

"I found his—"

"Girl, just give it up," Gia says, her tone sharp and dismissive.

My chest tightens, the heat of her words crawling up my neck. How dare she? Of all people, *her*?

"Somebody moved that arm," I say, louder now, my voice trembling. "Somebody locked me in the basement. And somebody—"

"The basement was not locked," Violet snaps. Her voice slices through me, cold and sharp. She glares at me, and it stops me mid-breath. She's always been the patient one, the steady one. But now she's looking at me like I disgust her.

"There was *no* arm," Gia chimes in, rolling her eyes.

"Just because you didn't see it doesn't mean it wasn't there," I shoot back, but my voice cracks, and I sound pathetic. Like a child who's lost her favorite toy.

It's over. I can feel it. The air in the room shifts as they start to peel away, one by one. Eli is the first to go, muttering something under his breath as he passes over the threshold. Then Violet, who shakes her head like she's washing her hands of me. Gia follows, whispering something to Violet as they leave. Their muffled laughter hits me like a blow to the chest. Garrett lingers a moment longer, his hands on his hips, like he wants to say something but decides against it. He shakes his head and goes back to tending to his wife.

I think I'm alone. Then I catch Roman standing on the edge of the room out of the corner of my eye. He's dressed now, in shorts and an old band T-shirt stretched tight across his broad chest. I meet his eyes, hoping he'll say something, anything. But he doesn't. He just stares at me, and the doubt on his face burns worse than all the rest.

I hobble upstairs, each step a jolt to my already bruised pride. I yank the passport out from under my pillow. My fingers tremble, but I tell myself it's from gripping it so tight or from the strain of holding the weight of everyone's doubt.

When I go back downstairs, Garrett is hovering over Lauren on the couch, fussing with her bandage. Roman spots me before anyone else. His eyes widen when he sees what I'm holding, and he pushes off the counter, standing straighter, his posture suddenly tense.

"What's that?" Roman asks, cautious, like he's not sure he wants the answer.

Gia and Eli filter back into the room, their whispers fading as their eyes lock onto the passport in my hand. Eli frowns, stepping closer to get a better look. Gia follows, her arms crossed tightly over her chest.

"It's your uncle's passport," I say, my voice louder than I mean it to be. I thrust it out toward Roman first, and he hesitates before taking it.

He flips it open, brows knitting as he studies the photo inside.

Garrett finally looks up. "What's going on?"

"Nolan's passport," Roman says, handing it to Gia, who snatches it like she doesn't believe it.

"It's definitely his," Gia mutters, passing it to Eli.

"Shit," Eli says, glancing up at me, his expression softening. "Sorry, Iris. I thought you were just . . ."

"Losing it?" I say for him, and he looks down, embarrassed.

Eli winces, rubbing the back of his neck. His contrition does little to soothe me.

Violet gently plucks the passport from Eli's hands. She studies it closely, her lips pressed into a thin line. Then she looks up, shaking her head.

"What?" I ask, my chest tightening.

She flips the passport around and points at the bottom corner. "It's expired."

I blink. "What?"

"This is old," she says, turning the page to show me the dates. "Look."

The words blur as I stare at them. Roman takes the passport from Violet and nods a second later.

"Yeah," he murmurs. "Expired a couple of years ago."

"Oh no, an expired passport!" Gia gasps in mock horror. "Somebody call the FBI."

Violet rolls her eyes. "No, seriously. What's next? Are we checking his grocery receipts for hidden messages?"

"This still doesn't mean he's not here," I mumble, more to myself than anyone else. But the words feel hollow now.

I want to argue, to push back, but the edges of my resolve are starting to fray. Maybe they're right. Maybe I've let this spiral into something it's not.

"Fine," I say finally, my voice brittle.

Everyone shifts, the tension dissolving as they start gathering their things for the hike. I stay rooted in place, my foot throbbing as the rest of me goes numb.

chapter
thirty-two

I curl up with my book on the deck until they're all packed and ready to go. Garrett carries all the gear out to the truck—a trekking pole, boots with thick, rugged soles, a humongous backpack, an insulated gallon canteen and a lightweight bucket hat. Gia must be borrowing her nylon Prada shorts from Lauren since she's also wearing her Chanel cap. Roman waves as he shoulders his backpack, then follows the women out the door. Eli helps Gia into the back row of the Rubicon, then sits next to her, their bodies right on top of each other's.

I knock on the door of the big bedroom, a glass of water and a bottle of Tylenol in my hands. Lauren says it's okay to come in, and when I push inside, she's topless. I quickly turn back out, apologizing, but she stops me, saying it's okay, that she wants to show me something. I stop at the edge of the king-sized bed, setting the water and pills on the nightstand. She angles her arm my way, showing me the intense swelling around the area where she was bitten. The puncture marks are even more defined now, like they've branded her. The rash has also spread across her stomach and chest, and now I see why she didn't cover up. It looks painful, both to the touch and just to move. It's hard to see her as anything but human. She may be rude and unpleasant most of the time, but she's made of blood and atoms and contradictions, just like everyone else. She bleeds. She cries. She's not infallible.

"Does it hurt?" I ask, holding on to her arm as gently as I can.

"It's like, burning. Stinging a little bit right here." My gaze follows where she points, around her rib cage. "I feel kinda nauseous too."

I reach onto the nightstand for the glass of water. "Brought you some Tylenol. Need anything else?"

Lauren rolls her eyes. "An Evian bath and body wrap at the Ritz."

She takes the water and swallows two pills. I follow her hand as she points to the dresser. I open the drawer and find her tops, neatly folded and stacked on top of each other. I pull out a tank top and pass it to her. She groans as she pulls it on, like every inch of her body aches. I feel horrible. She struggles a bit to pull it over her chest, the silence thickening, heavy and awkward.

I turn to leave but pause at the door, looking back at her.

"What?" she asks, her voice flat.

I drift back in and stop at the foot of the bed as she lies back against the throne of pillows with another groan.

"I was thinking . . . when that boat blew up . . ." I hesitate, rearranging my scattered thoughts. "Maybe it wasn't an accident."

Lauren's expression tightens with unease. "What are you saying?"

"What if Nolan meant for it to explode?"

She stares at me for a beat, then lets out an incredulous laugh. "You're serious."

"Just hear me out." I lean forward, adjusting the pillow behind her neck. "We're assuming he got a new passport and went to Italy. But what if he didn't? What if he's still here and rigged the boat so the fuel would leak?"

Lauren frowns, skepticism hardening her features. "But Roman was on the boat with you. You're saying he'd kill his own nephew?"

"I don't know," I cut in, exasperated. "I don't know what he's capable of. It just feels . . . off."

"It was just a coincidence," she says firmly, like she's trying to convince herself as much as me. "A freak accident."

I want to believe her, to let the idea dissolve into the chaos of everything else that's happened this week. But the timing. It was too perfect. Too calculated.

"You don't know that," I say quietly, thinking of the notes I've scrawled in my book, the faces of the missing women I can't get out of my head. "There could be something he's trying to hide. Something he would kill for."

"Like what?"

"Like if he saw me."

"Saw you what?"

"You know that spot where you guys went shooting?" I say, switching gears. Lauren nods. "Human remains were found there. They still haven't been able to identify the body because it was chopped up and buried in different places. The limbs were spread out over an acre of land. The teeth were removed from the skull too."

"I'm assuming this is relevant to me somehow and not just creepy," she drones, letting her eyes shut.

"There's a bunch of girls who have gone missing around here. Most of them happened over two years ago, but one was only a couple months ago. A few miles away from here, actually."

"When are you gonna give this up?" she mumbles without opening her eyes. "There was no arm out there."

I sit on the edge of the bed. "There *was* an arm. When I went out there alone, there was an arm in the ground."

She shrugs. "Well, none of us saw it."

"You guys didn't go out there right after I saw it. It took you at least twenty minutes to get back here."

"So you're saying that arm belongs to one of the girls in those articles?" Lauren asks, peering at me now, her voice tinged with mild curiosity, but mostly irritation. "If an arm had been buried in the back for two months, it wouldn't look like an arm anymore. It would have decomposed too much," she says matter-of-factly, and I remember her disturbing obsession with watching true crime.

"Then it could be someone else who hasn't been reported missing yet," I say, thinking out loud.

Lauren scoffs, shaking her head, but I don't back down. Right now, she's all I've got.

"There's a bunch of weird stuff in the basement, I tell her. "Garrett said it was Nolan's old woodshop, but there's so many tools down there. Knives, chisels, mallets, saws . . ." I show her the list of names I jotted down in the margins. "All these missing girls were found with holes in their skulls. Bludgeoned to death with some sort of blunt object. All of them. Two? Coincidence. Three, suspicious. Four? A pattern. He could've easily used any of those tools I saw down—"

"Okay, okay," Lauren says, sitting up straighter. She takes a minute to skim the names, then looks back up at me. "Let's just say you're right. Nolan was burying, what, another victim the night you got here? That's your theory?"

I chew my bottom lip. "Maybe."

"Well, a corpse didn't just walk out of the ground."

"There's another option," I say, and Lauren tilts her head, curious. I take a breath, the thought alone making me shiver. "What if his uncle is still here?"

Lauren frowns and tucks hair behind her ear. "What do you mean *here*?"

"We still don't know he's actually in Italy," I say, crossing my arms. "Garrett called him, right? But he doesn't answer, then sends a bunch of generic beach pictures. He didn't send a video, just some random sand and water. No date, no context, no proof he's actually there. He could be *anywhere*."

Lauren's mouth opens like she's ready to shoot me down again, but she hesitates. I keep going.

"Weird stuff has been happening that no one's copping to. The electricity randomly went out. I got stuck in the basement, but the door doesn't lock from the outside. It could have jammed, but I also saw this."

I scroll to a photo of a door jammer I saved on my phone. Lauren enlarges it to get a better look, then takes a beat, thinking it over. "You think he used this to lock you in?"

I nod. Lauren runs both hands through her hair.

"What if he knows? What if he saw me that night? When he was digging. Maybe he saw me find that arm too, and went out there and switched it with that doll before you guys got here. He could've heard me on the phone telling Roman what I found. Maybe he's the one who drugged me and has been doing all this other stuff trying to make me seem crazy so none of you believe me."

It sounds bizarre even to me, but maybe that's his thing: torturing his victims first, making them question everything, even their own sanity, before chopping up their bodies and putting them in the ground. Maybe it's a game for him.

Lauren covers her face with both of her palms and exhales loudly. "This is a lot."

"He's hiding something in the basement," I say, and she looks at me again, her eyes wide and conflicted, caught between disbelief and the mounting realization that she might have been wrong this whole time.

I tell Lauren about the door in the basement with the padlock, and she says she's coming too when I confide in her that I'm going to check it out before the others get back. I tell her she should stay in bed, but she points out that I'm the one who has only one good foot.

It takes us a while to make it down into the basement between my limp and Lauren's cramping. She's loud, moaning and groaning the whole way there. I use the walls to keep my weight off my bad foot, and we help each other down the stairs. We both use the flashlights on our phones and make a beeline to the makeshift woodshop. I grab the axe leaning against the wall, then lead the way to the door with the padlock. I grip it as hard as I can and swing with all of my strength, aiming for the center.

It takes three solid swings before I even make contact with it, and another two before the lock drops to the floor with a heavy *clunk*. Slowly, I grip the doorknob, and Lauren nods in fierce agreement.

I give the door a little push, and we both gasp and hop back a step, clinging to each other in anticipation of what our lights will find. It creaks open halfway, and we lean in together as we illuminate the area.

Dust and cobwebs cover the entire room. We creep around, but there's nothing inside but mundane junk. Dusty yard tools. Cans of paint and turpentine. Boxes filled with paperwork. No bodies. No arms or legs or heads or torsos. No blood. Nothing that screams *serial killer*.

After a moment, I glance at Lauren, and she shares my sentiment. Feeling a bizarre mix of disappointment and relief, we turn to leave. As I head for the door, I forget not to put too much weight on my injured foot, and I lose my balance. Lauren reaches out to catch me, but she's too slow. I slam into something, sending it tumbling to the floor, crashing at our feet.

Lauren bends over to pick it up, but the can of paint has already started to spill, the viscous green liquid spreading within seconds. She gives up, but as I push myself up, she notices something else with a gasp. I follow the beam of her flashlight, squinting to see what's caught her attention.

The glint of a pearlescent human incisor is unmistakable.

chapter
thirty-three

I spend the rest of the day doing more research as Lauren drifts in and out of sleep. Every time there's a random sound somewhere in the house, we both jump, our nerves on edge. The sun has already begun its descent when we hear the Jeep pull up on the gravel. We rush downstairs. Lauren runs right up to Garrett, pulling him aside while everyone else goes upstairs to change and shower.

"I think Iris is right," Lauren says, glancing at me, then back at Garrett. "About the arm."

He starts to object, but Lauren lifts the tooth, and he goes silent. He takes it from her, inspecting it closely. "Where the hell did you find this?"

"Basement," I say, watching him struggle with the realization.

"You know how when serial killers don't want the victim to be identified, they extract their teeth?" Lauren says, then lowers her voice to a whisper. "What if the tooth and the arm belong to the same person?"

"There was no arm," he says, annoyed now. "There was nothing but that creepy fucking doll out there."

"It was moved before you got there," I tell him, my voice firm.

Lauren backs me up with a nod. It's harder for him to deny her. He flips the tooth between his fingers, examining it another time.

"This is probably Uncle Nolan's," Garrett says, handing it back to me, but even I can tell he doesn't believe his own words. "He never goes to the dentist."

Garrett heads out of the room.

Lauren reaches after him. "Baby . . ."

But Garrett ignores her, disappearing down the hall. Lauren and I exchange a look as he asks Roman what he's making for dinner.

"It's a lot," she says in his defense. "I'll go talk to him."

I watch Lauren as she goes to her husband, hoping she can convince him to get out of here in the morning. As Roman whips up tacos, I try to put myself in Garrett's shoes. It took me an entire lifetime to accept my own mother was a manipulative abuser who neglected me since I was born. I can't even imagine what's going through his head. I'd be in denial too.

After dinner, I help Roman straighten up the kitchen. He gets me fresh bandages for my foot, then carefully cleans it for me. We debate which streaming service is actually worth the money as he wraps it again, and for a moment I laugh and forget that I might be in the home of a murderer.

Lauren goes to bed early. Around midnight, I hear noises coming from the stairs, small voices through the walls, and then it's quiet. As usual, I'm the last one up. I can't stop thinking about the girls in those articles, their faces all swirling around in my head, until there's a crashing sound from downstairs that breaks me out of my trance.

I look over at Violet, but she's still sound asleep. I force myself to relax. Then two more crashing noises rip from the room beneath ours. I swipe the covers from my body and slip my glasses on.

I limp as quietly as I can through the dark house. On the first level, I walk through the front room, then the kitchen, both dark and empty. I pause for a moment, listening, straining my ears. The house has gone silent.

I keep moving anyway, checking the other rooms. As I step into the rec room, I see the sliding glass door has been left ajar, the wind blowing in through the crack. A wooden chair in the room has a severed leg, and a broken lamp lies on the floor not too far from where I stand. I put two and two together and let out a breath. It was just the wind.

I start to slide the door shut, but then I hear another sound. This time it's a gasp that pierces the air. I slip through the crack and more sounds emerge. Muffled groans, like someone being strangled. The kinds of sounds I made in my nightmare, Nolan's hands tight around my neck, slowly squeezing the life out of me.

Swallowing hard, I grab a pool cue from against the wall and hesitate before stepping out onto the rear deck, not sure I should intervene.

A scream rings out, but it's strangled. I panic, thinking of Lauren and Gia. Violet was in bed, but it could be one of them. Another scream shatters the quiet, this one muffled as if a hand is clamped over her mouth.

I tighten my grip on the cue and creep toward the stairs, trying not to put weight on my leg. I go down the first step and pause. I hear her again. Now the sounds come in pulses. As I listen, my face goes warm in realization.

These are not the sounds of imminent death, of someone fighting for their life. These are the sounds of a woman caught in the waves of pleasure.

I blow out a breath of relief, realizing it's just Garrett and Lauren going at it again. It figures; she gets bit by a venomous spider, and then we find a human tooth in the basement, but all they can think about is getting each other off.

I turn back, but pause halfway to the sliding doors. My foot catches on something soft. I lift it up, and in the moonlight I recognize Eli's hoodie. I got it for him last Christmas. I hold it to my nose and take a long, luxurious inhale, his scent like a soothing balm quieting all of the anxious thoughts that have plagued me since arriving at this house.

I don't know what's come over me, but I can't give up. It just can't be over. Not like this. Not without him hearing me out. Not without him forgiving me. I use the sleeve of his hoodie to wipe my eyes, then realize the sounds have stopped.

I hurry back to my feet, not wanting Garrett or Lauren to see me like this. I shift to put his hoodie on one of the lawn chairs where the wind must have blown it from, but before I let it go, something gold flickers in the dark. A small square wrapper.

I know what it is, but I pick it up anyway.

Lauren seemed strong in her conviction about not having another child, but I think Garrett would agree to a vasectomy before going back to wearing condoms. And then it hits me. There's only one person I know who uses condoms with a gold wrapper. Used to. I almost drop down to my knees as I force myself to accept what's obvious—it's Gia and Eli down there making those sounds. The only thing that keeps me from collapsing is the sounds of laughter.

My mind races, ping-ponging between my options. Part of me wants to stand my ground and wait for them. I want to humiliate them like they've humiliated me. But I'm too angry. If I stay, I'll do something with this pool cue I know I'll only end up regretting.

"Can't believe we broke the chair," Gia says, her voice getting louder as they come up the steps.

I dart back inside and crouch behind the couch as their voices grow louder, drawing closer to the doors.

"That was all you," Eli says, and I can just hear his grin, the crooked one I stupidly thought only I could inspire.

Gia's laughter is light and fluffy, the sounds a woman makes when she's enraptured in postcoital bliss. I know that laugh. I know the way Eli makes you feel, like you're the only person left on the planet, the only star in the galaxy. Like the sun and moon rise with you.

"What are we gonna tell Garrett and Roman?" Gia asks, giddy. "I think Garrett said their uncle made that."

Eli laughs, and I fight back tears, furious tears. "We'll glue it back on in the morning."

I hear the door slide open and hold my breath.

"My hoodie," Eli says, turning back. Gia waits just inside the door.

"It's not here," he says, calling out to her, and my heart races.

His hoodie is still in my hands.

"You think someone's been down here?" Eli asks, not particularly worried, more like curious.

"Maybe the person Iris thinks has been terrorizing her snatched it up," Gia retorts, and they both laugh.

Eli laughs at her stupid joke, and it feels like my chest splits in two, right down the middle. I squeeze my eyes shut, and tears drip down to my neck.

"I had it on, didn't I?" he asks, still moving around on the deck.

A few seconds later, the lights come on in the room. For some reason, the illumination makes it feel like they can somehow hear me breathing, and I cover my mouth. Eli looks around a bit, asking Gia if he took it off here or outside.

"I don't remember. I was more concerned with a little something else."

"*Little?*"

Their laughter harmonizes, and my heart shatters into pieces so small, I know instinctively they will never be put back together.

"Just get it in the morning," Gia tells him, walking off. "I'm going to bed."

"Good night."

"Good night," she says, turning back around, her voice creamy.

She steps off again, but Eli grabs her by the waist and kisses her. It's loud and wet. I can hear their desire, the heat simmering between them like they want to start up again. But after a few moments they split off, Eli lingering a bit before giving up his search for his hoodie. He shuts off the light and jogs up the stairs.

chapter
thirty-four

My head pressed against the hard frame of the couch, the cool floor beneath me, I replay the sound of their kiss again and again and again. It didn't sound like Eli is just acting out some childish revenge, giving himself a hall pass because he thinks I cheated on him with Garrett. I heard longing in that kiss. I heard passion in that kiss. It might have been love I heard in that kiss.

I don't know how I manage to pull myself off the floor, but somehow I also make it to the edge of the lakefront. For a while, it's just me and the moonlight. I shouldn't be out here. Nolan could find me easily, and no one would even hear me scream. But I can't stay in that house knowing what just went down. I need the crisp night air on my face, my chest.

Violet calls out to me, and I glance back over my shoulder. She jogs toward me barefoot, wearing the same sleeping clothes as before, her hair piled on top of her head.

"What are you doing out here?" Violet asks, slightly out of breath from the run down. "It's late."

I can't tell how much time has passed since I've been out here. I look at her up close, her face scrubbed clean and shiny with moisturizer.

"Could ask you the same thing," I say, keeping my eyes averted in case they've gone red from all of my crying.

I don't want company. I don't want comfort. I don't want her to try and console me. I want to be alone, away from all of them.

"Had to pee. Saw you weren't there." She waits for me to say something. "Just wanted to make sure you were okay."

"I'm fine," I say, not shifting my eyes away from the water, but the words don't sound convincing, even to my own ears.

Violet sits down next to me on the rocky sand, and I instantly wish I had made more of an effort to seem okay. She doesn't say anything for a while. We both just sit alone with our thoughts until I feel Violet staring at me.

"What?" I ask without looking over at her. I'm thinking about that almost-kiss. I don't want to have to dodge another one of her advances. I'm exhausted, mentally and physically and emotionally.

She takes a breath, then releases it in a sigh. "That was fucked up. The other day. What I did in the water."

I glance at her but don't say anything. I have no idea why she's bringing this up now.

"I wasn't thinking. I should have been more sensitive to you, your situation." She stares down at her legs for a beat, reflecting, it seems, then shakes her head. "Your mom. You kept calling out for her. When you were having that nightmare."

When she meets my eyes, I see true regret swelling in hers. But I wave her off. "I'm over it."

It was a dumb prank with bad timing, but it wasn't a crime. I know she didn't do it to intentionally hurt me. It's by far the least horrible thing that's happened since I've been here. With everything else that's going on, I almost forgot it.

Violet turns her body so she's facing mine. "I was just trying to get you to loosen up, I swear. Didn't mean to trigger you or anything."

I nod as I shift my eyes back to the water, hoping she'll just move on. When she doesn't, I glance at her. Her eyes are on the ground, shoulders slumped, body slack with guilt. For a second, I wonder if she's really apologizing for the kiss under the guise of apologizing for the prank. I shift to stand up, her presence ruining my zen. Violet stops me with a look, her face full of quiet urgency, a silent plea for me to stay.

"There's something else," she says after a moment.

"Something else? What?"

"Okay, my intentions were good this time too. Just know that." Violet sucks in a big breath, and I hold mine, bracing myself for whatever's about to come. "I crushed up some pills and put them in your drink the other night."

I hear the words, but they don't compute. "What?"

"The night you blacked out," she says, losing eye contact.

I blink rapidly, my lids like a pair of butterfly's wings as her words sink in. Her confession is both a shock and confirmation—I *knew* someone drugged me. My pills had gone missing, and the way I blacked out, there was no way alcohol could have been the only thing in my system. But I would have never suspected it was Violet. I stare at her, trying to figure out how I could have missed this. I've never felt more betrayed than I do at this moment.

Not even when Genevieve pulled that trigger.

"I'm sorry," Violet whispers, her voice heavy with regret.

"If I would've known why, I wouldn't have done it, I swear. He used me."

"What are you talking about?" I ask, a cold dread washing over me, sensing whatever she's about to say will alter my brain chemistry and shatter everything I thought I knew.

"I got you to do that one shot, right? But then you wanted more. I've never really seen you drink like that. I was excited, so I texted Eli, and I was like, 'I'm getting your girl drunk.' We kinda had this bet going."

I stare at her in disbelief. "What bet?"

"That I couldn't get you drunk. So I had to gloat a little once I got you started. After a few drinks, you had a nice buzz going. I started telling him how relieved I was because, no offense, but you were sucking the fun out of everything. He said you've been cranky because you haven't been getting sleep. Mentioned your prescription. I thought you'd just go up to the room and pass out. He made it seem like it would help."

I narrow my eyes. "How could mixing sedatives with alcohol help me?"

Violet shakes her head helplessly. "I don't know, I just—"

"What if I'd already taken some?" I ask, my voice rising. "I could have overdosed."

"I know. It was stupid."

"You *drugged me*. You knew for this long and you . . . Why didn't you say anything after you saw how out of it I was? You just keep pretending everything was fine. You let me wake up thinking I was just drunk . . . thinking I was crazy."

Violet looks away, her lips pressing together. "I wish I didn't listen to him," she whispers, her voice barely above a breath. "I just knew you were stressed out, and then you were acting so weird with the dead body thing. But then you slammed into the door and hit your head, and I felt so, so bad.

It was my fault. I called him back and told him the pills were too much. You know how dramatic I am. Anyway, I went to check up on you, to get you some ice, and you were too out of it to get upstairs yourself. He told me to get Roman to get you in bed. That's how he said it. 'Get him to get her in bed.' I was drunk, I didn't think anything of it. I couldn't lift you, so I went to grab Roman. But I couldn't find him and told Garrett to take you up to your room."

Her words linger in the air as I try to parse through them. "I don't see what—"

"It was a *setup*," Violet says, the words ripping from her throat as if she's desperate for me to understand the gravity of what she's telling me. "It wasn't supposed to be Garrett. Eli knows how trashed Roman gets when he parties and how loopy those pills would make you. He thought neither of you would be able to remember exactly what happened. Or what *didn't* happen."

I stare at her, truly speechless. This is all too much. I replay her words over and over, but it can't be true. It's too far-fetched, too preposterous. There's no way Eli planned for any of this to happen the way it did. No way.

Violet swallows hard, then meets my eyes. "Eli only told all of us that he walked in on you and Garrett hooking up because it would give him an excuse to finally break up with you."

I frown, feeling my face warm. "What do you mean, 'finally'?"

Violet just stares at me for a beat, a pitying look in her eyes. "So you really don't know."

"Know what?"

She clamps her eyes shut, then gives me the most pathetic look I've ever seen. "Babe, Eli's been hooking up with Gia for almost a year."

chapter
thirty-five

I stare at Violet, my pulse ringing in my ears, the urge to slap her straight across her face so visceral I can taste it. The betrayal guts me. She knew this entire time that Eli was sneaking behind my back and never considered telling me so I could at least leave with some of my dignity intact. I know she's his friend first. I thoroughly understand the sense of loyalty she feels for him. But as a woman, I thought she would have enough decency, enough basic respect to tell me.

I let her talk, the anger and hurt churning inside me like a virus. She doesn't pause for a breath, detailing the whole story for me from the beginning. She tells me how Gia and Eli ran into each other in the city one day after she got a new job uptown near his office. They started texting from there. It escalated to grabbing lunch during his break. Then somewhere along the way—Violet isn't sure of the exact timeline—the relationship turned sexual. She says she only found out because she was with Gia when a nude mirror selfie of Eli pinged onto her phone.

I believe her; she has no reason to lie now. The way they kissed, the way they sounded so comfortable with each other, I knew it couldn't be the first time, but part of me was still clinging to the possibility of him only using her to get back at me.

Gia lives in New Jersey, just over the river. I do the math in my head. There are no intricate equations or theorems necessary. It's obvious when I look back now that he had the time with all of the ten-hour days he's been putting in. There probably isn't even a promotion he's up for. I hate that I have to do this, hate that now I have to comb through everything he's said to me. Anything could be a lie. It feels like it's all been one corpulent lie.

"Who else knows?" I ask, feeling like I've just come out of a tunnel. "Besides you, who else knows? Lauren? Garrett?"

"Lauren doesn't know. Pretty sure Roman doesn't either. Don't think it's something they've been broadcasting."

I take a moment to process this, but mainly all I want to do is run upstairs and strangle Eli. "So he dragged me out here to dump me? In front of her? Breaking my heart wasn't enough? He had to humiliate me too?"

Violet doesn't answer, just looks at me with regret and sympathy in her eyes.

Now Gia's constant negging and superiority complex make sense. She's always obnoxious, but this is the most unbearable she's ever been, and now I realize it's because she knew she had this over me the whole time. She was relishing in her secret, and I was too blind to see it.

"So it was supposed to be Roman?" I ask, so many more questions swirling in my head. "Eli wanted it to be him who took me up to my room?"

Violet shrugs with one shoulder. "I mean, he's had a crush on you since freshman year. It wasn't a stretch."

"But he wanted to catch us together? Not me and Garrett?"

Violet looks confused, cocking her head to the side. "What's the difference?"

"He was probably hoping Roman would try something. But Garrett didn't because he's obsessed with Lauren, obviously. So Eli tried to gaslight us."

"I thought it was weird," Violet admits thoughtfully and takes a beat to ponder this angle. "Garrett is obsessed with Lauren for sure, but Eli made it seem like maybe there was a chance something did happen between you guys. But when I asked you about it, I knew you weren't lying."

I take a second to think. After a few minutes, I turn to leave, but before I get more than a couple steps away from the edge of the water, I stop short.

"Wait." I turn back around, Violet on her feet now too. "Eli was visiting his grandmother in the hospital. He was never planning on coming here. He only came to bring me my glasses."

"No, Eli was always planning on coming a few days after dropping you off to catch you with Garrett. That's why he made that bet with me."

"The bet was his idea?" I ask, my stomach twisting in knots.

"He knew I'd take the bait," Violet says, her sigh reeking of regret. "He only fed you the story about his grandmother so he could show up here, catch you off guard and walk in on you with one of his friends."

I grab my abdomen, the nausea rising like hot water in a geyser. Eli set me up from the beginning, then manipulated everyone around him to orchestrate this moment just to be with her. With Gia. *Gia.* My mind races, replaying so many moments since I've gotten here, every lie I swallowed without a second thought. I can barely breathe as the depths of his deception sink in.

"Are you saying you don't even think his grandma is sick?" I ask, not sure I'm even prepared for the answer.

Violet gives me a sympathetic look. "At this point, I wouldn't put it past him."

"No," I say, because the contrary is too much to bear. "Eli wouldn't lie about something like that."

But then again, I thought he would never sleep with another woman behind my back for almost a year and then gallivant with her right in front of me minutes after dumping me.

Violet gives me one more look, her eyes filled with remorse, then heads inside the house. I linger by the water and run through everything one more time. I remember that Eli was the one who packed my meds in the first place, which confirms Violet's story—that his plan from the beginning was to manipulate her into drugging me. He knows how competitive she is; everyone does. He knew she'd eventually get me drunk. He knew I'd be out of it in the morning and wouldn't be able to remember anything. He thought he could easily gaslight me into thinking I was fooling around with Roman. Of course, Eli couldn't have known that I'd get hurt, or that Garrett would be the one to help me to bed, but once Violet told him I bumped my head, he capitalized on it. It went perfectly with his plan.

The longer I dwell on it, the more unbelievable it seems. To think that everything Eli did was so premeditated, so calculated, so diabolical . . . it makes me question whether I ever knew him at all.

I try to reconcile this new person with the one who's claimed to love me all these years, but it's undeniable. It was all a lie. Eli never cared about me. He only cared about himself. It was all a game to him, and I was just the pawn.

When I break awake, the time on the alarm clock startles me. I slept. Six hours straight with no medication. It's by far the longest stretch I've gotten in the last year without a tranq or two. I feel lighter somehow, like I've shed a layer of darkness that's been clinging to me for too long. My mind is clear, almost unfamiliar, like a place I'd forgotten I could inhabit.

But as soon as I swing my legs over the edge of the bed, I feel it. A migraine trying to split my head open like a cantaloupe.

I grab my phone from the nightstand, the sounds of soft chatter and clinking flatware drifting in from downstairs. I don't bother rushing down. I pull up a list of hospitals close to where Eli's grandmother lives on my laptop. It's a small town on the outskirts of Boston, so I pull up a few in the surrounding areas too. I call each one asking if a patient with his grandmother's name is currently admitted. Most won't give me a straight answer—HIPPA doesn't allow it without permission, apparently. A few politely refuse. None confirm anything. When I've exhausted my list, I climb out of bed in a robotic stupor and drag myself to the bathroom. I tilt my head back in the shower and let it wash away all my tears.

A half hour later, I step out onto the front deck. The air is thick, electric, the kind before a storm. The horizon churns with heavy slate clouds, their edges frayed like an unraveling thread. They drift across the sky, their swollen bellies flickering with distant flashes of heat and lightning.

Violet and Roman murmur good mornings, but I don't respond, my eyes scanning the area for Eli. I spot Gia on the water, lying on a floaty. I keep looking, then find Eli close by, snapping pictures of her with his phone.

"Which hospital is your grandma in?" I ask, my voice low and level, but beneath, the anger simmers. It takes everything in me to not snatch his phone and toss it straight into the water.

Eli turns to see me behind him, the flecks of green and gold in his eyes washed out in the gray light. "What?"

I flip curls out of my face. "I want to send her some flowers."

"Why?" He thinks about it, then says, "Is this your way of getting me to forgive you or something?" He doesn't miss a single beat.

"You arrogant asshole," I whisper under my breath in disbelief.

I watch him scroll through the shots he's snapped of Gia, his expression unreadable. There's something unfamiliar about him now, in the way he occupies the space around him. It's as if the mask has slipped, revealing the real man beneath—one who thrives on control, who maneuvers through chaos with unnerving ease, bending reality to suit his narrative whenever it serves him. I see it so clearly now, the subtle manipulation, the quiet baiting. But I won't let him draw me into his web of guilt. I've done nothing wrong. Garrett has done nothing wrong. I refuse to carry the weight he so desperately wants to hand me.

"We're not together anymore," he says, not quite meeting my eyes. "She doesn't need your flowers."

He steps away. I hop right on his heels. He doesn't get to end this. I do.

"You mean there's no room to send them to," I say to his back, and he turns around so quickly.

Eli's mouth drops open, lips parting as though to speak, but the words falter, swallowed by the silence that follows. It tells me everything I need to know. It seems so impossible now that this is the man I've been sharing a home with, a bed, my secrets.

"I can't believe this," I say, my voice trembling as I stare at him. The weight of it all presses down on me, disbelief coiling in my chest like a tight spring. "If you'd lie about your grandma having kidney failure, what won't you lie about?"

"What are you talking about? She—"

"I know about the whole setup, Eli." I cut him off, my words biting, my astonishment hardening into rage. "I know about your stupid, pathetic scheme to make it look like I was the one cheating when you're the one who's been sleeping around behind my back for almost a *year*."

Panic leaks through the crack in Eli's composure. A flicker flashes in his eyes.

"Looks like someone's off their meds," Gia chimes, her voice lilting with a singsong cruelty, the words slithering into the space between us like venom.

"Hey, chill," Eli says to her before I get a chance to light her up.

I glare at her, regretting every moment that I felt sorry for her. I thought maybe we could bond, our absent fathers the one thing we have in common. I never imagined we'd be sharing a lover too.

"This is what you want, right?" My eyes cut to Gia before locking onto his again. "Then go ahead. But when you realize she's not even half of me, don't expect me to come running back."

I don't wait for his rebuttal, don't need to hear his excuses or his denials. I limp away, each step on my uninjured foot heavy with fury and liberation. A sense of clarity washes over me for the first time in months.

I'm done being the one they try to tear down. I hope they crumble under the weight of their schemes. I'll rise, brick by brick, into something unshakable.

chapter
thirty-six

Gia's words echo behind me, her voice pleading for Eli to stay as I head for the deck. I feel him closing the distance between us but don't slow down. My foot protests with every step, a sharp, unrelenting throb, but the humiliation of him catching me would be worse than the pain. I force myself up the steps, my hand gripping the railing. Still, I miss one. My body lurches forward, my palms scraping the wood as I catch myself before I slam into the ground, chin first. My glasses slip from my face, sliding down the steps.

"Iris, wait," Eli calls out, his voice closer now.

I scramble back down to grab my glasses, but I don't see them. My head snaps over my shoulder when I hear him behind me. And there's another sound. A crunch. When I look down, I finally find my glasses. Beneath Eli's foot.

He bends down to pick them up, then hands them to me, his face etched with helplessness. One lens is shattered, the frame bent beyond repair. His apology starts to form, but I don't let it land. I fling the broken glasses at his chest and hobble up the rest of the stairs. Each step feels heavier than the last.

Upstairs, I slam the bathroom door behind me, locking him out. My hands tremble as I twist the faucet on, then the tub, letting the rush of water drown out the pounding in my head. And his voice.

"I didn't want to hurt you," he shouts through the door, but the words are like splinters, digging in where I thought I'd grown numb.

I sit on the toilet and roll my eyes, my blood simmering. "And *this* was the best you could come up with?"

"You already have so much going on. I didn't want me ending things to be the straw that broke your back."

Something inside me snaps at his patronizing words.

"You can't be that full of yourself." I yank the door open and charge toward him.

His back meets the wall. I see his next breath get caught in his throat.

"Don't put this on me," I hiss, my voice sharp enough to carve. "You cheated because you weren't man enough to tell me you didn't want to be with me anymore. What do I look like to you? Some kind of fragile flower or something?"

His voice drops to a low, unnerving calm. "No, not a flower. Fragile like . . . a grenade."

The words hang between us, the weight of them pressing down on us like the shroud of clouds over the sky. I glare at him, my bottom lip trembling, so many things I want to say, so many ways I want to watch him suffer. My rage bubbles just beneath the surface, but so do my tears, unwanted and uninvited.

Eli leans closer, his voice pushing past my defenses. "Do you have any idea what it's been like for me this past year? What *I've* been dealing with?"

I scoff, the sound bitter and sharp. "Oh, I'm sorry. Did *your* mother die too?"

He doesn't flinch, doesn't even blink. "No, but my girlfriend did. At least, the person I fell in love with did."

"You never loved me," I say, shaking my head. He tries to cut me off, but I don't let him. "To do all of this, you *never* loved me."

"No, I did all of this *because* of how much I loved you! I fought for us. I made sure you saw a doctor. I drove you to therapy twice a week. I kept the apartment clean when you could barely get out of bed. I did the grocery shopping, made sure you ate every morning, did midnight pharmacy runs whenever you needed me to. Don't tell me I didn't love you. I loved you more than I thought I could ever love someone."

I tilt my head back to keep the tears from falling down my cheeks. I force myself to stand tall, a monument to everything he almost destroyed with his betrayal.

"I held you when you woke up screaming. I walked on eggshells for months. Couldn't say the wrong thing or look at you the wrong way, even breathe in your direction for too long. And what did I get? You barely paid attention to me. Didn't want to talk. Sometimes you didn't even want me to touch you. You never thanked me for going out of my way to try to make you happy. But that was my mistake, right?" He pauses, waiting for me to concur or encourage him to continue, but I refuse to give him even that. "I can't make you happy."

I stare at him, incredulous. "So you just give up?"

"I can't make you happy," he says again. "You have to want it for yourself. You have to stop blaming yourself. Your mother was a horrible human being who never treated you right because she knew you were everything she would never be."

I turn away, unable to bear the sight of him any longer. The weight of his words settles in my chest like a stone.

A burden. That's what I've been to him. The realization claws at my insides, leaving me hollow and raw. How could I have been so blind? We've been living in different worlds, speaking different languages. While I thought we were building a life together, he was just tolerating me. Dealing with me. People deal cards, flipping them carelessly, building fragile houses destined to collapse. You don't *deal* with people you cherish.

Eli closes the distance between us with two long strides and swivels my body around to face him, but I refuse to meet his gaze.

"Iris, just—"

"Why her?" The words tumble out before I can stop them.

He sighs, shaking his head. "It was never about Gia."

"I was that bad, huh?"

"See, you're doing it again," he says, frustration lacing his words. "You blame yourself because it's easier to hate yourself than do the work it'll take to love yourself."

His words hit me harder than I want to admit, but all I can think is, how could I love myself when my own mother didn't?

"This wasn't about you. I felt . . ." Eli continues, his voice softer now. He fumbles, stopping and starting, his words disjointed, like he's struggling to piece together a defense. "I just needed . . . attention. And she was there. It happened. It was never supposed to be more than the one time."

I tilt my head, narrowing my eyes as I try to parse out the unspoken truth in his tone. "So you . . ."

"Nobody was supposed to catch feelings," he says.

I close my eyes, inhaling deeply, as if it might steady the chaos swirling inside me. "You're saying you love her?"

Eli hesitates, his lips parting before he clamps them shut again. He can't even bring himself to say it. "You were never supposed to get hurt, Iris. That's why I did all of this. Was it stupid? Fine, I'll take that. But I was just looking out for you like I always do."

I let out a sharp, humorless laugh. "That's such bullshit."

He flinches at my tone, his eyes widening as if he's shocked by my resistance. But this time he doesn't get to twist the truth and make me the scapegoat.

"You gaslit me. You gaslit Garrett. You tried to make it look like I slipped up because you knew exactly how I'd react. You knew I'd blame myself. You knew I'd be devastated when you ended things. You just didn't want it on your conscience."

Eli shifts uncomfortably, his head dipping for a moment before he looks back up at me, searching my face for something. But I keep my eyes locked elsewhere.

"It was supposed to be Roman," he mutters, almost too low for me to hear.

"I know," I say, my voice flat.

"He's always had a thing for you." He shrugs. "Thought maybe you'd hit it off."

But I see through him now, every word, every gesture. This isn't kindness or regret. It's a calculated move to position himself as the magnanimous, self-sacrificing hero. He wants me to see him as someone noble, not the man who betrayed me.

I hold his gaze now, letting him see the clarity in my eyes, the dawning realization of how insidious his manipulations have been.

"I became too much for you to 'deal with,' so you handed me off to the next highest bidder?" I tilt my head. "Is that how this works?"

"That's not—"

"I'm done with this." I step around him, feeling myself on the brink of tears again, but he blocks my path. "Get away from me."

I try to sidestep him again, but he seizes my arm, anchoring me in place. This time, I shove him off, the heat of my fury surging through me like an inferno. Eli tries to restrain me, but I can no longer hold back my anger. I hit him, once, then again, and again, each blow driven by the weight of my rage and the tears that spill. He grunts softly, flinching slightly with each impact. Finally, he releases me, and I crumble against the wall, winded and drained.

"I just want to go home," I whisper, my voice raw, like the words themselves are too heavy to carry. I wipe my eyes, but the tears come faster than I can stop them.

Eli stands there, silent, watching me for a long, unbearable moment. "Have you even tried to enjoy being here?"

"Is this some kind of retribution? Are you trying torture me the way I tortured you this past year?"

Eli exhales sharply, his shoulders sagging with resignation. "I just thought you could have a week to relax, to be yourself again."

"How can I relax in a house where everybody has it out for me and there's a murderer lurking around, but no one will believe me?"

He winces at the crack in my voice. "Thought you got over that."

I swipe at my face. "You weren't here."

"No, but I was there for eleven months of you—"

"There was an *arm* out back," I say, cutting him off, my words like razors. "And Lauren found a tooth."

He pauses, his expression flickering with something that feels like dread. "What tooth?"

I lead him into my bedroom, where my notes are scattered across the desk. As he flips through the pages, I explain everything I've found.

Eli's face drops as he reads. "How many are there?"

"Four pending identification," I answer quietly, but the weight of it feels heavier now that I'm speaking it aloud. "All missing teeth from their skulls. Same age range. Similar head injuries."

"Shit. They almost look like . . ."

"I think he's here. Nolan. Somewhere near the lake." I take a slow breath, then look him in the eyes. "I think he knows I know what he's done."

chapter
thirty-seven

The rain begins as a gentle percussion against the windows before deepening into a guttural roar. It gathers strength with a languid inevitability, the kind that warns of chaos before it comes crashing through. It reminds me of my mother. Unyielding, unrelenting, unashamed of the ruin she leaves behind.

I haven't eaten today. The hollowness in my stomach is strange. It doesn't ache. Hunger feels like a foreign concept, muted and unfamiliar. I tuck myself away in a quiet corner of the house, my book spread open in my lap. I've been combing through my frantic scrawls for hours, searching for any overlooked clue, any revelation that might push Eli the final inch toward believing me. He's close. I can feel it in the way his eyes lingered after I showed him the tooth.

My desperation fuels me as I pore over the pages with unbroken focus. But nothing new emerges, and I'm ready to give up when I remember the tools in the basement, the weapons.

All I want is to leave this stupid house. Tonight. But if I'm stuck here for another two days, I need to collect as much evidence as I can. The tooth should be enough to get the police to search the rest of the house, but photos could be invaluable. I grab my phone and rise to my feet, stretching my stiff limbs. If Nolan tries to hide or move them, I'll have proof. But before I can take a single step, Eli slips into the room.

"What are you reading?" he asks, his voice soft, hesitant, like he's afraid of the answer.

"Just rereading my notes."

His weight shifts, a nervous energy emanating from him. "Anything new?"

"Not really," I say, and it feels like I've disappointed both of us.

The words feel brittle in my mouth, awkwardly shaped, as though spoken to a stranger. The space between us feels vast, unfamiliar and unbearably polite. I'm suddenly hyperaware of myself, clutching my book like a lifeline, trying to convince a man who couldn't even love me to believe me. The heat of the humiliation creeps up my neck.

Before the moment can stretch any further, Violet appears in the doorway, her presence relieving some of the tension. "Food's done."

I shake my head reflexively, grateful for the reprieve, but unable to stomach even the thought of eating right now.

"I'll pass," I tell her, my voice low. The idea of sitting in the same room as Gia and Eli feels insufferable.

Eli tells her he'll be there in a minute. Violet nods, then leaves.

And we're alone again.

"I talked to Garrett about the stuff you showed me," Eli says, stepping closer.

The proximity of his body is a betrayal to my senses. My body, foolish and untrained, still reacts as if it knows only the old choreography of us. Leaning toward him, aching for the familiar comfort of his arms. It doesn't comprehend what my heart already knows. The love is gone, and yet this pull remains.

"What'd he say?" I manage, though my voice is wobbly.

"He got defensive. You're accusing his uncle of some heinous shit."

I stiffen. "He's the one who said he goes after young women."

"Yeah, well, being a creep is one thing. Chopping them up is another."

The words land heavy between us, an undeniable truth. I sigh, frustrated. Of course Garrett would take offense. It's a natural reaction, even if infuriating. Still, the thought churns in my mind: Would Roman be easier to sway? Could he convince Garrett to leave tomorrow?

"Did he at least hear you out?" I ask, pressing the edge of hope.

Eli shrugs, his gaze slipping to the floor for a moment. "He did. But he still wants to stay." A beat. He looks at me, studying my face. "It's only a couple more days."

"I don't want to stay a couple more days," I say, the words escaping in a sharp rush. They sound small, panicked, petulant. But I don't care. I can't wait for something worse to happen.

Eli nods, meeting my eyes. His own are clear, steady. "I'll take you back to the city."

"Really?" The word comes out barely a whisper.

"I believe you," he says, and I drink his words in, let them settle into my chest like a balm.

I believe you.

Three simple words, but they mean more than the other three he said all the time, the ones that turned out to be lies. Belief requires trust, and trust, *his* trust, feels like salvation.

"Can we leave tonight?" I ask, trying to temper my hope, but the longing is there, undeniable, pulsing.

He glances at the window, where the rain smears the glass like wet brush strokes. "Can you wait till the morning? Looks pretty bad out there. I'd rather not drive through that in the dark."

I nod, slowly.

One more night. I can do that. As long as he believes me, as long as I'm not alone in this, I can make it through one more night.

"Maybe we can just go to the local police station tonight then," I suggest, my voice tentative. "We can drop off the tooth. It might be evidence. And I want to tell them about the arm. Maybe they can send someone out to dig up the yard once the rain stops."

Eli leans against the window frame, peering through the rain-slicked glass, his brow furrowed in thought. For a moment, he doesn't answer. Then, with a slight nod, he says, "Yeah, let's go before the rain gets worse."

Relief swells in my chest. "Okay. I'll grab my jacket."

"Pack your things too," he adds, his voice calm but firm. "I want us on the road first thing in the morning. I'd rather hit the main road before traffic picks up."

I nod and resist the sudden, reckless urge to wrap my arms around him, as if affection could tether him closer, make him come back to me.

"Alright," he says, breaking the silence. "You pack. I'm going to grab something to eat. I'm starving." He pauses at the doorway, glancing over his shoulder. "You want anything?"

"No, I'm okay."

He shrugs and disappears into the hall, leaving me alone with the sound of the rain.

I take a detour to the basement before going upstairs, the damp air clinging to my skin as I descend. My phone's flashlight beams through the darkness, and I navigate my way to the far corner. The weapons are still there, just as I remembered. I crouch down, angling my phone for pictures. Most of the shots come out grainy, but it's enough. It'll have to be enough.

Back in my bedroom, I gather my things, double-checking the room for anything I might have missed, then set my bag by the door for the morning. My jacket waits on the edge of the bed. I grab it and pause by the window as I slip my arms into the sleeves. The rain is relentless, an unbroken curtain of gray. The road to the city feels impossibly far away. I think of how long it took to get here, and my resolve wavers.

The wary thought is solidifying in my mind when I hear the faint creak of the door behind me. I turn, expecting Eli.

"Eli changed his mind," Gia announces, her voice a dagger aimed directly at my chest.

"What?"

"He's not taking you anywhere tonight."

My head shakes automatically, refusing the words before they can settle. "But he just—"

"I know." She folds her arms, cocking her head in mock sympathy. "But then I asked him to stay. So he said he's staying. With me."

It feels like the floor drops from beneath us, but unlike Gia, who floats, I plunge.

"This isn't what you think it is," I say, my voice steady despite the heat rising in my chest. "I'm not trying to take him back."

Gia lets out a sharp, disdainful laugh. "As if that's even possible."

"So why are you being such a bitch?"

Her eyebrows shoot up, feigned surprise masking the satisfaction flickering behind her eyes. "Okay. Somebody's big mad."

I take a breath, grounding myself against the fight she's trying to provoke. "You can have him. But he's taking me to the precinct."

I push past her, taking a step toward the door, but Gia moves fast, sliding in front of me.

"Get out of my way," I snap, low and seething.

She smirks. "Don't go begging. Don't you think you look pathetic enough?"

The words land sharp and cruel, but I don't let them pierce me. I take her in fully for the first time since I heard her with him out in the woods. She drapes herself in confidence, but it reeks of performance.

A hot, bitter laugh rises in my chest. "You don't think he'll do to you what he did to me?"

Gia's expression hardens, her jaw tightening. "He didn't do anything to you. You're the one who's been fucking up his vibe for years now. Now he's free."

"If he can lie to me, he can lie to you."

"A happy man doesn't stray," she says, her lips curling into a victorious smile.

I narrow my eyes. "And a desperate woman can't see when she's being used."

Her face flashes with something—anger, maybe, or fear—but she recovers quickly. "You're just bitter because you couldn't make him happy."

I shove her aside, my patience snapping like a frayed cord. But just as I step into the hall, her fingers claw at my jacket, yanking me back. I shrug her off with enough force to make her stumble.

Then it's all fire and fury. Yelling, insults flying like pumice stones in the skies of Pompeii, the room vibrating with the weight of our animosity. Gia lunges, her nails grazing my arm, and I shove her back, harder this time. She recovers quickly, her breath coming fast as she launches into another round of accusations, her voice shrill with rage.

Roman's voice booms from the doorway, cutting through the chaos like a whipcrack, his tone a warning as he holds her at arm's length this time.

Gia squirms, muttering curses under her breath, but she doesn't fight him. "Let me go."

"Not until you calm down," Roman says firmly, his gaze flicking to me as if daring me to say otherwise.

I cross my arms, trembling with leftover adrenaline, but I nod.

Roman watches Gia for a moment longer, gauging her mood before speaking again. "If I let you go, there will be no more fighting. Got it?"

Gia rolls her eyes but nods, her movements jerky and defiant. "Fine."

Roman waits a beat, then releases her. She smooths her hair, adjusting her skimpy top with deliberate nonchalance before throwing a final glare my way.

"Pathetic," she mutters under her breath as she strides out of the room.

Roman steps into the hall after her, his shoulders tense. And a scream pierces the air.

All three of us freeze.

The sound echoes again, sharp and panicked, coming from downstairs.

The three of us rush down together, our footsteps thundering.

In the kitchen, Violet stands wide-eyed and trembling, her gaze locked on Eli. He's standing by the counter, motionless, his face pale and stunned. His hands grip the edge of the counter like he might collapse without the support. The room is heavy with something unspeakable, something horribly wrong.

chapter
thirty-eight

"What happened?" I ask Violet, my voice sharp enough to slice through the suffocating stillness of the room. Eli stands in front of me, his neck red and blotchy, sweat beads forming on his forehead. I can't tell if he's seen something, if he's been hurt. There's no blood, no signs of an injury.

"I don't know. He just started shaking. I think he might be choking or . . ."

I take a step closer, my heart climbing into my throat as he clutches his. "Eli."

His eyes meet mine, wide and glassy, two pools of fear edged with the desperation of a drowning man. He sways on his feet, his hand pressed to his neck as though if he could just will his body into compliance, the air would return. His lips part, but no sound escapes, only a rasp, raw and jagged. He drags a breath, then another, but it isn't enough. The muscles in his neck strain, his chest rising and falling in erratic, futile rhythm. His fingers claw at the hollow of his throat, nails scratching against skin in a desperate, wordless plea for air.

"What's wrong with him?" Gia's voice breaks through, frantic and useless, but I ignore her.

"Eli," I try again, his name trembling in my mouth like something fragile. "Tell me what happened. Please."

He tries. His lips shape a word, a sound, but it dies in the hollow of his throat.

And then I see it. The signs scream at me. The violent flush creeping up his neck, the way his lips are beginning to turn purple, the swelling. Oh God, the swelling. His throat is closing, collapsing inward like a dying star. He's going into anaphylactic shock.

Eli's knees give way, his body folding into itself like a marionette whose strings have been cut. I lunge forward, catching him before he crumples to the floor. His name tears out of Gia as she drops to her knees beside him. Her voice is raw, piercing, shredding the moment into jagged pieces.

Eli's breaths come in shudders, shallow and weakening, his eyes glazing with the distant sheen of panic.

The world tilts. I cradle his weight against me, my hands useless, trembling, as the enormity of it crashes down. The silence bellows, deafening, and the room seems to shrink around us, pressing in, suffocating us both.

"What the fuck is happening?" Violet cries from where she stands over us, her voice quaking with fear. "Why can't he breathe?"

I force myself to move, to think. His words flash through my mind. *I'm starving.* And the puzzle starts to take shape. I try to roll him onto his back, but Gia shoves me aside.

"What are you doing?" she snaps, her hands fluttering uselessly over him.

"Shut up," I bark out, struggling against the weight of him. "Get away from him."

"Would you shut up for one second?" I fire back, my patience shredding as panic claws at my throat.

I try to turn him onto his back, carefully trying to lower him to the floor, worried about his head, his airway. He's too big, too heavy. Violet places her hands on his shoulders to help.

Gia glares at me, her face twisted with fury. "You're just mad because he chose me."

"If by 'chose' you mean lied to both of us, then sure, congrats. You win."

Her response is sharp, physical, a shove that sends me stumbling backward.

"I'm trying to help him!" she screams, her hands trembling as she pries at his mouth, desperate to force him to breathe.

"Stop! Don't do that!" I grab her arm, yanking her back as her panic spirals into madness. "You're going to make it worse. Are you trying to make it worse?"

"Gia, stop." Violet's voice quivers as she speaks, quiet but firm. "You don't know what you're doing."

Gia's face crumbles, her bravado cracking to reveal sheer terror. "Then what do we do?"

"Did he eat anything with nuts?" I ask both of them.

Gia frowns hard. "How am I supposed to know?"

Violet's helpless shrug only adds to the suffocating tension in the room.

I whip my head toward the hallway and scream for Roman and Garrett. The walls echo with my desperation.

"Get his EpiPen," I tell Gia. "It's in his bag. Go!"

Gia scrambles to her feet, her movements wild as she sprints toward Eli's room. I yell again, louder this time, my voice breaking on the names.

Eli's skin gleams with sweat, beads gathering at his temples and slipping down his pallid face. His chest barely moves. I press my hand to his forehead, damp and cool, as if his body is already slipping away from us.

"We need to get him on his back," I say, my voice sharper now. "I'll support his head and neck. You take his hips."

Her nod is shaky, but she grips his body as I instruct.

"Ready? Go."

Together, we heave him onto his back, grunting with the effort. His weight is immense, his body almost completely limp. I guide his head onto the floor, careful, tilting it back slightly, his hair sticky with sweat. His face looks wrong, so wrong. Eyes closed, lips pale.

"We have to keep his airway open," I whisper.

Violet stares at me, her eyes shimmering with unshed tears. "It's getting worse. What do we do?"

"Call an ambulance," I order, my voice firm. When she hesitates, frozen by the gravity of it all, I yell, "Go!"

Violet jolts from her shock-induced trance and sprints out of the room to grab her phone.

Roman, Lauren and Garrett run into the room at the same time, shocked to see Eli sprawled on the floor. I prop his legs up on a chair, then check his pulse. Nothing. My chest tightens. I tilt his head back and start compressions, hard and fast, counting under my breath. We only have a few minutes left.

"I'll do it," Garrett says, kneeling beside me.

He takes over, giving Eli much stronger pumps while I blow air into his mouth. We alternate a few times, but each time I pull back, Eli's eyes are still clamped shut. My heart pounds as I blow harder, faster. Tears drop from my eyes onto his face, but I keep going. He will not die like this, not if I have anything to do with it.

Gia barrels into the room clutching his backpack. I frown at her, having expected to find the pen in her hand, ready to stab it into his thigh. The longer we wait, the less effective the epinephrine will be.

"It's not here," she shouts, frantic. "It's not in here!"

I snatch the bag from her hand and dump everything out onto the floor. I desperately shuffle through Eli's things. Lauren joins in as I struggle to find the pen. But Gia's right. It's not here.

I glance at Eli's face to see how the compressions are coming, but they don't seem to be helping. His body is slack, lifeless. His face is a mask of terror, frozen mid-struggle, as if the panic hasn't left him even in unconsciousness. His throat is swollen, the lines of it taut and constricted, and though he's not breathing, it's as if his body is still caught in the fight, choking on air that won't come.

I've always known it was a possibility, something like this happening always a shadow at the edge of my mind ever since he told me about the severity of his allergies. But I never thought it would actually happen. I can barely wrap my head around the idea of splitting up, of losing him from my life, and now I have to somehow grasp the possibility of losing him forever. It's impossible. This can't happen. Not now. Not like this.

"Check his pockets," I shout, and Lauren jumps right into gear, patting down his body.

She checks one side, and I empty the other. I pull out his phone, and Lauren finds his wallet and car keys. But no pen. There's *no pen*.

Roman rushes out to check the Jeep, hoping maybe Eli brought the EpiPen with him on their outings and it simply fell out at some point. Violet paces close by, talking on the phone with the 911 operator, her voice shaking with anxiety as she provides details. I give her the correct terms to say and go back to helping Garrett with the resuscitation.

Each compression feels like a desperate, futile attempt to rewind time. Lauren searches his bag again. I turn to Gia, who's shaking uncontrollably. I tell her to go upstairs to check all his pockets—his jeans, shorts, hoodie, *everything*. She nods and takes off.

I sink to my knees beside Eli, watching as his body betrays him. Garrett keeps pressing his hands to Eli's chest, relentless, each compression a desperate rhythm. Time stretches thin, each second heavy enough to shatter something inside me. The world folds in on itself, every sound dimming to a low, unbearable hum, like the universe itself is mourning.

I know what comes next. I've heard him explain it in calm, clinical tones, never imagining it would be like this. First, the organs fail, one by one, like lights winking out in a distant house. Next, the heart gives out. And then . . . nothing.

I hear Garrett's voice, telling me to keep going, that Eli needs more air, but I kneel there, frozen. I can't lose him. Not like this.

chapter
thirty-nine

Roman steps in to take over CPR for me until the ambulance arrives, sirens wailing, flashing red through the rain. We all pile in the Rubicon, and Garrett trails behind the ambulance. No one says a word, our collective anxieties mounting, thickening the air, making it hard to breathe. The rain pounds against the windows. This storm isn't slowing down any time soon.

Garrett grips the wheel hard as he pushes the Jeep to keep up with the ambulance, his knuckles going white. Suddenly, the car starts to hydroplane, the tires skidding across the slick road. My stomach drops as I grab onto the door handle, everyone silent as we swerve in the dark. Garrett regains control of the Jeep and continues driving with his foot flat on the gas.

I don't breathe again until we screech to a stop in front of the emergency room's automatic doors.

We all hop out into the storm and rush inside. Our clothes are soaked by the time we make it to the other side of the doors. As we huddle together in the waiting room, it seems as if we're the only ones in the building, an eerie quiet hushing every sound around us. As I glance around the bright room, I think of the first time Eli told me about his severe allergy to nuts. He said any nut, any quantity could stop his heart. It was our third date, the night I fell so hard for him. I was considering a dessert topped with walnuts to share, but he stopped me from ordering it. I got raspberry sorbet instead. On the ride back to campus, he told me about his EpiPen and his two spares—one in his medicine cabinet and one at his mother's house. I remember how intimate it was when he taught me how to use it. He took my hands in his, guiding me through the steps with a patience that was so tender, I think I fell in love right there. His voice was calm and reassuring as he explained the details. Every touch was deliberate, every instruction imbued with a sense of urgency that was both practical and deeply personal. I watched him closely, the seriousness of the moment blending with a closeness that was much more intimate than the sex we'd already had. It felt sacred, him putting his trust in me like that, his life in my hands.

The thought of Eli slipping away, of him leaving me with nothing but the fractured remnants of what we once had, is unbearable. The sharp, aching weight of it presses down on my chest as I slump in the waiting room. The fluorescent lights hum relentlessly, the faint beep of distant monitors threading through the silence, a cruel soundtrack to this endless purgatory. Time doesn't move here; it stretches, suffocates, swallows you whole.

My mind is a storm of contradictions. Eli's suffering, his gasping breaths colliding with the bitter sting of his betrayal, the lies that still fester beneath my skin. I want to hate him. God, it would be so much easier to hate him. But I can't forget the way he was there for me before everything fell apart. Before my mother died, before the sleepless nights and the suffocating grief. Before the anger and the emptiness. He listened to me when no one else did. There was a time when it was magical, when we were something more than this.

Finally, the doctor rounds the corner, and everyone leaps to their feet. Everyone but me. I can't move. I stay rooted to the seat of the chair, unable to breathe, unable to think, because I already know. I can see it in the way she hesitates, in the soft slope of her shoulders.

"I'm sorry," she begins, and her voice is gentle, but it still cuts. "We did everything we could . . ."

The rest dissolves into static. The words don't reach me. I hear Violet's muffled sobs and Gia's sharp cries. I hear the way her voice cracks as she pleads to see him, shouting at the doctor like she can claw him back if she just screams loud enough. Security moves in, takes her by the arms, pulling her away from the door. Family only, they say, and she screams louder.

Garrett wraps Lauren in his arms, her tears soaking into his shirt. Roman stands against the wall with his face in his hands. The doctor says something about how it was too late, how he went too long without oxygen, but the words don't register. They slide off me, weightless and meaningless.

I stare at the floor and wonder when it happened. When he left us. Was it when his eyes fluttered shut on the floor beneath me? Or was it later, when they wheeled him through those sterile hallways and did everything they could? When was the exact moment he slipped away? And why wasn't I enough to keep him here?

chapter
forty

"You did this, didn't you?"

The accusation cuts through the rain, sharp as shattered glass. I turn to see Gia slam the Jeep door behind her. Everyone but her and Roman has already fled back inside the house, but Gia marches toward me, her fury a tempest of its own. The rain has plastered her curls to her neck, the heavy strands framing a face contorted with grief and rage. Roman stops beside me, my hand anchored on his arm as I balance on my good foot.

"What?"

"You did this," she screams. Her voice shakes, raw and unhinged, every syllable a boulder hurled in my direction. "He didn't want you anymore, so you poisoned him!"

She's close now, so close I can see the anger shimmering in her eyes, so close I can feel her grief breaking apart like waves against my chest. My body stiffens, holding me upright, but my mind reels.

"He wasn't poisoned," Roman says, his voice steady, solid, a tether to the present. "He had an allergic reaction."

"I didn't even know he had allergies!" Gia shouts, her voice cracking. "But *you* did."

Her words hit like a slap, cold and unforgiving. I meet her glare with one of my own. "You didn't know he had a life-threatening nut allergy, but you knew how he liked to be kissed, didn't you?"

For a fleeting second, I see it. A crack in her armor, the truth flashing across her face. She knows I know. About the lies, the stolen moments, the things they thought they'd hidden so well. But she doesn't back down.

"You knew," she spits, her voice trembling under the weight of her despair. "You killed him. I know you did."

"Get out of my face," I say, my voice low, steady as a tide. But she doesn't move. She leans in closer, crowding me with her fury, her pain.

"He didn't love you," she whispers, grabbing the front of my shirt and shoving me back into the Jeep's door.

The impact jolts through me, a spark igniting the fire already burning in my chest. But I don't give in to it. She's hurting. She needs someone to blame. That's all this is.

"He stopped a long time ago," she continues, her eyes locked on mine with a relentless, unyielding ferocity.

Roman grabs her, pulling her aside so I can hobble into the house. But when I step around her, she rips from his hold and blocks my path. I glare at her, my fists clenching at my sides. I wish it wasn't so easy for her to get under my skin, but her cruelty is merciless and methodical. Tears burst from my eyes, and the only relief is that they get washed away quickly by the rain.

"He wouldn't stop complaining about you. How much you disgusted him. How tired he was of taking care of you, like some helpless child." Her words come fast now, sharp-edged and soaked in venom, each one aimed to wound. "When we were together, he was happy. He just wanted to be happy. And now he's . . ."

I brace myself for more, but Gia dissolves into tears. Loud, guttural wails. What she doesn't understand is that I get it. I feel the same pain. This is a moment that should bring us together, not something that should rip us even further apart. We've both loved Eli, and now we've both lost him. Blaming me won't bring him back or assuage her guilt.

I went through the exact kind of rage after my mother left me. I was forced to not only grieve the loss of the person but also mourn the future, what could have been. It's obvious by their rendezvous in the woods, and the brutality of her emotions, that she's been planning her future with Eli next to her. She might even have been in on Eli's scheme to break up with me.

But I don't hold this against her. Not in this moment. It isn't the time or place.

"The only reason he stayed was because he felt sorry for you," she says. "Because of her. Because of your mother."

The rain drums harder against the ground, relentless, drowning everything but her words. They pierce me, one by one, leaving jagged wounds in their wake. My nails dig into my palms. Every muscle in my body screams to lash out, to meet her cruelty with my own, but I hold the storm inside.

"Fuck you," I whisper my chin quivering.

"No, fuck you, Iris!" Gia screams, lunging at me, her hands swinging wildly. "You did it on purpose. You—"

"Get her away from me," I say to Roman, my voice breaking, trembling with the weight of my restraint.

It's not a plea. It's a warning.

Roman yanks her back, harder this time, dragging her toward the house. She fights him every step, writhing beneath his grip.

"*You let him die!*" she screams, her voice splintering in the air between us. "You let him die because you knew he loved me more than he ever loved you!"

For a moment, I'm frozen. Not by rage, but doubt. Did he love her more? Did he ever truly love me at all? The questions tear through me like wind through broken branches, leaving me hollow. I'll never know. I'll never get to ask him.

"The only reason he didn't leave you was because your mother killed herself," Gia shouts when I reach the door. "It's been an entire fucking year. *Get over it!*"

Ignoring the pain in my foot, I lunge at her, fueled by a fire I can no longer contain. I grab her hair, yanking her head back as I slam her into the door. The rain blurs everything, but I feel the solid press of her body against the glass, the raw power in my grip as I prepare to hit her with my curled fist.

Roman yanks me off her before I can. I try to fight him, but it's no use. Not even my wrath has a chance against his brute strength. He wrestles me toward the house, his voice low and urgent, but I don't hear him. My heart pounds in my ears, the sound louder than Gia's screams still ringing out behind me.

When we're inside, Roman stops, turning to face me. His expression softens, and for the first time in hours, the storm inside me begins to settle.

"She's just feeling everything all at once," he says quietly. "It's easier to be angry. You know?"

I swallow hard, my throat tight, and nod.

"I'm sorry," he says after a moment, his voice barely audible. "I know you loved him."

I take a breath, shaking my head. "What does it matter if he didn't love me?"

Roman's eyes meet mine, steady and kind. "Loving and being loved are two different things, no?"

The words linger in the air, soft yet unshakable, like the echo of a bell. They settle into the cracks inside me, quieting the static in my brain. It feels profound in a way I can't quite grasp at first. But then it hits me. Eli didn't love me, not the way I needed or wanted him to. But the love I felt for him, the way I carried it and nurtured it, even though he's gone—it still mattered.

Loving him *mattered*. Even if it was never reciprocated, even if it wasn't enough to keep him here. It mattered.

Before I can thank Roman, the words die on my tongue as Gia steps in from outside, still shaking. With anger or from the rain, I can't tell.

chapter
forty-one

Morning comes, but the storm doesn't relent. Rain lashes the windows harder than before, streaking the glass in chaotic patterns that blur the view of the waterlogged yard. The sky is a sullen gray and presses low against the horizon. The wind bellows with a renewed ferocity, shaking the walls as if to remind us that the worst is yet to come.

It's impossible to tell where the night ends and the day begins; the storm erases the boundary, folding time into itself. I hoped for clarity with the dawn. I was foolish. The vacation is over. Everyone knows it, but this house holds us prisoner.

Everyone breathes and blinks as if the world hasn't shifted, as if time hasn't splintered into a before and after. It isn't fair. Eli should be here, laughing at something silly Garrett's saying, stealing the last of the coffee from the pot. Instead, I sit here on the couch for hours, oblivious to everything around me, the day bleeding away and slipping toward evening. The tooth is still tucked away in my pocket like a cruel talisman, its weight more significant than it has any right to be.

I shift across from Roman in the living room, the kitchen visible just beyond him. The air between us is thick, not just with humidity but with everything unsaid. Thunder grumbles low in the distance. I shift again in my seat, the leather sticking to the backs of my legs.

Roman breaks the silence. "So, why can't you sleep? Before all this, I mean."

I pause, caught off guard by the question despite its simplicity. His eyes search mine, curious. For a moment, I'm acutely aware of how undone I must look. Barefaced, the puffiness under my eyes betraying endless sleepless nights. Vanity prickles at the edges of my thoughts, but it's fleeting. I'm too tired for pretense, too hollowed out to care.

"Every time I close my eyes, I see her," I admit, my voice almost too quiet with the rain. My eyelids fall shut briefly, as if shielding me from the memory. "My mother."

When I open my eyes, Roman's head tilts, his expression softening with interest.

"Isn't that good?" he asks, his voice careful. "I mean, isn't it kinda nice to see her in your dreams?"

I never see the good moments, though I know they existed, buried somewhere in the recesses of my brain. There were rare flashes of tenderness, but they're drowned out by the hurricane she carried inside her. When she visits me now, it's always the worst of her. The gun. The blood. The sickening finale of it all. I never tell anyone this, not the grotesque details, not the way she sometimes tries to pull me down with her into an endless black abyss.

Instead I shrug, clinging to the fragile hope that the nightmares will leave me if the guilt ever does.

Roman watches me for a moment, his gaze unflinching, as if he's trying to see past the walls I've built. "Iris, your mom was sick. There was nothing you could—"

"I know," I interrupt, cutting him off. The words rush out before I can stop them. "I know. It's just . . ." I hesitate, my voice faltering as I search for the courage to say the thing that's haunted me for years. "Sometimes I get scared that . . ."

His brow furrows, his curiosity shifting into concern. "Scared that what?"

I hesitate again, my throat tightening. "I don't know. What if it's hereditary? What if I start hearing things, seeing things like she did?"

The question hangs between us, fragile and trembling, like the moment before lightning splits the sky.

Roman doesn't speak right away. His gaze lingers on me, his eyes softening with uncertainty. He doesn't know what to say. I can see it in the way his lips press together, in the way his shoulders rise and fall with a breath he doesn't quite release.

The silence is enough. I don't need reassurances or empty platitudes. I'll save the spiral for my therapist next week. For now, I sink back into the couch, the storm's unrelenting rhythm filling the spaces where our words end.

Garrett slips into the kitchen and stands at the sink, his shoulders hunched over, his back turned to me. He twists the faucet handle, his movements mechanical, his mind far away. The storm outside howls, rain battering the windows, but inside, the kitchen feels too still, too quiet except for the gurgle of the water filling his glass.

I watch him, his eyes shadowed with something deeper than exhaustion. Grief. Of course, he's grieving too. His silence is heavy, as if he's holding his sorrow somewhere deep, where no one else can reach it.

Eli wasn't just mine. He was Garrett's, too. They were brothers in all the ways that mattered. And though I was the one who shared Eli's bed, it hits me now—his loss isn't any less sharp for everyone else here.

Garrett takes a gulp of water before recoiling, his face twisted in disgust. "What the hell is wrong with this water?"

Remembering what happened to me in the bath, I rush over to the sink, my stomach tightening with dread. His glass is contaminated with a viscous liquid, faintly yellow-brown with a sheen that catches the light in a sickly, unnatural way.

My hands grip the counter as he flips the faucet back on. What comes out isn't just discolored. It's alive with dark, swirling flecks that spiral like ash in a dying fire. The smell slams into me, raw and rancid, an odor that clings to the back of my throat. My knees threaten to give out as the memory of the bathtub water floods back. My breath catches in a shallow, panicked gasp.

Thick sludge, darker than the water itself, begins to ooze from the faucet, creeping out in slow, thick strands. The kitchen feels smaller, the walls pressing in as the air grows heavier with the stench. Garrett is frozen, his hand still gripping the glass, his face pale.

"What is that?" he whispers, his voice barely audible over the rain pounding against the roof.

Roman moves beside me, his jaw tightening as he leans in to examine the water. His face twists into something between horror and disgust, his nostrils flaring as he steps back.

"Jesus Christ," he mutters under his breath, just as something solid lurches from the faucet.

The nail is blackened, curling at the edges. The skin bloated, peeling.

A pale, decaying finger.

My shriek rips through the air, sharp and raw. Roman catches me, his arms a lifeline as my body trembles uncontrollably. Garrett stumbles back, his glass shattering on the floor. And then he doubles over, vomiting into the trash can, his body recoiling in horror.

The cacophony draws the others. Gia, Lauren and Violet rush into the kitchen, their expressions veiled in confusion. The storm outside rages on, the wind slamming against the windows, as if the house itself is crying out in protest.

"Bro . . ." Roman's voice is low as he pulls Garrett to his feet, steadying him with a hand on his shoulder. "You okay?"

Gia's fingers fly to the napkins in the holder on the table, snatching them up. Garrett wipes his face, grimacing, gathering whatever is left of his composure.

"What happened?" Lauren's voice is tight, sharp, as she steps forward, her eyes scanning him.

Garrett shoots me a look. It's strange, laden with something I can't place. A flicker of something soft, sorrowful. And just before he speaks, I catch it. It's an apology.

His head shakes. "There's a . . ."

Lauren's impatience sharpens her voice. "A what?"

"A finger," I say, the words tasting bitter as they slip from my lips.

Garrett drops to his knees, his body convulsing again. This time, his aim is worse. The trash can is forgotten as everything he's been holding down splatters onto the floor.

Lauren kneels at his side, her hand rubbing his back in quiet comfort, face a mask of worry and grim determination.

"There's a finger in the water," I whisper to her.

She doesn't hesitate. She leans over the sink, her eyes already wide with dread. The others follow suit, edging closer, their faces dropping, twisted in disbelief and revulsion.

The finger floats in the murky water, white and grotesque. This is where the arm has been this whole time.

As if on cue, everyone's eyes snap over to me, their faces slack with shock and disbelief. No one speaks. Just a brutal silence, the kind that settles deep in my marrow.

I try not to picture the rest of the body. The arm. Its swollen flesh. The rotting, peeling skin. The bones beneath.

"That's what's been in the water?" Lauren's voice rises, a screech of disbelief. "I *drank* that."

The realization crashes through me, a tidal wave of nausea and terror. My breath seizes in my chest as the bile rises, bitter and hot, clawing its way up my throat. I've been drinking this. I've bathed in it. For *days*.

"How did a finger get in the water?" Violet asks, but no one has an answer.

"The water supply is on the roof," Garrett says, his voice rough, empty.

I stand there, piecing the shards together. Nolan must have hastily discarded the arm after he saw me find it, tossing it onto the roof when he swapped it out for the baby doll. It's the only explanation I can come up with, but even as I rationalize it, the thought of him, of what he did, turns my stomach. The gravity of it presses down on all of us.

"We have to get out of here," Gia says, and for once, I'm with her. "We need to call the cops and get the hell out of this place."

Beneath the revulsion, a flicker of vindication burns through me. I've been saying it all week, telling everyone something was wrong. No one listened. They called me crazy, dismissed me with those condescending smiles, whispered behind my back like I was losing my mind. And now, here it is, the proof floating right here in the sink like a macabre trophy. I was right. I was right all along.

"I want to leave tonight," Lauren says, her voice cracking as she follows behind Garrett. The fear in her voice is raw and trembling, as though the ground beneath her is shifting. She's finally reached her breaking point.

"Look out the window," Garrett says, pointing at the rain, the storm now hammering the house with a ferocity that makes the walls shudder. We spill into the front room, standing there, waiting. "If we leave tonight, we won't get far. The area's probably already flooded. If we get out on the road and get stuck, then what?"

"Well, we need to get the cops here," Violet says, her arms wrapped tightly around herself as though shielding her body from the weight of everything that's happened.

"Let's just all calm down, alright?" Roman says, though the strain in his voice betrays his own nerves. He runs a hand through his hair, pacing the room, trapped in the pull of his thoughts. "We'll get on the road first thing in the morning, once the rain stops."

"The man is a *serial killer*," Lauren says, grabbing his arm with a force that makes him stumble slightly.

Roman balks, confusion written all over his face. "What?"

"Nolan killed that girl. Whoever's arm that is on the roof, he killed her. And he probably killed the rest of them too."

Roman stares at her, his eyes narrowing as disbelief floods his expression.

Garrett shakes his head, his voice hoarse, filled with uncertainty. "We don't know that."

"Then who put it there?" Lauren fires back.

"I saw him the night I got here," I say, feeling everyone's eyes settle on me. "He was in the back wearing the same jacket he's wearing in a photo I saw in the other room. I thought maybe he was covered in mud, but it wasn't mud. It was blood."

Garrett still isn't convinced. "We don't know that he had anything to do with any of those other missing girls."

"Well, we don't know that he didn't, so I'm with Lauren," Gia says. "I say we get out of here tonight."

Garrett collapses onto the couch as though the weight of the room is too much for him to bear. His face is a tangle of stress and disbelief. The urge to blame him for inviting us all here and leading us into this nightmare is aggressive. How could he not know his uncle has been killing women and burying them in the backyard? How could Roman not know either?

But then, just as quickly, a thought stirs within me, cold and unwelcome. I hadn't known about Eli, hadn't seen the signs of his betrayal, not even when it was happening right under my nose. Suddenly, I understand. You can share a bed, a life, a history with someone and still be blind to the parts of them that are dark, buried too deep to see until it's far too late.

"We'll get out of here first thing in the morning," Roman says again before crossing the room.

"What if that's too late?" Violet asks, scurrying after him.

"Nothing's going to happen with all of us here," Garrett says, backing up Roman.

"Says who?"

"Says common sense," Garrett says, looking around at all of us. "One against six? You really think someone would try that?"

Violet backs down, though she's clearly not satisfied with his answer.

I'm not either.

"It's not 'someone,'" I tell him. "It's your uncle."

The room falls silent, everyone retreating into their own thoughts for a moment.

"It's just a little rain," Garrett says, catching Roman's eyes.

Roman considers this for a beat, then slowly nods his assent. "Alright," he says. "Let's get everything in the car. You call the cops."

chapter
forty-two

The air in the room shifts. There's a sharpness now, a sense of urgency threading through the commotion that envelops the house. The walls feel too close, too oppressive. My nerves, still frayed from yesterday's near-collision on the slippery roads, twitch at every movement, but they're drowned out by an overpowering instinct to flee.

The house bursts into motion, a frenzy of packing, hasty movements and half-finished tasks. Everyone scatters, footsteps echoing, a symphony of panic. I help Violet stuff clothes into bags. Somewhere down the hall, Lauren's voice rises above the disarray, tinged with panic, searching for something. She can't find her Chanel bag.

I barely blink before Garrett is on his way, an unspoken agreement forming in the tension of the air.

"I'll check in here," he calls out.

The rest is all a blur. The movement of bodies, the sound of zippers and rustling bags, all of it merges. My hands work as if on their own—folding, stuffing, securing—each motion deliberate but mechanical, a way to ignore the panic tightening its grip around my chest. The urgency of everyone else's actions fades as the rhythm of my own packing becomes all that matters. One breath. One movement.

When we're all done, the house falls quiet for a moment, the frantic energy dissipating. The others rush outside, their footsteps hurried and uneven, a chorus of voices. I follow, the rain nipping at my skin, and climb into the back seat. My body is stiff as I settle into the worn fabric, my foot still aching. Roman and Violet stuff the last of the bags into the trunk. I tighten my arms around myself, unable to look at anything but the small space between us. Gia, at the opposite end of the seat, rests her head against the window, her eyes closed.

Lauren slides into the front, the silence of the car pressing in around us. Something shifts in the air, the absence of one voice hanging heavy between us.

"Where's Garrett?" she asks, her eyes on the empty driver's seat.

"Maybe he's still upstairs," Gia offers, her voice tinged with uncertainty.

Lauren shakes her head, her brow furrowing. "He came down before me."

Gia glances toward the window, her eyes squinting through the relentless rain, while Lauren shifts restlessly, rummaging through her bag, then her pockets.

"Shit."

"What's wrong?" Gia asks.

"I don't have my phone," Lauren mutters, her fingers brushing the floor beneath her seat in a futile search. "One of you call him. Thought it was in my bag. I must have left it in our room."

"I'll get him," Roman volunteers, and without waiting for a response, he climbs out of the car, his feet slipping briefly on the gravel before he steadies himself and makes his way back toward the house.

"Be careful," Violet calls after him, her voice laced with a note of fear.

Roman nods, acknowledging her words, then disappears into the house.

"I'll call your phone so he can grab it," Gia tells Lauren.

She nods in agreement, but as Gia reaches for her pockets and checks her bag, a shadow of doubt crosses her face.

When Violet and I check for our phones, we find them missing as well. The silence between us deepens, thick and uneasy. We exchange a look, one that says everything without a word.

No one dares to voice it, but we all know something's wrong. Something is very wrong.

Gia and Lauren head back inside the house, slipping through the front door, while Violet and I stay, rifling through the bags in the trunk.

"None of them are in here," Violet announces, her voice low, matter-of-fact, as though stating the obvious could somehow make it less terrifying.

A chill crawls down my spine, and the words rip from me before I can stop them. "I knew it."

"Knew what?"

"Someone else is here," I reply, my gaze locked on hers.

Violet doesn't respond, just opens her mouth a few times, as if searching for something to say, but nothing comes. She knows it too. She knows I'm right.

A distant scream cuts through the storm, raw and desperate, sending a tremor through the air. Violet's eyes meet mine in a wordless exchange, the weight of that scream pulling us both into a new, unspoken reality.

We race to the back of the house, our feet pounding against the slick ground as we make our way to the deck. At the top of the stairs, Gia stops short, her gaze fixed on something below. Violet, faster, reaches the crest of the stairs first, leaving me trailing behind. And then I see it.

The body.

Lauren, crumpled at the foot of the stairs.

Even in the dim light and without my glasses, there is no mistaking it, the unnatural angle of her neck. Twisted. Broken.

Gia's scream pierces the air. I realize, as the sound peals through the night, that she hasn't stopped. Her guttural wails seem to split the sky, an agony so visceral it feels as if the earth itself is trembling. Violet moves to restrain her, but Gia rushes down the slick steps, slipping on the final stair, her body lurching forward. She grips the railing just in time, sparing us from another disaster.

"Her head's bleeding," she cries, crouching beside Lauren, her voice a wail of disbelief. "Oh, my god, there's so much blood."

Roman emerges from the house and kneels beside Lauren. He presses two fingers to her neck, seeking a pulse that won't come. I stay frozen where I stand, my body refusing to move, unwilling to face the horror up close.

The thought of it, the blood, the finality, it all stirs something dark and violent inside me, something I thought I had buried a long time ago. I close my eyes, then open them.

My mother's face flashes in front of me. And then, against

my own will, I think of the deer. I see her slack face, her wide eyes. And then all the blood.

I shut my eyes again, and in the darkness, my mother's final moments play on a loop. Over and over and over again until I can't tell where reality ends and the memory begins. My body trembles uncontrollably as tears spill down my face, mingling with the rain. They feel different. Heavier.

Roman straightens out, and Gia starts wailing again when he announces there's no pulse. She refuses to leave Lauren's side. She cradles her bloody head as the rain beats down on us. I stare at Lauren's body twisted on the ground, knowing Garrett won't want to leave tonight anymore. And I feel bad for thinking of myself at this moment, but I can't fathom staying here another night. We'll have to call another ambulance and wait for them to arrive, then take another trip to the hospital. I think about driving Eli's SUV back to the city, stick shift or no, but then I remember my glasses are broken. I won't be able to see anything, especially in the dark. And even if I decided to risk it, driving in this weather is impossible.

"First Eli, and now Lauren slips and cracks her head open?" Violet says, tears in her eyes as she meets mine.

I stare at Gia holding Lauren, wondering if anyone would be crying like this if it had been me that slipped down the stairs. Would anyone have held me like this? The more I look at Lauren's body, the more something seems off.

"What if she didn't slip?" I whisper before I even get the chance to fully collect my thoughts, my voice barely more than a breath.

Violet turns toward me, brow furrowed in confusion. "What do you mean?"

"Eli always has his EpiPen with him. Always."

Her voice falters, cracking under the pressure. "What are you saying?"

I think back to the boat. The explosion. The unnatural stillness of it all, how it felt like someone had been waiting for the perfect moment. Someone tried to kill Roman and me. The pieces fall into place, slow and sure.

"I don't think it was an accident," I say, louder this time. Even as I say it, the truth feels almost too much to bear. But it's there, undeniable in its finality.

Nothing about this house, about what has happened to us, makes sense. And now, our phones all vanished without a trace. Gone. It can't be coincidence. *It can't.*

"This isn't either," I tell Violet, my eyes on Lauren as my head starts to shake. "Nolan knows we know."

She shakes her head like she doesn't want to believe it. "Iris, that's—"

"He saw me that night." Rain lashes against my skin, but I barely feel it, the cold nothing compared to the creeping realization tightening its grip around my throat. "He's known this *whole* time."

"Then why would he wait until now to do something?"

I take a moment to really consider her question. "Maybe he was hoping I'd leave. That's why he's been messing with me, taunting me. But I ended up staying, and now you guys finally believe me. Just think about it. As soon as we decide to leave—boom, two of us are dead? It's too convenient. It has to be him. He's scared we'll tell the police."

Violet shakes her head. "How would he even know—"

"Maybe he has hidden cameras in the house. Or maybe he's been sneaking in and listening to us. Something. All

I know is, he doesn't want us to leave this house with the truth."

A crack of thunder claps through the air. Violet doesn't refute me this time. She takes a moment, trying to process it all. Eventually, Gia's cries soften to weak sobs, and my mind stays on Nolan. I know he did this. He could have pushed her. He could have snuck up behind her and bludgeoned her in the head before she ever saw it coming. He had everything he needed in the basement.

I shout over the rain, telling Roman to get Gia so we can get out of here. He struggles to pry her away from Lauren's side, and my heart breaks seeing the agony on her face as she's pulled away from her best friend. Roman climbs back up the stairs with Gia in tow, limp in his arms. Even in my hatred for her, I can empathize with what this must feel like. Friendship is quieter than passion, the rare love that asks for nothing yet offers everything.

"Wait," I say, my voice a soft rasp. "Where's Garrett?"

Roman's answer is quick but not comforting. "I didn't see him."

"What do you mean, you didn't see him?" Violet asks, and I can tell by the waver in her voice, her fear is the same as mine.

"You three go wait in the car," Roman commands, rain darting at the bones of his face. "I'll check again."

"But—"

"I'll find him," he says, the firmness of his voice leaving no room for argument. "Wait for me in the car. Leave if you have to."

The force of his urgency grips me, chills me to my core. We're in danger. Immediate danger.

I don't want to separate. The idea of it feels wrong, my instinct telling me to stay close, to stay together. But then I think of Lauren. When Roman finds Garrett, when he has to see her body splayed at the foot of the steps, when he realizes all that he's lost . . . I'm grateful, in a way, that I won't have to watch it. That I won't have to see the last shreds of his heart crumble to dust.

chapter
forty-three

The world narrows to a single, unyielding moment. Time fractures—splinters of the past, of every choice that led us here, stabbing at my ribs. Each step is heavier than the last, my foot dragging like a chain around my ankle.

Gia and Violet are ahead, their bodies slipping into the storm, vague silhouettes against the fury of the night. They don't feel the weight of this moment yet, not like I do. They're running, scrambling for safety that doesn't exist. Not really, not anymore.

I make it to the car door, just a few feet from escaping, and stop. My breath hitches, and my gasp feels torn from somewhere deep within me. My eyes lock onto the sight ahead, my mind reeling, fighting to make sense of it.

It's impossible. It must be a mistake. Some trick of the light, some illusion spun by the relentless downpour that distorts everything it touches.

I squint hard, hoping to tear the image apart, but the truth doesn't yield. The meaning of it presses into me, sharp and cold, until I feel it deep in my bones, settling into my marrow.

We're trapped. There's no room left for doubt, no escape from the ugly reality that has just set in.

Nolan is hunting us.

Killing us off one by one.

"Hurry up and get in so we can lock the doors," Violet shouts, waving me over, urgency radiating from her every movement.

I try to respond, to form words that will cut through the suffocating fog in my mind, but my heart is a hammer, relentless, drowning out everything else.

"*Iris!*" Violet screams, her voice jagged and raw, piercing through the haze. It snaps something loose in me. "What are—"

"The tires . . ." I manage, the words incomplete, fluttering out on a shallow breath. My throat constricts, and the rest tangles somewhere deep inside, refusing to surface.

Violet leaps back out of the Jeep. Her gaze follows mine, and then she sees it. The breath she takes is sharp and audible. Both of her hands fly up to her mouth, as if trying to trap the sound, to hold in the panic.

All four tires. Flattened. Destroyed.

The rain streaks across the ruined tires, pooling in the blackened rubber like a taunt. My eyes weren't playing tricks on me. This is real. This is *final*. The escape we'd clung to, fragile and thin as a thread, has snapped. We are stranded. We are at his mercy.

"We'll just use Eli's car," Gia says after taking in the damage for herself.

The five of us could all fit. But there's no use.

"The keys," I say, remembering. "They're in his pocket. I put them back in his pocket."

"You fucking *idiot*," Gia shrieks, her voice cracking apart as she collapses into fresh tears.

I don't react. Her vitriol crashes against the walls I've built around myself in the last few hours. They splinter but don't break through. Let her scream. Let her cry. I've stopped caring about what Gia thinks of me. I'm the only one who has the right to rage. She's the one who slept with Eli. She's the one who crossed a line that was never hers to cross. Whether or not he was happy doesn't matter. That was never her decision to make. She doesn't get to rewrite what happened. She doesn't get to paint me as the crazy one, as if I'm the problem, when all along it's been her.

"Iris, I'm sorry," Violet says, her voice soft, hesitant, but I don't hear her. Not really. Something else is already churning inside me, my thoughts racing backward, snagging on a detail that sets my nerves on edge. "We should've left when you . . ."

Her words fade, swallowed by the storm in my head as I turn and limp away, heading back toward the house as fast as my injured foot will allow. Pain sears through me with every step, sharp and white-hot, but I grit my teeth and force myself forward. Agony is secondary now, a distant hum beneath the urgency pounding in my chest.

"What are you doing?" Violet calls, her voice rising as she and Gia scramble to catch up. "Roman said to—"

"I don't trust Garrett," I say, the words clipped, thrown over my shoulder without slowing down. Roman told us to stay in the car, to leave if we had to. But I can't. I won't leave him here.

"Garrett?" Violet's voice wavers, disbelieving, like I've just said something impossible. "Why?"

"Why is it taking Roman so long to find him?" I shoot back, my breath catching as the possibility blooms in my mind, dark and sinister.

Maybe Garrett is with Lauren. Maybe he found her at the bottom of the stairs, her lifeless body crumpled and broken, and now he can't bring himself to leave her side. That's possible. It's the kinder explanation. But my gut is screaming something else entirely, its voice low and insistent, pulling me toward a truth I don't want to face, but have to.

"He's been helping out Nolan," I say. I cling to it because I need to. It has to be true. It's the only way to make any of this fit together. "He told him that we found the finger, and now he's trying to kill us all."

Violet opens her mouth, but before she can respond, Gia cuts in. "You think Garrett is helping his uncle kill off all his friends, including his other nephew? That makes zero sense. They're not even close like that."

"How else could Nolan have known about Eli's allergy?"

"We don't know for sure it wasn't an accident," Violet says, her voice steadier, like she's trying to keep us all from losing it completely.

"Lauren is dead, asshole," Gia hisses at me, her eyes burning with a rage so strong, it looks like she wishes she could kill me herself. "Garrett would *never* hurt her."

"Eli's too careful about what he eats for something like this to just happen. And he always carries his pen with him," I say, my voice rising, matching hers. Then it hits me like a punch to the chest. "What about the police?"

Violet and Gia exchange a look, and I can see it happening, the pieces slotting into place for them too, the same gruesome realization crawling across their faces.

"He called," Gia says, but her voice trembles now, her certainty slipping.

"They should have been here by now," I say. I take a breath, and the words come out like a final verdict, heavy and absolute. "Garrett didn't call."

My words land like a glacier, pulling all of us deeper into whatever this is. I can feel my mind spiraling, racing through possibilities. If Garrett's in on this, how far does it go? Did he kill Eli, or was it Nolan? It doesn't matter anymore. All I know is that Roman's in there alone, and it's two against one. We can't leave him.

I step through the front door, my body pushing forward even as my brain screams at me to stop. Every nerve in me feels raw and exposed.

"I'm not going back in there," Gia shouts from behind me.

When I look over my shoulder, Violet's fear is written in sharp lines. I tell them both to stay outside, to get in the car and lock the doors. I need to find Roman. I need to figure out what's happening.

I limp through the front room, the ache in my foot sharp and unrelenting, and make my way down the hallway. Halfway there, I hear Violet call my name. I freeze, the realization dawning cold and sudden. She didn't listen.

I turn back toward the front door, scanning the area for any trace of her. The darkness presses in. I flick the light switch, but nothing happens. The storm must have killed the power again.

"Violet?" I call out, my voice brittle against the silence.

No answer. I tread cautiously over the creaking floorboards, my breathing shallow. Just as I open my mouth to call for her again, a hand clamps down on my arm, its grip unyielding.

I whip around, grabbing onto a wooden chair within reach. I grip it tightly, ready to swing.

"It's me, it's me," a low voice pleads.

I squint into the dark. Roman's face takes shape, his features stark and etched with fear. Relief floods me as I lower the chair, my hands trembling. He's holding a mallet, his knuckles pale against its handle. He looks just as spooked as I feel.

"We have to go," I say, my voice hoarse. "It's Garrett."

"What?"

I steady myself, forcing the words to come out in order. "I think Garrett is helping your uncle. He's helping him . . ."

I stop when Roman begins shaking his head.

Without a word, he takes my arm and pulls me up the stairs. At the end of the hall, he pushes open one of the bedroom doors. The lights are still out, but I see it. The body sprawled on the floor, still, slack.

Garrett's face stares upward, suffocated under the sheen of a clear plastic trash bag.

My breath leaves me in a shudder. I stumble back into the hallway, my hands covering my mouth. The sight of him lifeless pins me in place. Guilt surges through me, swift and merciless. He wasn't the one helping Nolan. He wasn't the one trying to kill us. And now he's dead.

Tears burn hot as they trail down my cheeks. The image won't leave me. Garrett gasping for breath, the life stolen straight from him. My mind dredges up the memory of my dream, the suffocating weight of Nolan's hand on my face, the terror of fading to nothing.

"You were right," Roman says quietly, his voice heavy with resignation. "About all of it. He doesn't care who he kills, even if it's family."

I stare at Garrett's motionless body, my own trembling uncontrollably. It's too much to make sense of. He had a son. A boy who now has no one. Eli was right about my mother. She was cruel and selfish, a failure of a parent. But at least I had her.

"Do you think it's too late for CPR?" I ask, my voice breaking as the tears spill faster.

Roman shakes his head, his tone definitive. "I checked him. There's no pulse, no heartbeat. He's gone." He steps into the hall, his eyes locking onto mine, the urgency in them unmistakable. "We need to get out of here."

"We can't," I say, my voice barely audible.

"What do you mean, 'We can't'?"

"The tires." I swallow hard, choking on the panic rising in my throat. "Somebody slashed the tires on the Jeep. We can't leave. We can't call for help. He's trapped us here."

Roman's jaw tightens as he thinks, his silence taut with a fierce determination. "Then we take the tires from Eli's car. We'll swap them out and use the Jeep."

Hope flickers weakly, but it's enough. I nod, clutching the idea like a lifeline. Roman leads the way, and we hurry down the stairs and out the front door.

When we reach the Jeep, it's empty.

Violet and Gia are gone.

chapter
forty-four

"They were here when I left," I tell Roman, shaking my head.

This can't be happening.

He backs away from the Jeep, looking around as he calls each of their names multiple times. But there's no answer.

"Let's just get the tires on the Jeep," Roman says, heading over to Eli's SUV.

"Won't that take a while?" I ask, knowing I won't be of much help. "Shouldn't we find Violet and Gia first?"

Roman doesn't respond. He moves away from me, slowly, then pauses right before he reaches Eli's car. When he looks back at me, I can almost feel what's coming. My stomach clenches.

"What?" I whisper, bracing myself for the worst.

"These tires are slashed too," he says, his voice heavy with disbelief.

"No," I say, the small sound getting swallowed up by the torrential downpour.

I stagger over and crouch down to see for myself, desperate to deny it even when I'm looking at the deflated tires with my own eyes.

Roman takes me by the arm. "We'll have to go on foot."

I shake my head. That seems impossible. "We're in the middle of nowhere."

"We'll flag somebody down. Might take a few miles, but we don't have any other choice."

"Nobody's going to be out driving in this rain. We'll be stuck out here for hours. What if no one ever comes? What if we don't make it? No one will ever find us—"

Roman's hands grip my shoulders as he shakes me quiet. He tells me over and over to calm down, but I can't. He tells me I'm a survivor, that I've already survived so much, and this is nothing.

I suck air into my lungs and pull myself together. He's right. We have no other choice.

Roman moves ahead of me, his strides careful but determined. I linger just behind, my fingers clinging to his arm, nails digging into his skin. Together, we call out for Violet and Gia. When our voices echo unanswered, we exchange a look. It's brief but weighted, a shared acknowledgment of the fear neither of us can speak aloud.

As we pass through the kitchen, Roman slides a pair of knives into his pockets. For a moment, I hesitate, then reach for one myself, the cool steel trembling slightly in my grasp.

We step out onto the back deck, Roman taking the stairs down first. I stay above, scanning the shadows, my gaze flitting over the yard like a moth desperate for light.

Then my eyes catch it. Something that shouldn't be there.

My breathing falters. "Roman . . ."

I hobble toward the hot tub, every step dragging me closer to the inevitable. Roman turns and follows, his pace quickening as he sees where I'm headed. And then I see what it is: Violet floating on the surface.

I press a hand to my mouth, a choked sound escaping before the words force their way out. "He drowned her," I whisper, my voice breaking as the truth crashes over me. "That bastard drowned her."

Roman catches me as I crumble, pulling me into his arms. I can't stop shaking, my whole body a vessel for grief and terror. Violet loved the water. It's what made her feel alive. And now it's become her grave.

Roman holds me only for a moment. Then we circle the house's perimeter, sticking to the shadows, each step more tentative than the last. I fight through the pain in my foot, gritting my teeth as I limp after him. Roman moves with urgency, but the slick ground betrays him. He slips on a patch of mud, falling hard, and I lunge forward to help him up.

When we reach the front of the house, we call out again for Gia, our voices hoarse with desperation. Then we stop.

There she is, sprawled on the gravel, blood pooling beneath her like a dark and widening halo. Her throat is a clean, savage slash, and the sight of it steals the breath from my lungs. I scream, raw and guttural, the sound tearing from me before I can stop it.

Roman grabs my face, his palms steady against my trembling cheeks, forcing me to meet his gaze.

"Breathe," he says firmly. "Okay? Just breathe."

Somehow, I do. The air drags into my lungs like shards of glass, but it's enough. Roman pulls me forward, his grip unyielding, but I stop.

"We can't leave them like this," I manage, my voice barely audible over the roar of my heartbeat. "We . . ."

"We have to move."

I nod. I nod a thousand times, but I can't move.

Roman wraps my arm around his back and takes on the brunt of my weight. "We might find some help once we get back to the main road."

I nod again.

We're doing this. We have to.

chapter
forty-five

The forest swallows us whole, its maw dark and endless as we tread deeper along the gravel path that fractures the trees. The house is far behind, but not far enough, and the main road feels like a dream we'll never reach. Roman guesses it's at least another mile ahead, but distance is a cruel abstraction now. My legs drag beneath me, heavy with the weight of soaked clothes and raw exhaustion. The rain falls like a curtain, cloaking the path ahead in shadows, and the night breathes around us, alive with the sounds of hidden predators—the rustle of leaves, the snap of a branch. But it's the human predator that chills me most.

My hand grips the knife tighter with each stride, its handle biting into my palm. The pain in my foot grows sharp and insistent, but I swallow it down and press harder to keep pace with Roman.

Up ahead, something materializes through the rain. A hulking shape against the shadows. Roman slows, squinting.

I blink hard, my eyes straining to see it, and when we're close enough, recognition blooms between us like poison.

"That's his truck." The words rasp from my throat, barely audible above the rain. "It was parked out front the night I got here. When he was digging."

Roman's jaw tightens. He jogs ahead, vanishing into the gloom. "It's empty," he calls back. "I'll check it out."

He keeps moving toward the vehicle, and I follow behind. This is where he's been hiding.

The forest splits with a sound. A wet crunch of leaves, and then the snap of a branch. We both turn, eyes snapping toward the darkness. And there he is. Twenty yards away, his shape cuts through the rain like a blade. He walks with intent, his strides sure and unhurried, a predator savoring the chase. Something hangs at his side, the weight of it swaying like an extension of his arm. The jacket he wears is unmistakable, even through the haze. The same one from that first night, the one from the photograph in the study, smeared with the blood he didn't bother to wash away.

I limp closer to Roman, my steps hurried, breaths shallow. "That's his jacket too," I say, my voice a thread pulled too tight.

He doesn't waste time. His mind is already working, turning over a plan. "Don't panic. Listen to me, okay?" His words come steady, a quiet command. "We need to get inside his truck. That's our way out of here."

Nolan's voice splits the air, a jagged yell that carries Roman's name. It's close. Too close.

"Okay," Roman says, a calm in his voice I can't comprehend. "This is what we're gonna do. We take off again. Then you're gonna trip and fall. Get on the ground—moan, cry, whatever. Make him think you're hurt, that he's got you. I'll act like I'm distracted, trying to help you. He'll start moving closer, right? He'll think he can ambush us. When he's close enough, I'll tackle him to the ground. I have at least fifteen pounds on him. I can take him, okay?"

I nod, the motion jerky and frantic. "Okay."

"Once I have him down, you run like hell to the truck."

"What about the keys?"

"Check inside. He probably left them in the ignition. Can you do that?"

I nod again, everything turning to a blur, my breath hitching in shallow gasps. There's no more room for hesitation. No more time for fear. "Yeah. Yeah, I can do it."

Roman's gaze flickers over me and his voice softens, just barely. "Is your foot okay? You can make it?"

I glance down, the ache pulsing like a heartbeat, but I lift my chin. "Don't really have a choice."

We press on, moving as one. The gravel beneath us crunches in a muted rhythm, swallowed by the rain. Roman stays just ahead, his shoulders taut with purpose, and I keep as close as my aching foot will allow, teeth clenched from the pain. Mind over matter. A chant, a prayer, a tether to keep me going. My mind loops through the plan again and again, trying to smooth the edges and account for any crack where things could break.

What if Roman doesn't overpower Nolan? What if Nolan turns his efforts on me? My breath falters, and for a moment, I feel the weight of my own body dragging me down.

But then I remember the knife. My fingers brush against its handle, and though it offers little comfort, it reminds me I'm not defenseless. Besides, Roman is quicker and stronger than Nolan. He played defense in college, spent years mastering the art of tackling. He knows how to bring a man down.

It will work. It has to work.

"Little bit more," Roman murmurs, his voice low. "Just a little bit . . ."

We take a few more steps, the forest swallowing us whole, and then he slows. "Okay. Now. *Fall.*"

I stumble forward, letting my leg collapse beneath my body, and go down with a gasp. The jagged undergrowth bites into my palms, cold and unforgiving as Roman turns back and drops beside me, crouching low. His hand brushes my ankle as if to tend to a new injury.

We wait.

My heart pounds, every beat a hammer against my ribs. I strain to hear, to catch the rhythm of Nolan's steps over the rain. Roman's broad frame blocks my sight. I want to see, need to see, but I can only listen to the sounds.

His boots. The slow, deliberate approach. Each step louder, closer, heavier with intent.

And then I see it.

A flash of metal in the dim light, drawn back in one smooth arc. It glints as if it has been waiting for this moment. A fire poker, heavy and unyielding, poised to strike.

My head snaps to Roman, and he reads the signal in my eyes. Move. *Now.*

The world narrows to the sound of bodies colliding. A grunt and a thud so loud it seems to echo in the trees. Roman's tackle is flawless, a symphony of motion and strength. The poker clatters to the ground, slipping from Nolan's grip. I scramble to my feet, the storm still raging.

It takes Roman a few desperate attempts to wrestle Nolan into a chokehold. Their bodies twist in the slick underbrush, the rain turning everything into treacherous mud. Roman holds him steady long enough for me to lunge forward, my hands trembling as I search Nolan's pocket. The keys are slick with rain when I finally snatch them, my fingers clumsy and slow, the metal biting against my palm.

Nolan thrashes, his strength terrifying despite his age, and within seconds, with a single swift movement, he has Roman's forearm in a death grip, the knife hovering just shy of flesh.

"Go!" Roman shouts, his voice breaking on the word. "*Go!*"

The command jolts me like a shock of electricity. My body moves before my mind catches up. I take off, limping, stumbling, my breaths coming in ragged gasps.

Behind me, the sound of their struggle grows fainter, muffled by the trees and the rain.

I glance back just as I reach the truck. Roman and Nolan are a blur of movement, their fight dragging them farther from the path, deeper into the shadows of the woods. My heart drops when I see Nolan gain the upper hand, straddling Roman and pinning him down with his full weight. His hands tighten around Roman's neck. Roman's body bucks beneath him, his arms clawing for leverage.

I open the door to the truck, toss myself in and clutch the keys like a lifeline before starting the engine. But my feet are frozen, my brain trapped between two impossible choices. I can't leave him. I can't.

I can't go back either. The knife in my waistband feels laughable, a toy against a man like that. My body trembles with indecision.

The plan. Stick to the plan.

Roman's words echo in my head, but they feel thin now, empty and fragile in the face of what's happening in front of me. His face, pale and straining, his hands clawing at Nolan's arms. The crushing weight of Nolan's body, the way his hands close around Roman's throat.

It's the same as my dream. The same stranglehold, the same desperate fight for air. I know what that grip feels like, the way it chokes not just the breath from your lungs but the fight from your limbs.

I can't let him die like this.

I shove the door back open, the rain slicing against my skin as I climb down. But before my feet hit the ground, I see Roman twist, his hands finding enough leverage to wrench Nolan's grip loose. He scrambles upright, but Nolan is relentless. He attacks him again in an instant, driving him back into the mud.

Blow after blow, his fists land with sickening, wet thuds.

He's going to kill him.

I slam the door shut again and struggle to find the right gear, trying to remember what Garrett taught me. I make sure the truck is in Neutral and press the clutch pedal all the way down.

When I glance up, Nolan is on his feet. Roman is still down, splayed on the ground. I clench my teeth and start the engine, shift into first gear. I take a breath and slowly release the clutch, keeping gentle pressure on the gas pedal. It starts moving. I turn the wheel, and when I see Nolan heading toward me, I flatten the gas pedal. I careen directly toward him at full speed.

Immediately, he swerves to avoid the two tons of steel coming at him. I brake hard, stopping a few feet away from where Roman's made it to his knees. The engine sputters, and the truck lurches to a shuddering halt.

"*Roman*," I shout, flinging open the passenger door. "Get in."

Roman sways on his feet, then heads for me, staggering toward the truck. But Nolan charges at him again, relentless, an unstoppable force cutting through the storm. Roman spins, fists flying. Some are wild, some precise. A kick lands square in Nolan's gut, doubling him over with a guttural groan. Another sends him crashing to the ground.

"Roman, *get in the truck*!" I scream, but he doesn't stop.

He throws himself at Nolan, dragging him into the mud, their bodies a tangle of rage and desperation. Nolan slams Roman into the truck with a bone-shaking thud. Roman slumps, his head dropping, dazed.

I fling the truck door open and grab the fire poker. My foot screams with every step, but I breathe through it.

Roman pushes up to his knees now, his face bloodied, barely holding on. Nolan stands over him, his fists ready.

I lift the fire poker, gripping it tight as I close the gap between us. But then the hood slips from his head to his nape.

I stare at his face.

I recognize him.

chapter
forty-six

My mind shatters.

It can't be.

Time unravels, every second stretching thin as I try to reconcile the face before me with the one I swore I'd never see again.

The last time I saw him, he was sprawled on the floor, his head suffocated in plastic, his body completely still. He was dead. Roman had checked for a pulse. He said there was no heartbeat.

And yet I stare at Garrett, motionless, stunned as a viscous trail of blood snakes down his temple.

He grabs me, his grip viselike, wrenching me off my feet. The fire poker slips from my fingers, clattering uselessly to the ground. Roman roars, a primal sound that rips from his throat, tearing me from Garrett's grasp.

I hit the earth hard, the breath knocked from my chest. Gasping, I cough against the pain, but it barely registers before Garrett slams Roman's head into the nearest tree trunk with a sickening crack.

Roman swings his fists, but Garrett is relentless, overpowering him, striking again and again. Blood blooms across Roman's face, obscuring his features until there's almost nothing human left. He collapses in the mud, a heap of blood and muscle.

"Oh, my god," I whisper, the words trembling on my lips. My hands shake as I try to steady them.

I'm alone now.

With him.

Not Nolan.

Garrett.

He lunges for me again. I sidestep him and catch the glint of a knife on the ground. I snatch it up, turning just as he reaches for me. He tries to pull me toward his chest, but I press the tip of the serrated blade to his neck.

He freezes, his chest heaving in short, shallow bursts. "Iris, put—"

"I knew it was you," I say, cutting him off, the words sharp and cold.

"Put down the—"

"What do you want?"

"I want you to put the knife down." His voice softens, almost pleading.

"What's *wrong* with you?" My voice breaks, trembling with rage. "Why'd you kill them?"

His teeth grind together. "I didn't kill anybody."

I shake my head. "Liar."

He tries to disarm me, but I step back, leveling the blade. "Stay back!" I scream.

"Okay, okay." He raises his hands, palms open, a performance of surrender. "See? My hands are empty."

I glance down at Roman. He's stirring, shifting slightly. He's still alive.

My grip tightens on the knife, the blade trembling just enough to betray my fear. "What do you want? Why are you helping him?"

"Helping who?"

I lift the blade, pressing the tip closer to his neck. Garrett flinches, his pulse quickening beneath the edge of the knife.

"Iris . . ." His voice shakes now, the control draining from his face.

"Where is he?" I growl through clenched teeth.

"Where is *who*?"

"Your uncle." The words are a hiss, venomous. "Where is Nolan? Why are you helping him?"

My gaze flickers to Roman, willing him to move faster, to rise and help me. In my hesitation, Garrett lunges toward me, his grip like iron, twisting my wrist until pain explodes up my arm.

The knife slips from my fingers, thudding softly into the moss and leaves below.

Before I can react, Garrett's fist connects with bone. Another ominous *crack*. Roman slumps to the ground again.

I wait for him to stir, to groan, to give any signs of life. My chest tightens, each breath snagging as panic claws its way up my throat.

"No . . ." The wail tears from my throat, raw and desperate.

Garrett reaches for me again, his hand closing around my arm, but I twist free, yanking myself from his grip.

And then I run. I run and run and run.

I tear through the trees crowding in around me, their branches clawing at my sleeves. My breaths rip from my chest in sharp, shallow bursts.

My bandaged foot buckles on the slick earth. I hit the ground hard. Mud seeps through my pants, gritty and cold. Pain flares in my foot, but I shove myself up and force my body forward.

Behind me, I hear him. His footsteps thunder closer, closing the distance between us.

Then they stop.

Silence folds around me, drowning out the sound of the rain and wind, everything but the hammering of my pulse. I limp to a massive oak, pressing my back into its soaked trunk. My chest heaves as I strain to hear through the rain's violent patter.

Then, faintly, footsteps. Measured. Deliberate.

I peek around the tree. A shadow moves through the drizzle, cutting between the trunks. Garrett's voice rises, calm and coaxing.

He says he's not going to hurt me.

It's the kind of lie you feel in your bones.

I pull back, squeezing my eyes shut, trying to calm my breathing, to think. The silence stretches taut again. The rain soaks through my hair, chilling me down to the bone. I open my eyes and peek again.

Nothing now. No movement. I've lost my sense of direction. The truck could be anywhere.

A shift in the air.

Behind me.

I whip around, but not fast enough. Heavy arms lock around me, steel-hard and unrelenting. A large hand slams over my mouth, muffling my scream. It's soft, uncalloused.

Garrett.

I kick him with my good foot, but he's too strong. My movements feel like nothing against him.

My mind flickers to my mother, to the echo of her body meeting the ground, a sound that still feels like a rupture in the world. Final. Irrevocable. Is this how I'll end too? Lost in the damp embrace of September, the mud pulling me under, the trees closing their arms around me, erasing all trace that I was ever here?

"Shh," Garrett breathes against my ear, his voice low and steady, like I imagine he speaks to his son when he wakes crying in the night.

I feel just as small, just as powerless, thrashing against his grip. I twist, wriggle, but his arms are unyielding, coiled around me like steel.

"I don't want to hurt you," he says, his words measured but strained, his breath warm against my temple. "Do you hear me? I don't want to hurt you."

I claw, I kick, I push every ounce of strength into my escape, but it's useless. My body betrays me, my muscles burning, lungs heaving. I collapse into his hold, helpless and defenseless.

"Look," Garrett says, his tone almost soothing now as he lifts the knife into the weak beam of light filtering through the trees. The blade glints, sharp and cruel. My body seizes, bracing for pain, for blood.

But instead, he moves the knife slowly toward my pocket, his voice low. "I'm putting this in your pocket. See? Just like this."

I flinch, expecting the blade to pierce my stomach. But it doesn't. He slides it in, and the cold weight grounds me.

"You were right," he says, his voice tinged with something I can't place. Regret? Resolve? "Uncle Nolan isn't in Italy."

My head jerks back toward him, my breath catching. His words hang in the air, heavy and incomprehensible.

"I found his phone upstairs," Garrett continues. "He never left."

The ground beneath me feels as if it shifts, the rain soaking through my shoe, mixing with my blood.

Garrett lets me go, his arms falling away. I stumble forward, too drained to scream, too stunned to bolt. My fingers brush against the knife in my pocket. Its weight is my only comfort.

"What does he want?" My voice is a hollow echo, my thoughts spinning.

"You're not understanding what I'm telling you," Garrett says. "He doesn't want anything."

"How do you know?"

He stares into my eyes, and for a moment, his expression softens. "Because he's dead."

The words crash into me, as sharp and cold as the rain. I stagger, trying to make sense of them.

"You . . ." My voice cracks. "You killed him?"

Garrett doesn't hesitate. "He was dead before we even drove out here."

"No." My head shakes, desperate to push the truth away. "I saw him that night. In the back. He was . . ."

But the words falter, my voice splintering as a shiver courses through me.

Nolan is dead. He's been dead this whole time. Garrett is the one I should have feared all along.

I see him in my mind, burying the arm in the backyard, in the dark. The jacket he wore then, the jacket he wears now.

A scream claws its way up my throat, but I break free instead. I don't make it far before Garrett catches my wrist, his grip firm but not enough to hurt me.

"You have the knife," he reminds me, his voice soft and steady. He pats his pockets, then lifts his hands in surrender, his palms empty. "I have nothing."

"Then what do you want?" I spit, the hilt of the knife slick in my hand. "Why were you trying to kill me?"

"I wasn't . . ." He exhales sharply, his jaw clenching. "I was trying to *save* you."

"Save me from what?"

Garrett doesn't answer immediately. His eyes scan my face, searching for something. When he speaks again, his voice is laced with frustration. "You really don't get it, do you?"

I glare at him, the demand for answers burning in my chest, and finally, he relents.

"I found his phone in Roman's room," Garrett says, looking around as if making sure Roman isn't near.

"What?"

"I was looking for Lauren's purse, and I found it there."

Too much has happened all at once. My mind spins, trying to catch up with my body, but it's impossible. Fatigue presses down on me, dragging me under its weight. I sag, barely able to hold myself upright as I struggle to piece all of this together.

I stare at Garrett, not understanding, not until his words fall into place. The realization hits me like a blow to the chest, rattling me to the bone.

He found Nolan's phone in Roman's room. The same phone that had texted Garrett a few days ago. The same phone that had sent pictures of the beach in Lake Como.

If Nolan was already dead by then, he couldn't have sent those messages.

Someone else sent them. Someone who knew I needed

proof Nolan was in Italy. Someone who was close enough to move unseen.

"He tried to kill me upstairs," Garrett says, fracturing the silence. "When I found the phone, the messages, I started to call the cops. Next thing I knew, everything went black. He hit me in the head with something, I think."

Which would explain the plastic over his head. My whole body trembles at the thought.

"So . . ." I take a breath, trying to steady myself. "The arm . . ."

"It's Uncle Nolan's."

All this time, I'd thought it was a young woman's body. One of Nolan's victims. But I was wrong. Nolan *is* the victim.

It strikes me, sharp and sudden, like lightning coursing through my veins: Roman was leading me into the woods to kill me. If Garrett hadn't intervened, I wouldn't be standing here.

I can barely speak. "But why? Why'd he kill him?"

"I don't know." Garrett's voice is strained.

My head shakes, frantically, as though I could shake the answers loose.

"Why'd he kill Lauren? And Gia? And Violet?"

"I don't know."

"Oh god," I say, my hand covering my mouth. "Did he kill Eli too? Did he—"

Garrett grabs me, gripping me hard. "Listen to me. I know you're scared, but we need to get out of here. We need to move before he finds us."

Garrett pulls me with him, tugging me back the way we came. But before we can take another step, I freeze.

"Too late," Roman whispers, and before I can react, he swings the poker toward Garrett's neck.

I scream at the crack of impact. Garrett crumples to the ground, a sack of fabric and skin.

Roman's gaze settles onto me, and I forget to breathe.

chapter
forty-seven

Roman lowers the poker. The metal gleams in the dark like a promise. I wait, expecting the blow. But it never comes.

Roman releases his grip, letting the poker drop to the ground.

I stare up at him in the dark, the ruin of his face. His flesh is torn and raw, blood dripping from his split lip, staining his chin. His eye is red and swollen, barely open, his skin shredded where his head hit the tree. I can't look away from him, this disfigured stranger standing in front of me, his expression unreadable as his hands fall limp at his sides.

The silence chokes me. I want to move. To scream. But I'm frozen, still piecing it all together. He must have something else in mind for me, something worse.

"It's your fault, you know." Roman's voice is unnervingly calm, smooth like velvet, but it carries a grim weight. It's a voice I can't place, the man who was once desperately trying to rescue me gone, replaced by someone unfamiliar.

I jerk my head side to side, trying to shake off the weight of his words. This isn't mine. None of it is. The guilt doesn't belong to me. But it clings, claws at my chest.

"Don't worry," Roman says, stepping closer, his presence consuming me. He's too close, close enough to touch me, and then I can feel his broken breath on my skin. "I won't hold it against you."

I stumble back, desperate to put distance between us, my chest tight with fear. "Please don't. Please, Roman. Don't do—"

"It wasn't supposed to be this way." He cuts me off, his voice a whisper, oddly tender. "The only person that was supposed to die was Uncle Nolan. But you just wouldn't let it go. Now they're all dead. Now . . ."

He stops, his gaze locking with mine. I feel it. Something jagged, something sinister. His eyes are haunted, as if he's already mourning me, the regret already swelling inside him. I'm the last thread he has to sever.

I rip my eyes away from his and peer down at Garrett, his body a limp mass in the mud.

He's gone.

I can't process it. This nightmare, this massacre. The numbness creeps in, thick and slick. How could all of this have happened so quickly?

Roman steps toward me, and my body is heavy with surrender. My legs betray me, cemented to the earth beneath. I shut my eyes, the dark my only solace.

It's over. I've lived every moment I was meant to live. There's nothing left to claim.

And then I feel him. His hands are a quiet tempest, pulling me into him. I gasp, a sound that doesn't belong to me, but his mouth silences it.

I can't breathe. I can't run. It's not a kiss. It's a storm more powerful than the one that envelops us.

His lips are rough, hungry, as though they've been starved for a thousand lifetimes. The taste of salt and blood is sharp like an open wound, rain the only thing between us. He kisses me as though he would carve me into his very soul, mark me for eternity if he could. He holds me by my neck, and as the world around us shudders, I wonder if I'll ever be anything again but ash in his hands. Then I open my eyes, watching him devour me. The taste of rain, blood and something darker clings to my lips, sticky and foul.

But I don't pull away. I don't scream. I don't fight. I surrender, letting him take whatever he wants from me.

I feel for the cold weight of the knife in my pocket. My fingers brush against the hilt, trembling. For a moment, I wait. I let him groan and growl, let him become feral.

I give him every last bit of me, my fingers tightening around the handle of the knife. When I feel it—the break in his breath, the shudder of his body—I draw it back. The blade sinks into his neck with a wet thud. His roar rips through the air.

Fresh blood, black in the darkness, pours, hot and thick. I rip myself away from him, pushing off with everything I have left. He reaches for me, desperate to catch hold, but I'm already gaining momentum.

The trees blur as I stumble over the slick undergrowth. My foot screams in pain, the injury tearing open again. Blood seeps from my heel, but I keep running, faster, harder.

I can't stop. I can't stop.

When I glance over my shoulder, Roman is rising to his feet, a hand clutched to his neck. The knife still lodged there, slowing him down.

I keep pumping. The world is a blur of shadows and pain, branches tearing at my skin, my foot burning like fire.

And then, there.

The road.

I see it, barely, the white truck in the distance a promise. I give all that's left of me. Every last breath, every aching step.

I finally make it to the door. Everything moves in slow motion. I toss myself behind the wheel and glance back again.

Roman's closing in. His steps stutter, but he's coming.

My hands shake as I fumble with the gearstick. Clutch in, shift to first. Garrett's words echo, but the engine coughs, sputters. It dies. I try again. Rain and tears and sweat and blood trickle down my face, into my eye. I turn the key, desperate. The engine roars, but I release the clutch too fast. The truck jerks. Stalls.

The door swings open. Roman grabs my shirt, yanks me from the seat. Blood runs down his face, the knife clenched in his other hand.

I kick him in the stomach, and he stumbles back.

I move. Quick. Quick. Quick.

Breathe, I try to breathe. My hands shaking, I grip the wheel. Clutch in. Turn the key. The engine growls. I shift into first, my foot steady on the clutch. Slowly, I release it. The car jerks forward. But this time, I don't panic. I find the sweet spot and shift my foot onto the gas pedal.

The tires grind over Roman's feet, a sickening crunch. His scream rips through the air, but I don't flinch.

I don't know if Garrett is alive or dead. I can't think about it. I can't go back now.

I flatten the gas pedal. I don't look back. I just go.

Just go.

chapter
forty-eight

The hospital is all cold light and sharp edges. Nurses swarm me like bees, tending to the scrapes and bruises on my legs, patching up the gash on my foot. Their hands are efficient, impersonal, but I cling to their presence, to the sensation of someone taking care of me.

I bow my head for a moment, thinking of the truck driver who stopped to help me, eternally grateful for his kindness. Without him I would still be stuck out on that cold, dark road. His headlights cut through the storm as soon as panic started to consume me. My vision was a blur as I fumbled with the stick shift, tears streaming down my face as the gears groaned in protest, the truck jerking and stalling relentlessly. I'd been heading in the wrong direction for miles when he pulled over just ahead of me. He handed me his phone without hesitation, then offered to drive me to the hospital. When I spoke to the police, I told them where to find Garrett, told them to check if he was still alive. They found him just in time, barely breathing, bleeding out on the forest floor.

I wait with my hands clenching and unclenching in my lap, the chair in the waiting room hard and unforgiving beneath me. Time drags, the faint hum of machinery filling the quiet, the wetness soaking into my marrow. Finally, a nurse appears and gestures for me to follow. She speaks in clipped, measured tones. Significant blood loss, fractured rib, stab wounds. But Garrett is stable now, she assures me. He'll recover.

Garrett will be fine. We'll both be fine.

The door opens. The room is too bright, fluorescent lights turning everything stark and raw. My gaze lands on Garrett, and the air punches out of my lungs. He's draped across the narrow bed, too tall for it, his legs hanging awkwardly over the edge. His face is a patchwork of bruises, one eye swollen shut, the other dull and unfocused, glassy from the morphine. Stitches track down his cheek like some cruel constellation. Dried blood clings to his jaw, flaking but stubborn, refusing to let go.

His chest rises and falls under the thin hospital sheet, shallow and uneven. Wires snake out from beneath it, leading to machines that beep softly in the corner, keeping time with his breathing. His hands rest on the bed, palms up, knuckles split and raw, trembling faintly, as if his body hasn't yet realized the fight is over.

I don't move. I can't.

The room is quiet except for the machines and the hiss of my own breathing. I want to reach out, to touch him, but I don't know where. Everywhere looks broken. Everywhere looks like it hurts.

Garrett's eye cracks open as I step closer, his swollen face barely shifting. For a moment, he gazes at me, his eyes heavy with the weight of pain and medication.

"Lauren?" he whispers, the name fragile like it might shatter in the air.

I hesitate, my throat tightening around the words. "She's gone."

The truth lands like a mountain between us.

His lips part, but no sound comes. Just a slow exhale that quivers in the stillness. His eye flickers shut for a moment, and when it opens again, it glistens.

"I want to sleep," he whispers, his voice hoarse and defeated.

"Okay," I manage, my voice barely a breath.

I linger for a moment, watching his chest rise and fall before I step out of the room, the weight of his loss heavy in the sterile air. Eventually, I leave him to his silence, and even this feels cruel.

Beneath the harsh glow of the hallway, my thoughts unravel like thread, tangled and frayed. A man in a rumpled, damp suit pauses in front of me. His hair drips, rainwater carving restless paths down his temples and pooling at his cuffs, his umbrella dangling uselessly at his side. He introduces himself, Detective Something, his voice low and precise.

"Can we step out for a moment?" he asks, gesturing to the corridor ahead.

I follow him without a word, my feet moving before my thoughts can catch up. The linoleum beneath me seems to stretch and waver. The air feels too thick, too close.

Before he can begin, I ask about the others. The names tumble out of me, sharp and desperate, splintering the air between us. I have to know.

His face shifts, the weight of his answer already hanging between us. "I'm sorry. They're gone."

For a moment, the earth seems to tilt off its axis. My knees threaten to buckle, but I force myself to stand upright.

He continues, asking for a statement, and I try to summon the pieces of the last few hours, to make sense of the chaos.

I recount everything, but the story comes out disjointed, my voice thin and worn. My thoughts are scattered. I'm so tired. More tired than I have ever been in my life.

"What about Roman?" I ask, the question clawing its way out of my throat. I have to know. "Did he . . ."

The detective's gaze flickers. "He pulled through. He has some pretty bad internal bleeding, but the doctors think he'll recover."

The words slam into me, knocking the breath straight from my chest. Roman, alive. Roman, saved.

But not Eli. Not Lauren or Violet or Gia. It's so unfair, so bitterly, cruelly unfair. Anger sparks in my chest, but it's an impotent rage, destined to burn out before it can consume anything.

"Actually, he's, uh . . ." The detective hesitates, his brows pushing together as if even he can't quite believe what he's about to say. "He's been asking for you."

chapter
forty-nine

I stop in front of Roman's door and peer through the glass. He's still. Asleep. Broken. His face is covered in bruises and rough stitches. For a moment I just stand there, watching. My breath fogs the window, blurring the edges of him until he's nothing but a smear of color, a shadow in the sterile light. Then I push the door open.

Inside, the stench is metallic and sour. I step closer, soft as if the floor might crack beneath my weight. He doesn't stir. His head lolls to the side, the tension gone from his face in a way I've never seen before.

I stop at the edge of the bed, close enough to see his chest rising and falling in uneven stutters beneath a thin hospital blanket. The thought cuts right through me, sharp and unstoppable: I could kill him.

It would be so easy. A hand on his throat, a pillow over his face. No one would question it. Not after what he's done. Not after the bodies he left behind. My fingers curl into fists at my sides, and I lean over him, close enough to smell the sweat and blood on his skin.

And then, beneath the gore, I see him. The man I thought I knew. The one I laughed with, trusted.

His eyes snap open.

I jerk back, and for a moment, neither of us moves. His gaze locks onto mine, and he does his best to smile.

"Thought you . . ." The words trip over my tongue. "Thought you were asleep."

He chuckles, the sound scraping through the quiet. "Saw the door open and figured it was that dumb cop again."

I don't know where to begin, so I start at the beginning. "Why'd you do it? Why'd you kill Nolan?"

"I . . ." His voice cracks. The words fumble in his chest, bruised and broken, and it takes him an eternity to find them. "Things got out of hand. One minute we were arguing, and the next his neck was in my hands."

He makes it sound so small, so simple. I blink, the weight of his words settling in, and realize with a jolt that I've never really known him. Not ever. There's an ocean between us now, an abyss of ice and fire, and I'm drowning in it. I can't even picture the Roman I thought I knew.

"I didn't plan to kill him," he says, his voice unraveling with the weight of things unsaid. "Didn't have time to clean up. That's why I couldn't let you go talking to the cops. Didn't want them sniffing around the house."

I hadn't expected him to talk. But he is, and I'm drawn closer, one careful inch at a time, like I'm threading my fingers through glass.

He reaches for my arm. I jump back, my heart slamming in my chest. His eyes flash with surprise, then something darker, deeper. Hurt.

"What?" His voice is low and wounded. "You're scared of me now?"

"Shouldn't I be?"

"You missed my carotid by an inch," he says, the corners of his lips curling with amusement, and even that feels hostile. "Maybe I should be scared of you."

I think of the poker, of that moment when his hand trembled, when he decided not to end it, end me. I taste the memory, the salt, the blood. I still don't understand it.

"Why didn't you kill me when you had the chance?"

My words seem to fill the room. And I know, I now know why I'm here. I need to know. I need to hear him say it. His eyes lock onto mine, and for a long moment, the world goes still, frozen between breaths.

He shakes his head, looks helpless. "I couldn't do it."

The way he says it makes my heart stutter. It breaks something in me, cracks the surface of the hatred I've been carrying in my heart.

"You killed all of them," I say, my voice thin, threadbare. "You—"

"I couldn't kill you." His laugh is brittle, jagged, like glass breaking in his throat. "I couldn't kill you."

"Why?" The question feels too big for my mouth. Too much.

Roman squints at me. "Don't you get it?"

"Get what?"

"I *love* you."

I stumble, the ground slipping out from under me like I'm falling through the very fabric of time.

"Oh, come on," he says, taking in the shock veiling my features. "I've always loved you. Everybody knew."

I stand there, caught in the stream of his words, my mind a whirl of confusion, disbelief, and a thousand other things I can't untangle. I don't know what to do, what to say. I want to scream. Run. Kill him. Cry. Sleep.

Everything feels impossibly heavy.

"You found the arm, and I . . ." His words falter, and the weight of them seems to suffocate him. He stops, gathers what's left of himself, and tries again. "I didn't know what to do at first. You're right. I had the chance. I had so many chances. If I would've just killed you first, no one else would've had to die. But I couldn't. So I tried so hard to convince you that you were making it all up. I did what I had to do. I even put that doll in the ground so everybody would think so too. That it was all in your head."

Roman breathes out, a bitter exhalation. He shifts in the bed, then lets out a groan through his clenched teeth, and I almost smile at his pain.

"It was nice that everyone else helped, especially Gia," he says. "She was such a bitch to you."

"Don't talk about her like that. She's . . ."

Dead. Everything she did, every ounce of cruelty, none of it matters now.

"All is fair in death, huh?"

I don't answer. I can't.

And then I remember.

"But you blew up the boat," I say, and a sudden, sharp flinch moves through his body.

"I didn't. That really was an accident."

An accident. I can't swallow the words; they stick in my throat.

"Anyway," he continues, wiping away the edges of reality with his gravelly voice, "when that didn't work, you started digging around, googling, putting shit together that didn't need to be put together. But then you came up with Nolan. You truly became convinced he was here. Shit, for a second, you almost had me thinking he rose from the dead. I figured no one else knew where he was, so why couldn't he be the one who killed all of our friends? So I went with it."

Roman holds my gaze, but I can't return it.

The silence wraps around us. His eyes want mine, but they find nothing. I don't know what to feel anymore. I don't know why I'm here. I don't know why I'm doing this to myself.

"I was never going to kill you. Not until Garrett told you what I did. You knew Nolan was dead. My cover was gone. I had no choice." A smile blooms on his battered lips, then quickly falters. "I still can't tell if you got away. Or if I let you."

I take a step back, my skin prickling.

"I didn't want it to be like this," he says, his voice dropping even lower. "I wanted to make love to you."

"Stop."

"I've wanted you for so long. Been trying to find you in other women. But it's never been right."

I don't acknowledge his words, though they claw at me, twisting inside my chest. For some reason, it makes me feel filthy.

The room is a hollow echo now. I turn away, my tears falling like they belong to someone else. I brush them away quickly, but he sees me.

"Don't cry."

"How could you do this?" My voice breaks, the words full of everything I can't hold back anymore. Anger, betrayal, the sting of it like a raw wound. The same kind I felt watching my mother shoot herself.

"Eli was the hardest," Roman admits after a long pause, his voice louder now, more honest.

"You asshole."

"I'm sorry."

"You killed him because you wanted to make love to me?" The words feel like acid on my tongue, and the thought of Eli, his last moments—confused, terrified, horrified—tears me apart.

"No, no. God, you think I'm . . ." He shakes his head, eyes wide, like he still believes in his own innocence, as if the blood on his hands doesn't count. "I tried to talk him out of taking that tooth to the police station, but he wouldn't budge."

It's surreal, listening to him justify it. I close my eyes, hoping the weight of this truth will ease, but it doesn't. The only comfort I find is that Eli isn't here to witness the vile metamorphosis of his best friend, his brother.

"I had to get rid of Eli. I figured we'd all be leaving in a couple more days. You'd realize you were freaking out over nothing. Everything would go back to normal. Maybe we could spend some more time together." He shakes his head like it's some sort of twisted regret. "But then that fucking finger ruined everything."

"Why'd you even throw his arm in the water supply?"

"You think I did that on purpose?" His voice is incredulous. "You had everyone hyped about an arm. I had to dig it out and get rid of it fast. I just threw it up there." His head shakes again. "Everybody was spooked after that, so I had to change course."

My jaw tightens. "You didn't have to kill them."

"Everything just started going wrong. Garrett kept trying to call the cops once I told him what happened with Uncle Nolan. Gia saw me drowning Violet . . ."

"Why'd you push Lauren?"

He shakes his head like it's just another detail he can't be bothered to explain. "I didn't touch her. She must have slipped."

I can't listen to any more. I can't bear it. He makes it seem like a natural progression, like it's all just a string of events that couldn't have been stopped. But I know they could have. It didn't have to end like this.

"Maybe it's better this way," Roman says with that strange warmth in his voice again. "Garrett couldn't live without her. So I guess they're together now, right?"

I don't answer. He thinks Garrett is dead.

I thought he was too when we left him in the woods. It's a miracle the cops found him at all. But I can't shake the feeling, a nagging instinct, that tells me not to tell Roman.

Garrett is the only one left who can help me tell the truth.

Roman shifts, his gaze sharp, unnervingly intent, as if he can feel the secret slipping through my fingers. Maybe the truth rests somewhere tangled in between the lies, and maybe the lies are the closest thing to the truth I will ever get.

Roman asks me something, but I turn and push out of the room. His voice flickers in the air, a final plea, but I don't turn back. I've heard enough, heard too much.

There's nothing left here for me to find.

The elevator hums, mechanical and indifferent. It rises, carrying me back to the floor where Garrett rests, and I press my hand into my pocket, feeling the cool, jagged edge against my skin. And then I feel it.

The tooth.

My fingers curl around it before the weight of it crashes in. A small thing, so tiny in my hand, and yet it feels as if the world shifts with it. I stop and stare at the little shard of enamel.

Roman's words echo in my head, distant and urgent. Eli was going to take me to show it to the police. But Roman said he strangled Nolan. There's no reason for it to be in my palm. Here.

A slow pulse pounds in my temples. The news articles, the ones I couldn't stop reading, they come rushing back. The remains, found. The teeth, gone. Always gone. Unidentifiable.

The pieces shift and fit together like a puzzle I've been holding upside down. And just like that, everything snaps into place. The realization burns through me, rattling my bones, searing the truth into the core of me.

Roman didn't just kill Nolan.

He's the one who murdered all those young girls.

He killed them all.

chapter
fifty

The elevator doors slide open, but I don't move.

I've wanted you my whole life. Been trying to find you in every other woman I've been with. But it's never been enough.

Roman's words have taken root somewhere deep inside me. My body trembles, a slow wave of recognition crashing over me, too heavy, unbearable. My mind flickers to all the missing women I saw online, their faces haunting me. I remember seeing myself in them, and now I see why. Roman's been hunting for me, a version of me, and leaving the others in his wake. What had they done? Why did they have to die? What part of them—of me—was so wrong that it had to be erased?

I force myself to not spiral, to snap out of it. The doors close me into the box of steel, and the world feels too small, too tight. I feel like a fish underwater trying to breathe air. I press the button again, and the doors open. I step back out onto Roman's floor, my footsteps heavy against the tile.

As I peer in through the little square window, Roman looks like he's sleeping again. Underneath the gore and bandages, his face is soft, vulnerable, the sharp edges of his cruelty dulled in his exhaustion. It's bizarre looking at him like this. How could the same man capable of such horrors look human now?

The truth seems so inviting, like a clear sky after a storm. We convince ourselves that once we reach it, everything will make sense. The pieces will fall into place, and the world will be as it should. But the truth isn't so simple. It's sharp and jagged, a splinter in the mind, digging deeper the more we try to pull it out.

They say it will set you free, but what if that's just another lie? What if some questions are not meant to ever be answered? Or worse—some answers change, slip away, like sand through your fingers. I wonder now if I even want to know. If knowing is better than this restless, gnawing ache of not knowing. Maybe some things are better left in the dark, safe from the pain of their revelation. Or maybe the dark is what will swallow me whole in the end.

I try to breathe, to anchor myself, but the ground feels like it's fading away, slipping from beneath my feet. And when his eyes open and meet mine, all I see is the same depthless blackness.

"Knew you'd be back," he says, his voice cracked with exhaustion.

"I know why you killed him," I say, the words trembling on my lips. "Why you killed Nolan."

Roman's face shifts. It's not the agony or the injuries that change his expression. It's something else. Something deeper.

"Why?" he asks, his voice barely above a whisper.

"Because he found out who you really are," I reply, my voice steady, though everything inside me is breaking apart. "What you really are."

He stares at me, wide-eyed, frozen in place. I see it. The terror, raw and unmasked. I know he knows that I know. The silence between us is the heaviest thing I've ever felt. The kind of silence that tells the most truth.

"You murdered those women. The ones from the headlines. You . . ." My chest tightens, my heart pounding. "You said you strangled Nolan."

Roman doesn't respond. He just stares at me, vacant. Blank. A stranger's eyes.

"He couldn't have lost a tooth when you killed him," I say, stepping closer to the bed, rage filling every inch of me. It drowns my fear, any uncertainty left inside me. "So who did the one I found belong to?"

Roman frowns. "What?"

"You said you had to kill Eli because he was going to take me to the police so I could give them the tooth," I continue. "You said you couldn't let that happen. You knew they'd search the house. They'd find out who you were."

No response. No reaction. He's frozen. Speechless.

"You killed all of them," I say, and the words feel like they're shattering the entire planet.

Still nothing. He's staring at nothing, like he's already gone. Like I'm not even here.

"Was it worth it?" I ask, my voice rough, desperate for something, anything other than this silence.

But he doesn't answer. Not a word, not one movement. Not even a blink.

"You should've killed me when you had the chance," I whisper, the words a threat, and still he says nothing.

Which tells me everything.

I leave the room, the air too thick, the walls too close. My body aches in places I didn't know could hurt, and my mind feels worn, scraped raw. I'm exhausted, hollowed out, like the world has taken everything it could from me. Tomorrow, I'll untangle what's left of this life. Tonight, all I want is sleep. Sweet, merciful sleep.

Outside, the rain still falls steady, unrelenting, as if it, too, is trying to wash everything away. I see Detective Something heading to his car, his coat pulled tight against the storm. My steps are slow, uneven, the ground slick beneath me.

When I reach him, I stop. I don't speak. I don't have to. I hold out my fist, the rain sliding down my wrist, pooling in the creases of my fingers. Slowly, I open my palm. The tooth. The truth. It sits there, small but immense, a fragment of all that's been broken, of all that cannot be undone.

He drives me to a hotel close by, the hum of the car engine the only sound between us. The rain drums against the roof, steady and rhythmic, like the heartbeat of a captive bird. When we arrive, he offers to walk me in, but I shake my head. I don't need anyone else tonight. I tear off my clothes. Climb into the bed, still damp, still shaking, and pull the blanket over me.

For a moment, I think of Eli, of Roman, of my mother, and of the aches they've left behind, the kind of pain that seeps into your marrow and makes a home there, permanent and unshakable. I think of all the ways they claimed to love me and all the ways they never really did. How Eli told his lies with a smile so soft, it was impossible not to believe it was the truth. How Roman doesn't love me—not for the person I am but for the idea of me, the shadow of something he could shape and mold and keep. And my mother, who couldn't love anyone, not even herself, let alone a daughter who tried so hard to be enough, to be worthy of the one thing she'd never give. And yet I loved them, all of them, loved them in the way that consumes, in the way that scars, in the way that feels like stepping into fire and staying there because you don't know how to leave, because you don't want to, because loving is the only thing you know how to do, even when it leaves nothing behind but ash. Maybe that's the difference. Maybe that's what sets me apart, that I keep loving, that I never stop, that I don't know how to stop. Maybe that's the only truth I'll ever have, that loving is its own kind of curse, its own kind of grace.

I close my eyes and force myself to not think about tomorrow, the day everything fell apart. The day I lost what was never mine to keep. Tonight feels different. For the first time in a long time, I feel the crushing weight of the past slip from my shoulders, like a heavy blanket being lifted from my chest. The realization eases over me, quiet but undeniable: It's time to move on. Time to stop carrying the ghost of my mother, all her broken pieces. For the first time, I breathe easy at the thought of her. It's over. It's all over.

The world falls away in pieces, dissolves like sugar in water, slow and quiet, and sleep comes not like a thief but like an old, old friend, soft and steady and sure, wrapping itself around me like a lullaby, pulling me under into its dark and endless depths, into a silence so vast it feels holy, into a stillness so complete, so whole. There is no ache here. No weight. Just silence. A stillness that feels endless, that feels like peace. And for the first time in longer than I can remember, I let go. Nothing follows me. Nothing hurts. Just sleep. Deep and dark and infinite. The sweetest thing I've ever known.

★ ★ ★ ★ ★